Runaway

Safe Havens 2

Sandy James

Sandy James
sandyjames.com

Printed in the United States of America
First Printing: September 2013
ISBN: 978-1-940295-02-2

Chapter One

San Francisco Bay—October 1883

"They might be thieves and breed bastards like rabbits, but at least *my* family didn't try to murder me." Ty Bishop flexed his fingers, trying to restore some circulation to his tied wrists.

His gaze wandered the dank, dark cave as he calculated how much time remained before the tide rose enough to turn the cave into a watery tomb.

Sitting atop a large boulder, he pressed his back against the strong back of his best friend, Jake Curtis. Both were bound at wrists and ankles, and any movement by one affected the other. The beating they'd both taken before being subdued made every muscle in his body ache, but Ty put his pain and fear aside and scanned the cave for what seemed like the millionth time.

Large, jagged rock walls. Bars of sand and shells that shifted as the water rushed in and out in a steady, swaying rhythm. The smell of rotting fish and stale air. He tried to breathe easy and block the image of the walls pressing in on him—his typical response to being trapped in closed spaces. There was more than enough air. He just had to constantly remind himself of that fact.

Glancing over his shoulder, Jake gave Ty a shake of his head. "What can I say, buddy? I come from bad stock."

Their captor, Derrick Shay, ran his hand through his graying ebony hair. His dark eyes gleamed with amusement as he absentmindedly brushed some sand from the sleeve of his jacket.

"I must admit I like seeing that spirit, Mr. Curtis. Shows there might be some Shay blood flowing through your veins after all." He turned to his companion. "What say you, Robert? Do you believe that laugh-in-the-face-of-death bravado comes from *my* side of the family?"

Robert Putnam's smile now seemed reptilian, so in contrast to what Ty had wrongly judged as a friendly face. Of course, on first meeting, both Derrick and Robert had also appeared genuinely pleased to see that Jake had replied to Derrick's invitation to come to San Francisco to meet the family he'd only recently discovered. Hell, the men had fallen all over themselves to welcome Jake into the Shay family, even hinted he might wish to drop his adopted name Curtis and accept the mantle of being a part of the Shay dynasty.

Then things had gone decidedly wrong. Clearly Derrick and Robert were cut from the same evil cloth.

"He's got some Shay blood for sure," Robert replied. "Couldn't have inherited that kind of courage from his whore of a mother."

Jake strained against his bonds, causing both of Derrick's beefy henchmen to grab him and Ty by the shoulders and push the two restrained men harder against the boulder.

"Grace isn't a whore!" Jake shouted, his words echoing off the cave walls. "Your brother raped her! He raped a fourteen-year-old girl!"

Derrick gave him a derisive snort, the only indication he'd even heard Jake's angry reply, accompanied by an exaggerated appraisal of the cave. "Look where she led you—where your greed and hers led you. You should have kept your head tucked low in Montana. Had you not sniffed out money that doesn't belong to you—"

"*You* sent for *me.*"

"Simply to assess the threat you posed to my fortune. Had you not risen to the bait, you and your friend would not be here. A shame you both will drown on your little...*fishing trip.* I imagine it might take days—even weeks—for your bodies to wash ashore. I shall be sure to claim any body parts the sharks leave untouched and send those pieces to your loving families."

Ty paid little attention to the conversation, focusing instead on finding any kind of plan to get him and Jake out of this mess. The tide was already coming in, the slowly rising water swirling around Derrick's ankles. Silently testing the strength of his restraints, Ty's already dwindling hopes fell. Good, tight knots in thick ropes.

"If you'll both excuse us." Derrick gave them a condescending bow. "We'll be on our way." A glance down to his sodden feet. "I fear I've already ruined a perfectly good pair of shoes, and my father is waiting to hear that these loose ends have been properly tied up." He clapped Robert on the shoulder. "You have assured your place in this dynasty, my friend. My father will not forget all you've done today, and your reward will be substantial."

"I'm pleased to help the senator in his time of need, and I am ready to sign the contracts that tie your family to mine." Robert bowed to Jake and Ty and picked up the lantern resting on a smaller rock. "I bid you both *adieu.*"

"As do I," Derrick added with a nod to his goons. "To the dingy."

Ty and Jake kept their silence as their four tormentors crawled into the boat and then labored to row out of the cave. They called back one last time, a laughing farewell that made him want nothing more than to be able to get his hands on his Colt. But it had been taken from him back at the Shay mansion.

As his eyes adjusted to the dim light that managed to come through the cave's entrance, he tried to think of any possible way out of the tangle. Not a single one came to mind.

"Can you get loose?" Jake leaned harder against Ty, pressing their backs firmly together. Fingers brushed across the ropes binding Ty's wrists.

"Nope. Can you get a grip at all?"

After several moments of frustrated struggling, Jake's hands drifted away. "Too cold to feel my fingers."

Wiggling his wrists and then his ankles, Ty finally sighed in resignation, his exhale hanging like a small cloud in the frigid air. "That, and I'm bound tight enough the blood's not even flowin'."

"I heard drowning's not a bad way to go."

"There's a *good* way?"

He hadn't meant to shout. Jake was merely speaking out of nervousness. He didn't want to die any more than Ty did. Jake had more to live for anyway. A wife, a daughter—both waiting back home in White Pines, Montana.

"Sorry, Jake."

"Don't apologize. Was a stupid thing to say. If we get through this, you know there'll be hell to pay with Emily."

"Your wife will be happy to tell you 'I told you so' for the rest of your miserable life."

"And I'll gladly listen."

The sounds of rocks tumbling down a hill, hitting ground, and then splashing into water shut them both up for a few strained moments.

"Hear that?" Ty whispered.

"Yep." Jake nodded toward a steep, rocky slope near the cave's entrance. "From there."

"Why would they come back?" The tide would keep rising, and if their captors returned, they'd likely be trapped in the cave's waters.

"Can't be them."

Ty waited a few more moments before the quiet became agonizing. "Must've been a sea lion." He could hardly contain the disappointment and near despair in his voice. "Damn, but I wish they hadn't found that knife in my boot."

The tension in his muscles almost unbearably taut, he pulled against his restraints again. That failing to have an impact, he rubbed his bindings against the rock, not caring that the tender skin scraped raw while the heavy ropes stood stalwart. It wasn't in his nature to go passively along with anything—let alone the Shay family's plans to murder him and Jake—but he was rapidly running out of ideas.

More rocks tumbled down the hill, the bounce and splash echoing off the cave's walls.

Squinting, he tried to focus on the top of the slope. A dark, slender figure formed at the peak. "Someone's there."

"I see him." Jake pushed back a little harder against Ty. "Friend or foe?"

"Can't decide, but I sure as hell am praying *friend*."

The shadow stepped over the edge and slid feet first down the mountain of rocks and shells, tempering the descent by dragging and shifting his weight down the slope before resting at the bottom in a crouch. Then he stepped into the stretch of deep water separating his perch from the boulders where they sat hog-tied.

Ty followed their visitor with his eyes as the man smoothly stroked across the still pool, cutting a V through the water, leaving ripples in his path. Reaching the opposite side, he pulled himself up onto the smooth stones before shaking the water from himself like a wet dog.

Thrilled that this was probably the only chance he and Jake had at rescue, Ty threw caution aside. Surely Shay's goons wouldn't have come back to possibly be imprisoned in the flooding cave, and he wasn't about to die at twenty-three. "Over here, mister! We're over here!"

The figure rose, standing to full height, slight though it was.

A woman. Their savior had come in the form of a thin woman dressed in only wet undergarments that were plastered against her skin. A long, dripping braid hung over her shoulder, and her breath raised small puffs around her face.

She stepped carefully across the rocks and shells. "I'm coming. Hang on." A colorful curse slipped out as she quickly jerked back her foot as if she'd stepped on something painful.

"Who *is* she?" Jake whispered.

"Don't rightly give a damn," Ty replied. "So long as she's got a knife."

"As a matter of fact, I have *two*," her sweet voice replied as she struggled to wade across the water surrounding the large boulder Ty and Jake sat upon.

When Shay's men had hoisted them there, the water reached their ankles. This woman found herself thigh-deep as she trudged closer.

Climbing the rocks with catlike dexterity, she knelt at Ty's side. She unsheathed a knife strapped to one shapely thigh.

This was a dream. That was the only way to explain the beautiful and decidedly ethereal spirit that graced his presence. He sat quietly, studying her as she worked at sawing through the ropes, and he wondered why he'd be dreaming that some goddess had come to their aid.

A smattering of freckles over the bridge of her nose fascinated him. Her braid swayed against her chest and arms as she worked. The color appeared black in the dim light. Instead of wasting precious time pushing her hair back, she flipped her head, sending the heavy plait flying like a whip. Her skin was pale as milk, almost ghostly white against the grey of her wet and mud-smeared undergarments. A lithe body. Long, slender arms.

"Who *are* you?" he finally asked. Hoping to break the spell she'd woven around him, he put his mind away from the temptation kneeling at his side and focused on getting him and Jake out of the cave.

She didn't reply, answering him instead with another curse he seldom heard from women, especially one so dainty and feminine.

"What happened?" he asked.

"Took a chunk out of my thumb." She wiped that thumb against her soaked pantalets, leaving a trail of blood behind. The sea water seeping into that wound had to hurt like fire, but she never complained and returned to hacking and sawing at the ropes.

Jake squirmed against him, and just as Ty was about to see if it might be better to turn the knife over to him and let him have a go, a loud snap echoed through the cave. The rescuer grabbed a second knife sheathed to her other thigh and handed it to Jake, who fumbled with it for a moment before he set to working on his bound ankles.

His wrists free from Jake's, Ty pulled and tugged to get the ropes loose so he could use his hands. Ice-cold fingers refused to obey his commands.

"Here, let me," the woman said. She jerked at the ropes until his hands were free. Her small hands encased him, rubbing gently to return the circulation. "You're so cold."

Her skin felt like silk, and her touch, although cool, had turned his tongue so thick, he couldn't even reply.

She released him and slid down the boulder where she turned to face him. The water lapped against her hips now. Carefully pushing the knife between his ankles, she worked to free him, not even whispering a complaint about the agonizing chill of the water.

About to offer his thanks, Ty glanced down at his savior and the words froze in his throat. The view was exquisite, causing a low growl to rumble from his chest. Her clothes molded to her body, revealing her tempting shape. Thin but muscled thighs. Rounded hips. A narrow waist. Her breasts strained against the thin cotton, the dark outline of her nipples making his body respond despite the entirely inappropriate circumstances. About to snatch the knife away to give him something to do besides ogle his rescuer, Ty breathed a sigh when the ropes separated. With a triumphant cry, she glanced up.

Large eyes held him captive. The color was masked by the darkness—but they were light, either blue or green. Framed by black lashes, those eyes dominated a round face. When she smiled up at him, dimples creased both cheeks.

She was exquisite. He would have been content to stare at her forever had the water not continued to rise.

The woman grabbed his hand and pulled. "We have to go. Now."

Jake had waded over to stand next to her. "Who are you?"

She flipped her braid over her shoulder one more time. "Pray let me introduce myself. I am Cassandra Shay. I have come to rescue you."

Chapter Two

Cassandra Shay.

Ty was absolutely speechless.

Jake, on the other hand, waded over until he towered over Cassandra. Hands on his hips, he glared down at her with hard, angry eyes. Their rescuer never flinched, nor did she take a telling step back.

Damn, but she looked so small, so fragile. Yet her spine was obviously forged of steel.

"Cassandra Shay?" Jake's shout echoed through the cave.

"Actually, I prefer Cassie, if you'd be so kind."

Jake's scowl grew darker. "You're a *Shay?* Why in the hell are you helping us?"

Ty watched a mask of calm settle over Cassie's beautiful face and wondered why having a man a good foot taller bellowing at her would receive such a strange response. For some odd reason, her courage pleased him.

She met Jake's glare with wide eyes, but nothing else about her revealed any fear, except perhaps the way she clenched her hands together.

"I discovered what Derrick and Robert were planning," she replied. "I...I couldn't simply...leave you." Crossing her arms over her chest, she rubbed her upper arms as if trying to gain some warmth.

"You're a Shay!"

Watching Jake take out all his anger and frustration on Cassie didn't sit well. Ty's own anger rose in response. While he normally preferred to sit back and watch events unfold rather than jump in feet first, this time he couldn't take that tack. The need to protect her reached deep down inside him, finding a place both primitive and possessive. The cave was freezing, she was trembling—either from the chilly air or Jake's anger—and he couldn't tolerate her discomfort.

"I don't rightly care who she is. I want to get the hell outta this cave." Ty squeezed his body between Jake and Cassie, his chest moving Jake back while Cassie's hands fisted in the back of his damp flannel shirt. "She ain't the one who tied us up and left us here to die."

Jake's open mouth attested to his surprise.

"We must go." The soft voice behind him was accompanied by a few tugs on his shirt. "The tide is coming in. We must go now."

"Then let's go," Ty replied. He reached behind him to grasp one of Cassie's hands. It had changed from cool to icy-cold so quickly, he feared for her safety. "We need to get you outta here before you freeze to death."

"I may be small, but I am sturdier than I look." Her chin rose defiantly. "I found you, did I not?"

Ty found himself fascinated with her fancy speech, wondering if all rich young women spoke in such a fashion. He'd never known a woman like Cassie Shay.

"What I'd like to know is *why*," Jake growled. "You're in cahoots with Derrick, ain't you?" She wasn't even given time to reply. "This is just some game to you, ain't it?"

Since she didn't respond, Ty figured she found the questions either insulting or unworthy of a reply. Instead, she gently pulled her hand from his grasp and headed back to the pool of water. Wading in, she waved for them to follow. Without even waiting to see if they complied, she swam her way across.

What choice did they have but to trail after her?

The water's icy chill hit Ty hard, making him hiss for breath and setting his teeth to chattering. But he swam across, glancing back over his shoulder to be sure Jake was behind him and ignoring the drag of his heavy, wet clothes. By the time they all reached the opposite side, Cassie had already started to climb the tall rock and shell pile.

"Where you goin'?" Jake asked, his tone no less harsh.

Her head whipped around, sending her braid flying. "I intend to hie myself away from this wretched cave before I drown or freeze to death. You're quite welcome to follow." A dainty shrug. "You may, however, suit yourselves."

The friends exchanged worried frowns.

"Out of the fryin' pan?" Ty whispered.

"Right into the fire," Jake replied.

"Better to burn than drown."

A curt nod from Jake and the men hurried to follow Cassie, who now stood on the top of the large hill, arms folded over her chest as she shivered and obviously waited for them despite her threat.

Scrambling up the shifting wall of sand, shells, and rocks wasn't an easy task, and both men were out of breath by the time they reached the summit.

A bewitching smile crossed her blue lips as she watched them. "Not so easy as it appears, is it?"

Ty thought about grabbing her and kissing that sassy grin right off her face. He tried to catch his lost wind and ignore the cold seeping into his bones. Slender Cassie had to be suffering greatly from the cold, yet she never complained.

"Where now?" he asked between long sucks of cold air that made his chest ache.

She turned and pointed to a small opening in the wall that appeared narrow, dark, and utterly terrifying. "That tunnel leads to the surface."

"Tunnel?" The world suddenly started to close in on him, pressing closer and closer. His returning breath rushed out and refused to be replaced.

"More like a carved out cave." Cool fingers closed around his hand. "Are you unwell?"

The concerned tone of her voice broke through his terror, but he still couldn't catch his breath. How could he possibly force himself into that dark entrance? "I…I don't like to be…to be…in small places."

She nodded. "I understand. My momma feared small places as well. I wish I didn't have to take you through there, but… I fear no other way out of here exists. Except perhaps there." Another nod, this time toward the entrance their captors had used to leave. "We would find ourselves slammed against sharp rocks if we choose that route. I doubt any of us would survive."

He closed his eyes, clenched her hand, and tried to bring his panic under control. The fact that she spoke of them as if their fates were now entwined seemed a great comfort.

Jake slapped him hard on the shoulder. "He'll be fine."

Easy for you to say. He wasn't the one with nightmares of being buried alive almost every night.

That hole looked mighty small. Big enough for someone as slight as Cassie—but someone Ty's size? His shoulders would surely get stuck. Years from now they'd find his rotting corpse still wedged between stone walls. A shudder ripped through him.

Cassie gave Ty's hand a squeeze. "I shall take the lead. You may hold my ankle until we reach the surface." She looked to Jake. "You may bring up the rear."

A deep, shuddering breath did little to help Ty find his courage. "I…can't. Won't fit."

Her eyes narrowed, and the squeeze on his hand became the grip of challenge. "You *can*. And you will most assuredly fit. Trust my judgment. Your name is Ty Bishop. Correct, sir?"

She had to have learned that when she'd discovered Derrick Shay's plans, so he tossed her a brusque nod.

"Please look at me, Mr. Bishop."

That was about all he *could* do. "And?"

Her smile was downright cocky. "*And*, if a little bit of a girl such as me can do this, then a burly cowboy such as yourself can surely make his way out of this wretched dungeon."

Pride. How clever of her. The one thing that could get any man to face even his worst fear. Threaten to injure his precious pride.

"Fine," he snapped.

Her smile seemed as bright as a lighthouse beacon. "Think of it this way, sir. I got in here through that cave, so surely we can all make our way out the same route."

Hell, it would be better if he didn't *think* at all.

Without waiting for a response, Cassie jumped, grabbed the edge of the tunnel, and hauled herself up until she could enter.

Ty had never seen that kind of strength in a woman. Fragile creatures, he'd always thought—although Jake's mother, Grace, and his wife, Emily, certainly weren't fragile.

The hole was small enough Cassie could barely wiggle back around to stare down at Ty and Jake with her large, doe eyes. "I shall start climbing. Mr. Bishop, you may grab my ankle and follow." She quirked a brow at Jake. "Could you please make sure he keeps following?"

"What if he tries to turn around and go back?" Jake asked. "Ty don't like tight, dark spaces much. Tends to go a little loco."

Her smile grew until the only word to describe it was mischievous. "I assure you that will *not* be a problem."

"Why?" God help him, Ty couldn't keep from asking.

"Because you will find that you have insufficient room to turn around." On that chilly pronouncement, she began her assent, stopping when all that was still visible were her slender, white ankles and mud-covered feet. "Are you coming, sir?" Her muffled shout drifted down, the impatience in her voice plain.

With a grunt, Ty hoisted himself into what he prayed wasn't his tomb.

Cassie sighed, feeling guilty for the ordeal she'd have to put Ty Bishop through. The poor man was terrified.

She understood—closed spaces weren't what frightened her, but she truly understood fear. Her mother had explained why it bothered her, how she always felt as if the walls were slowly closing in until she couldn't draw a breath.

Oh, yes, she understood—the same terror assaulted Cassie whenever she thought about being forced to marry Robert Putnam.

If she hadn't stumbled across the plan to kill the two men she'd just rescued, she would already be miles away from San Francisco. Even now, her horse waited with Old Tim—the stablemaster she'd known her whole life. Now that she was so late, she prayed the man would still be waiting when she finally got to him. The plans had been so carefully made, surely he would know a couple of hours didn't make much difference. Her mare, Duchess, should be saddled, packed, and ready to make an escape.

If only her grandfather had listened to her. Or even her uncle. Neither gave much notice to women and their opinions. When they thought matches could bring them something, they didn't hesitate to marry the women in the Shay family off as though they were nothing more than chips in a high-stakes poker game.

Cassie had been lucky, making it to the ripe age of twenty-one without having been forced to take someone as a husband.

She didn't want to marry at all—*especially* not Robert Putnam. He was far too old for her. He had a mean streak a mile wide that she'd been unfortunate enough to experience firsthand. And he had a liking for any maid who came within arm's reach.

Married to Robert?

Not for all the Shay money.

Not for all the money in the world.

Once her grandfather announced the engagement, Cassie had secreted away as much money as she could while forming plans on where she could hide from the enormous reach of her relatives. A few destinations seemed promising, but before she could make up her mind, her uncle had moved up the wedding date. If she didn't flee now, she'd be forever bound to a man who would beat her and cheat on her. She couldn't abide him, and a marriage would mean she would never be able to bolt from the family whose actions disgusted her.

Preparing to leave, she'd almost been caught searching for maps in her grandfather's study. Hiding in a small cupboard, she'd overheard the threats being made against the two men who'd come from Montana—one of them claiming to be Stephen Shay's son. Not only had that news been a shock, but to also find out her uncle and Robert were planning to murder the men? In her heart, Cassie knew she couldn't live with herself if she didn't try to save them.

Now, she found herself climbing through the narrow cave she'd discovered years ago as she boldly explored the Shays' San Francisco holdings, helping two men she didn't even know. She almost grumbled to herself when she felt Ty's cool fingers that had held tight to her ankle slip away. The walls on either side were too close for her to turn to check, not that she could see anything anyway. The tunnel was pitch-black.

"Don't let go, sir," she demanded.

"Get me out of here!"

"Hold on to me. We've almost reached the end. I promise." Cassie extended her leg until her bare toes brushed against what felt like his arm. "Please, sir. Hold onto me. *Please*. Let me lead us out of here to safety, just as I promised."

"I hate it! I want outta here! Now!"

The panic in his voice reached her heart. Something about the man had called to her from the moment she saw him. "Calm yourself. I *will* get you out," she crooned as if talking to Duchess when she'd spooked. "I promise. Trust me. Please. We're almost there. Just hang on to me, and I shall make haste."

Fingers brushed against her leg, sliding up to her knee before digging painfully into the flesh of her thigh. The man was terrified, so she didn't scold him. A bruise or two and some improper familiarity wouldn't kill her. His breaths were loud, frantic, so she moved her leg, silently urging him to follow. Thank the Lord, he did.

The first rays of light dotted her vision, and she smiled. "See the light? We've almost reached the end."

The hand on her leg tightened, but Ty didn't reply.

Cassie hauled herself up and out of the entrance to the tunnel, a difficult task considering the death grip the man held on her leg.

He followed her up and out, collapsing on the rocks.

"Careful, Mr. Bishop," she said. "We are quite close to a cliff."

Blue eyes stared back at her—far too handsome blue eyes. His light brown hair was still wet and mussed, a bit longer than she normally preferred. His face was hard with sculpted lines that reminded her of the marble busts she'd seen in museums.

For the first time in her life, she found herself attracted to a man.

A curse almost slipped from her lips, the type she liked to say when no one could hear. Ladies weren't supposed to use common words, but sometimes letting one of the harsher ones loose took away some of her tension. Her grandfather would be scandalized if he heard her use such vulgarity. That thought only made the digression sweeter.

A crude word would serve to remind her that this was neither the time nor place to be suffering from some foolish, girlish infatuation. She'd done well by these men, getting them out of the cave before they drowned in the tide as her uncle and Robert had planned. She owed them nothing more. The time had come to take care of her own problems.

The other man—Jake Curtis—was her half-brother and would most assuredly hate her the moment he knew that, judging from what he said about what their father had done to his mother. She believed him, of course. Her father had been ruthless—just like *his* father. Her mother had tried her best to shelter Cassie from their wraths and the constant meddling of her other male relatives. But the frail women simply couldn't match the Shays.

Jake made it out of the tunnel and collapsed at his friend's side with an exhausted grunt.

Gathering the clothes she'd left behind earlier into her arms, she held them against her chest. She'd considered how indecent she would look when she'd stripped to her undergarments, but the weight of her gown in the water might have drowned her. The silly thing would have probably gotten her stuck in the tunnel.

Trying to shield herself from their gazes, she pressed the clothes to her body. "I shall leave you gentlemen now." Her words shook with her shivers.

Would she ever be warm again?

Ty leveled a frown at her that stung, considering what she'd done for him. "Leave?" he demanded in a harsh tone.

"Yes, Mr. Bishop, *leave*. Not that it's any of your concern, but I need to be on my way. Should my uncle—"

"Derrick Shay's your uncle?" Jake asked.

Cassie nodded. She didn't want to get into a discussion of familial ties, nor did she want to delay her escape a moment longer because a new fear suddenly gripped her heart—fear that if she didn't force herself to leave soon, walking away from Ty Bishop would become more and more difficult. "Yes. But I must go and—"

"Go? Go where?" Ty slowly got to his feet. "Back to the Shay mansion? Your uncle will whup you good for helping us."

"He shall not even know."

"No? How else could we possibly have gotten outta that tomb?"

She shook her head, her still-wet braid brushing against her back, sending more shivers down her spine. Her underclothes were soaked. With the sun setting, the autumn air was growing decidedly chillier, and she was already dangerously cold. She wouldn't start dressing in front of Ty and Jake. It had been bad enough they'd already seen her camisole and pantalets plastered against her body. "They surely believe you're both dead."

"There'll be someone watching," Jake insisted as he also rose from the rocky ground. "You know a Shay ain't gonna leave nothin' to chance. He'll want to be sure we're dead. When the tide goes out and no bodies float away, Shay will know someone got to us. And it ain't gonna take much for him to figure out that someone was *you*."

"It will not make a difference. I shall be long away from here by—"

"Away?" Ty bellowed.

"If you would pray stop interrupting me with your shouts, Mr. Bishop, I will explain." She gave him a chastising frown.

His blue eyes narrowed, but the corners of his mouth twitched into a halting smile. "By all means then, *Miss Shay*…"

"I had already made plans to leave. I shall not stay in San Francisco long enough to incur my uncle's wrath."

With that, she turned to walk away from the cliffs, praying silently that Old Tim still waited with Duchess, that he hadn't decided she'd changed her plans and put the mare back in her stall.

It was getting dark, but she could still cover enough miles before the darkest hours to get her a good distance away from San Francisco—away from her grandfather, away from her uncle, and away from that hideous Robert Putnam.

A strong hand wrapped around her upper arm, dragging her to a stop. "Where are you goin'?"

She whirled to face Ty, angry and afraid her escape wouldn't work. Tears stung her eyes. "I don't believe that is any of your concern, sir."

"*Where?*" he demanded, his features growing stern.

"It is not your concern!" Cassie had to tamp down the urge to let him see her sometimes gloriously hot temper.

Ladies didn't shout. Yet the more she thought about what she faced, the more she could feel her panic rising. The men were right—her uncle would surely know she'd let his intended victims free. Punishment in the Shay family was swift and severe, and she had no intention of getting caught.

"You saved our lives. We owe you a blood debt."

She shook her head. "You owe me nothing."

Jake stood to her other side, his big hand settling on her shoulder. "A woman shouldn't be travelin' alone. Let us escort you—make sure you get safely to where you're going."

"But I don't *know* where I'm going!" Her hand flew to cover her errant mouth.

She hadn't meant to confess that, and now that the words were past her lips, neither man would allow her to leave on her own. They might be rough-around-the-edges cowboys, but they were men. And no man would allow a young woman to venture off alone, especially when she had no idea of her destination.

Ty stared down at Cassie, not sure why her fear should hit him so hard. But it did.

Damn, this wasn't a good time to find himself drawn to a woman. He'd never been much of a ladies' man. Hell, he hadn't been a ladies' man *at all*. A tumble now and again with a clean whore pleased to take his money was the extent of his experience with the fairer sex.

As he held tight to Cassie Shay's arm, he knew there was something different about this woman—something that called to tender feelings he'd wondered if he even possessed. Now, he knew they were there, and this woman was the one to drag those emotions to the surface.

A Shay. She was a *Shay!* How in the hell was he supposed to react to that?

Hazel. Her eyes weren't green or blue. They were hazel, reminding Ty of the summer grass on the prairie.

There was no way on God's green earth he'd allow her to head out alone. Didn't she realize the danger?

Probably not. She was a Shay and had probably been sheltered and pampered her whole life.

"We're going with you," he insisted. "Don't matter if you want us to or not."

The woman thought it over a good, long while before she nodded. Instead of speaking, she dropped her clothes and began to tug them on.

Jake politely turned his back and tried to squeeze the water out of his shirt.

Ty stood where he was, mesmerized by the sight of her rolling a stocking up her shapely leg.

She suddenly stopped. "You may turn your back, sir."

"Bossy bit of fluff," he mumbled as he did what she asked.

By God, the girl had plenty of grit. While he waited for her to dress, he tugged his shirt from his denims and wrung it to squeeze out whatever water he could, which wasn't much. The damp, cold clothes would probably make him catch his death, but he wasn't about to return to the Shay mansion to retrieve his other belongings.

"There are some dry clothes in the stables," Cassie said. "You may turn around now, gentlemen. If you would be so kind as to follow me…"

She marched away before either man could answer.

"Yep," Jake said, giving Ty a hard slap on the shoulder. "You're right. She's a bossy bit of fluff. So do we follow?"

"Oh, hell, yeah. Not letting that filly outta my sight."

Jake's laugh must have reached Cassie because she suddenly stopped and glanced back over her shoulder. "Have you changed your minds then?"

The relief in her voice hit Ty like a slap, but he also saw it as a challenge. Instead of responding, he gave her a shake of his head and savored the frown she tossed back at him.

Marching away again, she never looked back to see if they followed.

Chapter Three

"Thank God!" Cassie spied Old Tim standing in the barn door, holding a lantern and peering out into the growing darkness. Waving her arms, she tried to get his attention. "Over here, Old Tim!"

"Old Tim?" Jake asked.

Why she felt the need to explain herself to the men who trailed her like bounty hunters was beyond her. "His son's name is also Tim. Old Tim. Young Tim. The names are simply a habit we adopted."

"Miss Cassie? That be you?" Old Tim held the lantern higher, but he'd never see her from such a distance. His eyesight had been fading for years.

"Yes, yes. It's me. I have two friends escorting me, so please don't be frightened." The man was clearly nervous, and she didn't want him to panic when he saw the men who'd followed her to the barn. Despite what she'd said, she had every intention of leaving without their gallant escort. She didn't need their help. She could find her way in this world alone.

"Lord above, I was worried 'bout you!"

"I know. I was…delayed. I came to get Duchess and my things."

"It's past dark now. You're still planning on leavin', girl?" He reached for her hand as she hurried to the door.

Ty and Jake stood a few feet behind her, both rigid enough she easily picked up on their tension, especially when she placed her hand in Old Tim's. He gave her a hard squeeze, at least as hard as his arthritic fingers could manage.

"Yes, I shall still be leaving tonight."

"*We're* still leaving." Ty's voice was as harsh as the winter wind.

She turned to Ty, who had taken a step closer behind her, hands set against his hips as he hovered over her like some avenging angel. "It's quite all right, sir. There really is no need for you to follow me. Old Tim will help me now. You may go home now instead of accompanying me."

"Oh, I *may*, may I?"

The condescension in Ty's voice raised her temper, but she was a lady, so she quickly put a lid on her annoyance.

He inclined his head at Old Tim. "He won't be telling everyone about us?"

"Of course not." Cassie turned back to the stablemaster. "These men were never here. Do you understand? My uncle would… Please, Old Tim. They were never here."

He squinted as he stared at them, sizing them up as he did a prized horse.

They stared back, and she wondered what they thought of the gray-haired man in the rough clothing. To her, he looked like the grandfather she'd always wished she'd had in place of the one who'd tormented her all these years.

After a few moments, Old Tim tossed Ty and Jake a curt nod. Then he directed a fatherly glare at her. "At least wait 'til light."

If she gave him the chance, Old Tim could eventually talk her out of her plan. It hadn't seemed so rash until the moment of leaving arrived. Having Jake—and especially Ty—nodding along with the stablemaster's order to wait, she knew they could easily wear down her resolve if she gave them half a chance.

Why could they escape and not allow her to do the same simply because she was female?

Then she pictured Robert's face and thought about spending the rest of her life married to the man. "I must leave tonight. Nothing has changed. Nothing will *ever* change. Please, you mustn't worry about me. I shall be fine. There's sufficient light for me to get away from this place. I promise to stop should I feel Duchess cannot find her way."

Picturing a clearing where she could start a cozy fire, Cassie firmed her resolve. She could do this. She *would* do this.

"You decide where you headin', girl?" Old Tim asked as he still warily eyed Ty and Jake. "You ain't goin' alone now?"

She shrugged. A few destinations came to mind, but she'd planned on visiting at least two before she decided. Planning to spend the rest of her life in a distant place, one couldn't afford to make hasty decisions.

Crossing to her tethered horse, she ran her hands over the pack attached to the back of the saddle.

"Did you put in a flint?" she asked, ignoring the way all the men frowned at her. "I'm chilled through. I can start a fire when I stop for the night."

Her fingers brushed the tight roll of money and the Bible she'd hidden in the men's clothing. She'd folded everything up in the bedroll she'd left for Old Tim to pack. As soon as she got away from here, she could change into her disguise, and she'd have money to aid her flight. The Bible had been a gift from her mother, and not a day passed without her reading it.

Pretending to be a boy would be easy enough. The thought of what she had to do to her hair was the only thing that troubled her. But vanity was a sin, so she'd hack it off as soon as she donned her male masquerade. Hopefully, it would grow back once she found herself settled.

She reached under her skirts to pull out the knife she'd tied to her thigh and quickly slid in between her clothes. The other knife rested against the small of Jake's back, last she'd noticed. Probably not worth the battle sure to erupt should she ask for its return.

Ty glared at her. "Good plan, lady. Start a fire burnin'. Send up a signal to everyone within miles. Are you wantin' to get robbed?" His angry eyes raked her from head to toe, making her feel for a moment as if she stood before him naked. Her face flushed hot. "Or worse…"

A shiver raced through Cassie—and not because her underclothing was still damp. Images of the fate that could await a woman without an escort flashed through her mind, but she simply strengthened her resolve. She could defend herself. Why, she'd even learned to use a gun thanks to Old Tim. Besides, no one would know she was a woman.

"You needn't worry about me, sir. I'll be fine." Her tone sounded nervous, even to her, and she hated showing them any weakness.

"You ain't goin' alone," Jake pronounced before he glanced over to Old Tim. "We had horses when we got here. They in this barn?"

Old Tim nodded. "Got two new horses this morning. A bay and a paint. They yours?"

"Those would be ours," Jake replied. "Which stalls?"

"Down that row. Master Derrick told me they be horses he bought. Never trusted that bast—" He gave Cassie a worried frown. "Sorry, girl. Keep forgettin' he be yer uncle."

"No harm," she replied. "'Tis not the first time I have heard that name applied to Uncle Derrick. Nor, do I dare say, shall it be the last."

She turned to Ty. "You should go get your horses. You will also find dry clothing hanging in the tack room, should you wish to change before you ride out." If he and Jake were occupied with saddling their animals and getting into dry clothes, perhaps she could—

A strong arm encircled her wrist as Ty dragged her down the aisle of the barn.

She stumbled to keep up with the fast pace.

"Not letting you leave without us," he said. "And don't think, lady, that I don't know what you had planned. I can read that pretty face like a damned book."

Pretty face?

Ty thought she was pretty?

A smile broke out on her lips before she could contain her response.

He hauled her back to where Jake had taken the two horses out of their stalls and tied them to the gates. The paint already had a blanket and saddle thrown on his back. She guessed the bay was Ty's.

"May I ask his name?" she inquired.

"Horse," Ty replied. "He is what he is. Don't rightly need any other name."

"That's quite sad." Cassie stroked the horse's soft muzzle. "A proper mount needs a proper name."

As he smoothed a woven blanket over the animal's back, Ty chuckled. "So like a woman. Making somethin' easy into somethin' complicated."

"Duke," she blurted out before she could stop herself. "I believe I shall call him Duke."

After setting the saddle in place, he tugged at the cinch while he frowned at her. "Duke? Why Duke?"

She shrugged, not wanting to admit it was to match her Duchess. Such a childish and entirely silly thing for her to do, and she wasn't about to admit her folly. Lord, she'd probably never see the man again once she was able to get away on her own.

Why did that thought make her sad?

"Her mare be Duchess," Old Tim tattled when he came to stand by her side. "Makes this stallion her mate."

Traitor.

She stumbled to cover her embarrassment. "I–it merely seemed a fitting name for such a–a proud animal."

Since the men weren't changing into dry clothes, she wondered if she could find something suitable in the tack room. Perhaps if she changed now…

Ty stopped his work to gape at first at the old man and then at Cassie Shay.

Why in the devil did her deciding to name his horse to match her mare send a wave of pleasure over him? The woman was rapidly turning his brain to gruel. If the three of them were going to get away from the Shays, they'd need his wits—and Jake's—at their sharpest. Perhaps she had some intelligence as well. At least as much as any woman could possess. They were, after all, a frilly, shallow lot.

Although she *had* found a way to get him and Jake out of the cave...

They'd escort her wherever she wanted to go—assuming she ever revealed where that was. One thing was damned sure—she wouldn't be riding out of here alone.

"Did you wish to change your clothes?" she asked, a hopeful tone to her voice. "The tack room—" she pointed to her left, "—has many shirts and trousers. No doubt you will find something suitable."

"Nah," Jake called from behind his horse. "No need. I'm getting' dry. I wanna get the hell away from here as fast as we can."

Ty nodded.

"B–but, you're both wet. Surely you'd wish to—"

"Her horse ready?" Ty asked Old Tim.

The stablemaster nodded.

"Get on your horse, lady. Time to ride."

"But...but..." She wrung her hands as she sputtered her protest.

"Told you," Ty interrupted, assuming she'd try to talk them out of following her again, "you ain't riding out alone. Get on your horse. We're leavin'."

Whirling around fast enough her skirts billowed around her legs, she stomped toward the tack room she'd pointed to. "I have to change first."

"Change?"

She slammed the door on his question.

The sound of shuffling made him turn to quirk an eyebrow at Jake.

His friend's response was a grin and a shake of his head—probably because he was used to dealing with a woman and sympathized with Ty's plight.

"What's she up to now?" Ty finally asked Old Tim.

"I reckon she's changing to some boy clothes. Wears 'em when she's out exploring or ridin'."

Ty tried to picture slender Cassie dressed as a boy. As if she could ever pull off the ruse. Everything about her screamed femininity. No man in his right mind could overlook her...attributes. Of course most men hadn't been blessed with a view of Cassie Shay in wet underwear, either. That image—the tempting swell of her breasts and the gentle curve of her hips—would be forever branded on his brain. The simple thought of another male seeing her charms made his blood boil, and if that wasn't the damnedest thing...

Her face poked out from the door she cracked open. "Old Tim?"

"Yes, girl?"

"Can you please fetch me a sharper knife? Mine is a bit dull for my task."

As Old Tim hurried to hand her a rather large hunting knife he had sheathed at his side, Ty turned a worried look to Jake. "Knife?" he asked as Cassie slammed the door shut.

Jake's face bore a concerned frown. "Not sure what she's up to."

"It's that hair of hers," Old Tim said, pointing to his own gray hair. "She be wantin' to get rid of that long hair."

In fast strides, Ty reached the tack room and slammed the door open with his shoulder.

Cassie, who had been sitting on a barrel and pressing the sharp edge of the knife to her braid, jumped to her feet. "Jesus, Mary, and Joseph! You scared the life out of me."

Not even caring about her words, he hit her wrist with his forearm hard enough to knock the knife from her hand.

As it clattered to the floor, she cried out, clutching her abused wrist to her chest and cradling it with her other hand. "You hurt me."

He felt like a brute, but the thought of her cutting off her braid had twisted his stomach into knots. "I'm sorry. I just... Why in the devil would you want to cut off all that hair?"

Cassie glanced down to the men's clothing she now wore. "I needed a disguise to keep safe." Still holding her hand against her chest, she flipped her head enough to make the braid whip in the air. "I do believe I might have some difficulty disguising myself as a boy with this trailing down my back. Don't you agree?"

He snorted. "No one with half a brain would ever believe *you're* a man."

She gasped. "Why, I... I believe I make a very nice boy."

"Lady, there ain't a thing about you that ain't downright—" God, he was an idiot. He'd almost blurted out just how pretty she was, and he wasn't about to hand that kind of power over to any woman.

"That *ain't* what, Mr. Bishop?"

"Don't say that."

"Say what?"

"Ain't. You were brought up better than me. Don't like hearing you use ignorant words."

Those large eyes stared at Ty as if she had no idea what to make of him. "Then since you seem determined to keep me from cutting my hair—" she rubbed her wrist to probably make him feel guiltier, "—what exactly do you suggest I do with it?"

His eyes scanned the room before settling on a tweed cap hanging from a nail. He grabbed it and moved to stand in front of her. Lifting her braid, he held it on top of her head as he put the cap on her.

"There," he said, stepping back. "Now you look like a...boy." He choked on the last word, knowing she'd never be anything but a beautiful woman to him. Perhaps she could fool a few others, though.

"I thought you said—"

"Enough. We're leaving." He picked the knife up, grabbed her belt, and slid the knife under it so she could keep it close. Then he took her injured wrist, pulled it until she had to take a step closer to him, and looked to see if he'd really hurt her. There were no bruises, only a small red mark where his arm had hit.

He felt terrible. Never in his days had he struck a woman. But the thought of Cassie cutting her long hair made him lose his senses.

Cradling her hand in both of his, he rubbed his thumb over her wrist. "I'm sorry. Didn't mean to hurt you none."

She just looked up at him, a flush rising on her cheeks.

"Feelin' better?" Ty couldn't make himself stop caressing her soft skin.

Teeth tugging on her bottom lip, she nodded. But she never tried to pull away, only kept those incredibly beautiful eyes fixed on him.

He pulled a little until she was only a hand's breadth away. As he rubbed her wrist, his fingers came perilously close to the rough shirt she wore, close to the swell of her breasts. She seemed oblivious to his trespass, keeping him mesmerized with her gaze. He wanted to kiss her. He *needed* to kiss her.

Slowly, giving her a chance to resist, he lowered his head to hers.

Her eyes widened before closing as she leaned in closer, rising on tiptoes.

The moment their lips touched, the door slammed open again.

"What's keeping you?" Jake shouted before he fell silent.

Cassie had taken a step back, and her hand had gently withdrawn. Her face was tinted by a blush, and she shyly stared at the floor.

Jake's gaze shifted from Ty to Cassie then back again. "Sorry I interrupted."

Throwing his friend a shake of the head, hoping he'd drop the whole thing, Ty stomped out of the tack room and headed to his horse.

This trip was a bad idea—a *terrible* idea. He'd realized that the moment he'd recognized just how drawn to Cassie he was, when he recognized that this woman was different than any other woman he'd known.

That was his problem! She fascinated him because she was *different*. That explained the pull and the desire that twisted his gut. She was simply different.

Ty kept telling himself that ridiculous lie as he watched her hurry to the front of the barn, Old Tim right behind. He mounted his horse, turned to be sure Jake followed, then nudged Duke—damn, but he'd already accepted that silly name—to get him to move. As he passed Cassie, he caught the tears in her eyes as she spoke in low tones to the stablemaster.

"God be with you, girl." Old Tim helped her mount her mare.

"You have been so good to me." She sniffled as she reached down to take his hand. "Please remember me."

The old man's eyes filled with tears. "I could never forget you, Miss Cassie. You be like my own grandchild."

"I love you," she choked out. Then she slapped Duchess with the reins and trotted out of the barn, never looking back.

Her shoulders shook, probably because she was weeping. About to go after her, Ty stopped when Old Tim grabbed Duke's reins.

"You be good to that girl," he warned. "I can see the fire 'tween you. You be good to my girl."

"I will," Ty said with a nod before he gave his horse a nudge with his heels and followed after Cassie.

Chapter Four

Cassie reined in Duchess when the horse shifted nervously. She wanted nothing more than to throw herself out of the saddle and rub the ache out of her abused backside. She'd always considered herself an accomplished rider, but holding a saddle well wasn't the same thing as riding for extended periods. The stories of the cowboys in the dime novels she'd dared to read always spoke of adventure and daring.

They never mentioned sore backsides or legs as wobbly as strawberry jelly.

As the sun rose on the horizon, Ty and Jake talked softly enough she couldn't make out their words. They'd purposely placed themselves several yards away, saying that they needed to discuss *something*.

More like someone...me.

So like men—excluding women from important plans, telling them who they should marry and how they should live. Her grandfather and uncle had simply called her to the study and told her she would marry Robert Putnam in three months' time.

Shifting uncomfortably in her saddle, Cassie thought about forcing her way between Ty's and Jake's horses and interrupting. They were, after all, discussing what the next leg of this journey would be. She had her own plans, but she'd only be able to fulfill them if she could get away from her stubborn escorts. Then she could follow her dream, go to a nice unsettled area, and start a farm of her own. She'd raise animals and tend her own garden in peace and solitude, away from the intense scrutiny she'd always known. Away from the ridiculous demands of her family. Away from Robert Putnam.

People seemed to envy her because she was a Shay and her family was wealthy. She never considered it a blessing, only a curse. She couldn't be herself or follow her own desires and dreams because her family dictated every move she made. She was sick to death of it.

Marry Robert Putnam?

She'd sooner join a convent.

Do convents take Presbyterians?

Ty and Jake nodded and shook hands, making her wonder how soon she could start her trip toward her ultimate destination. The hours she'd spent on horseback had given her time to narrow down her choices. She could settle in the most exciting of her possible new homes—the Dakotas.

Before she could consider things for too long, Jake turned his horse, gave it a gentle kick, and rode away.

She could only gape as Ty trotted Duke over to where she waited. "May I ask where Jake is going?"

"North."

"And pray tell, where are *you* going?"

"East."

He nudged his horse, moving back toward the barely visible road where he trotted away, not even looking over his shoulder to see if she followed.

Cassie stayed as still as a statue. If Ty intended to ride away, she wouldn't stop him. The thought of him leaving made her stomach roil, but she tried to lie to herself and blame the nausea on the fact she hadn't eaten for almost a full day. A betraying tear slipped down her cheek, but she quickly wiped it away with her sleeve.

This was what she wanted—to be alone and make her own way in the world.

Wasn't it?

About to turn Duchess and head back toward the last town they'd passed through an hour ago, she was surprised to see Ty tug his reins to stop his horse.

"C'mon, lady. We need to get movin'."

He isn't leaving me.

That thought brought a smile to her face. Until she remembered she wanted him to leave.

Didn't she?

Sweet Lord, she didn't know *what* she wanted anymore. Fatigue bore down on her, and more tears threatened.

Ty came trotting back to throw a tight-lipped frown at her. "We gotta get movin'."

"I shall be glad to decide whether to follow you or not just as soon as you explain why Mr. Curtis has gone one direction and you are going another."

"Look, lady—"

"My name is Cassie. Actually, *Miss Shay* might be more appropriate under the circumstances. But I'll settle for Cassie."

The man rolled his eyes heavenward as if seeking divine guidance in dealing with her. Since she'd see that reaction more times and from more people than she cared to remember, she waited patiently for him to get past his annoyance and answer her.

"All right, *Cassie*. Jake's heading north, and we're going east to make sure we ain't followed."

"You're afraid of my uncle."

Ty's hand shot out to grab Duchess's reins, and he jerked the horse close enough that Cassie's thigh pressed up against his. "Get it straight right now, lady. I ain't afraid of no man."

"I told you more than once, sir, my name is—"

Her words were smothered when he cupped her neck and dragged her close enough to settle his mouth on hers.

This wasn't the kind of kiss Robert had stolen in the garden. No simple touching of lips. Ty ground his mouth against hers, demanding her surrender. She sighed, leaned closer, and slipped her hands to his shoulders.

He growled, grabbed her by the waist, and pulled her from her horse onto his lap.

Instead of gentling the kiss, he ravaged her mouth. And it felt magnificent.

Her blood turned to molten lava, racing through her veins and pooling low in her belly. She couldn't catch her breath, and her heart slammed hard enough, he surely felt it against his chest.

Something deep and primitive in Ty surged up when he realized Cassie had never been properly kissed. He'd wanted to kiss her from the first moment he saw her, despite the entirely inappropriate location. The kiss he'd tried to steal in the barn had left his nerves frayed, and that pouty pink mouth of hers had tortured him. Once she started scolding him about what he called her, he gave in to the urge mostly to shut her up. Now that he had her in his arms, he intended to take full advantage. The moment his lips touched hers, his body responded, tightening and hardening with desire.

His tongue teased the seam of her lips, but she didn't seem to understand what he wanted. He nipped at her bottom lip. As her lips parted in a gasp, his tongue surged inside her warm, sweet mouth. His tongue caressed hers until her hesitation disappeared and she kissed him back. She didn't know what she was doing, but he was just the man to teach her.

Slender arms looped around his neck, and Cassie pressed her chest against his. She tasted like more.

He gave her tongue a gentle suck, coaxing her to follow his back into his mouth. And God, how was he supposed to bring a halt to this if she kept stroking his neck, tugging on his hair, and flattening her breasts against him?

He snatched the cap from her head, letting her long braid escape its restraints. He wanted to untie it and spread that hair over her shoulders. Was it curly? Straight? Soft as it appeared?

Dredging up strength he didn't know he possessed, Ty finally pulled back. When she followed with her mouth, he gave her one more hard kiss to show her how much she pleased him. He reached for her wrists and slowly tugged her arms from around his neck.

Cassie stared up at him, appearing bemused. Her lips were wet and red, begging him to kiss her again.

He swallowed his desire and smirked at her. "Now that I've got you quiet…"

Damn, but the woman was pretty when she got riled. Judging from the fire shooting from her eyes, she was furious.

"You will *not* be taking those liberties again, Mr. Bishop."

"Oh, but I promise you, Miss Shay, I *will*." She tried to squirm out of his lap, but all she succeeded in doing was enflaming him more. "Just sit still and listen."

She folded her arms under her breasts. "Fine. Now if you would be so kind, please tell me why we had to separate from Mr. Curtis and where exactly you plan on taking us."

At least she was saying *us* now instead of *you*. "If the Shays are following, they're looking for two men or two men with a woman. Not one man traveling alone or a man and his…" He snorted a laugh. "… little brother."

"And where are this man and his…*little brother* traveling to?"

"White Pines."

"I beg your pardon?"

"I'm taking you to White Pines. Where I live. We'll catch up with Jake there."

She threw a worried glance to Duchess. "Where is White Pines?"

"Montana Territory."

Putting both hands against his chest she tried to push herself away. He held on tight until she stopped resisting.

"But–but you cannot expect me to go to Montana." Another worried glance to her mare. "That must be at least five hundred miles away. How can the horses—"

"We're catchin' a train soon."

A yawn slipped from her, big enough to make her whole body shake.

Ty couldn't resist. He kissed her forehead. All she did in response was yawn again, her mouth wide enough he could see her back teeth. "Can you keep those sleepy eyes open for another hour or two, Cassie?"

Just as he suspected, her spine grew a little straighter. "I can stay alert as long as you need me to, Mr. Bishop."

"Ty. Call me Ty."

Cassie shook her head, but he grabbed her chin and brushed a quick, no-nonsense kiss over her lips. "Call me Ty."

"As you wish. *Ty.*"

He jostled her around to settle her back on her horse. Then he handed her the cap.

She tucked her braid up and pulled the tweed cap over her head.

With a firm nod, he turned Duke and started the short ride to where they could catch the train, listening intently for her to follow.

***

Ty helped get Duchess settled in next to Duke on the almost empty livestock car. His bay sidled up to Cassie's white, pushing her toward the side and snorting at a gelding in the adjoining stall that sniffed at her through the slats in the wood divider.

How odd that his stallion seemed every bit as protective of the mare as he felt about Cassie.

Perhaps his horse was wiser than he was by not fighting the attraction.

Having given Cassie what little cash he had left to purchase their tickets, Ty wanted to make sure the horses would be well cared for before he went to find her. Assured they had water, hay, and enough room to bed down, he walked down the wooden plank and back toward the station.

Winding his way back to the ticket office, he found Cassie counting out bills from an enormous roll of money.

"Jesus Christ," he muttered to himself. Stomping over to her, he grabbed the cash, ignoring her indignant expression. "Are you loco?"

She stared up at him with curious eyes. "I beg your pardon?"

He shoved the money into her coat pocket before pulling the cap lower over her face. "Flashing money 'round like you're the damn queen of England. Beggin' to get robbed is what you're doing."

"I most certainly was not flashing my money—"

Ty grabbed the tickets the clerk was holding and shoved them at her. "Get what you wanted?"

Pushing them back toward him, she frowned. "Since it's obvious you have little faith in my judgment, should you not check them yourself?"

He waved the tickets off and tried to give her a stern frown, but all she did was grin in return.

So much for intimidating her.

"Check the tickets, Cassie."

With a resigned sigh, she scanned the top ticket before she slipped it under the second. "They seem to be in order. Sleeping berth number—"

"Berth? I can't afford to buy us both berths. I told you day car seats."

She pulled the few folded dollars he'd handed her when he sent her to buy the tickets out of her pocket. "I used my own money, sir, and I–I assumed we would *share* a berth. We must stay close. In–in case we encounter trouble." Her cheeks flushed. "I assure you I can afford—"

"Oh, I know what *you* can afford."

Resisting the urge to shout at her that he'd walk the entire way to Montana rather than ride with a ticket paid for by Shay money, he bit back his harsh words. Cassie could barely keep her eyes open, yawning every other minute. If they traveled in a day car, she wouldn't get much rest. And it wasn't as if her disguise was all that good. By cozying up in the same berth, he could keep a watch over her while she got some sleep away from prying eyes. Perhaps he could catch a nap as well.

She'd only bought one berth. Could that mean she wanted to be close to him as well?

"Fine," he blurted out.

With a victorious smile he wanted to kiss right off her face, she led him to the car.

An attendant looked at the tickets then motioned for them to follow him inside. Once he reached one of the booths, he stopped. The curtains had been pulled back, revealing two velvet-covered seats.

"Fold 'em out if you wantin' to sleep," he said. "Makes one big bed. Pillows and a blanket in here." He flipped open a small storage compartment above the seats. "Just give me a holler if you boys need some help. Dining car's two cars that way." He pointed to his left before he pushed past them to head back down the aisle to a wealthy looking couple.

"He didn't believe we would tip him well." Cassie stared down at her clothes. "I am used to much nicer attention from the porters."

"I imagine you are. You hungry?"

"I fear I'm far too tired to eat." She smothered another yawn with her dainty but dirty hand. "The beef jerky and bread Old Tim packed was sufficient for now—even if we ate our meager meal on the back of our horses." She gave him an embarrassed smile, as if she'd just confessed some mortal sin. Most likely, she'd never eaten a meal that wasn't served on a silver platter.

Ty nodded, grateful the stablemaster had given them something to chase away the hunger as they rode.

"I shall fall asleep on my feet soon," she said. Dark circles had formed under her eyes, like someone had given her a good punch in the nose.

"You need to rest," he said.

"So do you."

He wanted to suggest they fold the seats into a bed now so they could both sleep, but he'd already trespassed by kissing her. "Sit down. You can lean against me." He nodded at the heavy drapes. "Pull those shut, we can have some privacy."

"I didn't purchase a berth to sleep sitting up, sir." Her gaze shifted from the seats to Ty and back to the seats. "If you would be so kind, help me unfold these." She grabbed the high back and slammed it down.

He almost argued with her until he realized he was getting exactly what he wanted—privacy, sleep, and the chance to hold her close. In only a few minutes, they'd converted the seats into a small bed.

Cassie reached for her cap, but Ty put his hand on top of her head. "Get in first. Let me pull the curtains."

For once, she didn't argue. Hopping up on the bed, she crawled to the right and jerked off her boots.

He followed, turned to pull the drapes closed, and sat on the left side without even bothering to take off his boots. Opening the storage, he grabbed two pillows and a worn blanket. He shoved one of the pillows and the blanket at her before dropping the other pillow on his side of the bed. Snatching off his hat, he set it in the storage compartment, then stretched out and waited for her to get settled.

Before she could, the train lurched into motion.

Cassie ended up sprawled on top of him.

Gritting his teeth at the suggestive position, Ty had to resist the urge to wrap his arms around her and hold her where she was—at least he did until she scrambled to get away from him and her knee found vulnerable targets between his legs.

"Shit!"

"Please excuse me."

She quickly crawled to the other side of the bed and sat there, staring at him.

"What's the problem *now?*" he asked.

Instead of an answer, she took the cap from her head and tossed it at the storage compartment. Her braid fell, flopping against her back. "Will you please take your boots off?"

"No."

"But–but…they are filthy."

"We're both filthy. You got more dirt on your face than I got on my boots. Don't rightly care. Lay down, Cassie girl. Get some shut-eye."

As Ty waited for her to stop sputtering in indignation, he tried to make himself more comfortable.

Cassie shook out the blanket.

When she spread it over both their legs, he arched an eyebrow at her. He'd expected her to roll the damn thing up and put it between them so she had some separation, something to protect her virtue. Instead, she shrugged out of her coat, laid it aside and practically fell to his side. After a few minutes of her turning this way and that and then punching her pillow again and again, he finally lost his last shred of patience.

Snaking an arm around her waist, he dragged her back up against his front. "Go to sleep," he ordered.

After only a few minutes, her body relaxed and her breathing slowed. He waited a good while to be sure that no one would bother them before he allowed himself to let his guard down. He pulled her a little closer until he could rest his chin on the crown of her head.

Yes, they were both grimy and dusty from traveling, and their clothes smelled like a stable and some lingering fishy odor from the cave. He didn't give a shit. Judging from how quickly she'd fallen asleep, a little inconvenience didn't bother her, either.

Cassie had ridden through the night without a single complaint, despite her weariness and how difficult it had to have been for her to leave her plush home behind. Just helping them escape from the cave had to have taken a toll on her fragile body, but they'd also asked her to sit her mare for a good ten hours.

The woman was clearly made of strong stuff despite the taint of Shay blood that ran through her veins.

Pressing his thighs up to mold against the back of hers, Ty tried not to think of just how right it felt to hold this woman close. She was a complication he wasn't remotely ready to deal with. After all, he'd come to San Francisco with Jake to help his friend claim his birthright. The notion of finding a beautiful woman and fetching her back to Montana had never once crossed his mind.

He reminded himself she was a Shay—the granddaughter of Senator Hiram Shay, one of the most powerful men from one of the most powerful families in the whole country.

He reminded himself that he was nothing but a dirt-poor cowboy with a scrap of land his adopted father had given him and nothing more to offer a woman, especially a woman who'd known nothing but wealth.

And he reminded himself that her family would come looking for her. Soon.

Despite all of that, he wanted her anyway.

Chapter Five

Cassie's stomach refused to be ignored, rumbling and complaining loud enough she was amazed the noise didn't wake Ty. He slept with his mouth partly open, each breath sounding like a funny little snore. Waking him from such a sound sleep seemed almost cruel, so she decided to fend for herself.

Sunlight still poured into the berth through the small dirty window, so they hadn't slept the entire day away. She'd have to listen for the conductor to call out the next station because she'd dozed right through any of his other announcements. How far they'd traveled remained a mystery, although she now knew their ultimate destination was Missoula. From there, they would reach Ty's hometown by horse.

As she crawled from the berth, she jostled Ty. Holding her breath, Cassie waited for him to awaken and scold her for trying to leave. Thankfully, he slept like the dead. She breathed a relieved sigh and dragged her coat and cap with her as she left, donning both once she was in the aisle.

Firmly tucking her braid under the cap, she decided to venture to the dining car to get something to eat. No one would give a dirty, disheveled guy a second glance. Just another poor young man traveling on the Northern Pacific Railroad in search of his fortune. Piles of gold. Wild women. Strong whiskey. And a good, rousing brawl, so her dime novels claimed.

She smiled at her silly little fantasy.

Used to moving around in her family's Pullman, she quickly found her balance in the swaying car. Walking the length, she struggled to open the heavy doors separating her car from the next, then she worked her way through another long aisle of sleeping berths, most of which remained converted into seats and were filled with people chatting or watching the scenery pass by. Another set of next-to-impossible doors helped her reach the tempting aroma of the dining car.

Judging from the empty seats at the counter, she'd slept past the noon meal. A few people sat at the booths, nursing coffee or smoking cheroots. Cassie took a seat at the counter and waited for the man stirring whatever he was busy cooking to take her order.

The man sitting next to her gave her a long look, so she pulled her cap lower over her eyes. While she normally would have struck up a friendly conversation simply to pass the time, now she tried to lay low. If Ty was right—which he probably was since he had more worldly experience than she did—her disguise wouldn't bear up to intense scrutiny.

"Can I buy you a sandwich?" the man asked. His voice was soft and quiet.

"N–no. Thank you." Ty had warned her not to tell people she had money.

"You look like you could use a good meal. Kinda skinny and all."

"I–I'm n–not all that hungry." Since her stomach chose that inappropriate moment to let out a loud rumble, she wasn't surprised when the man laughed right in her face.

"I can see that." He gestured to the attendant. "A ham sandwich, an apple, and some coffee."

"Tea," Cassie quickly corrected and then scolded herself for letting the stranger order for her. What would a man do? She was supposed to be a man.

Shouldn't she grunt or something? "Uh…thanks." Her grunt sounded more like a snort. "Sir."

"My name's Andrew Pearson. Call me Drew. And you are?"

Her head shot up until she met his gaze. She wrung her hands in her lap, entirely aware that she'd been a fool to not make a few plans on what to do if someone took the time to talk to her. "My…um…my name? You want my *name?*"

His chuckle was warm and kind, even if he was making sport of her. "That would seem to be appropriate since I just introduced myself to you." The smile seemed a bit too knowing, and she suddenly feared Drew saw right through her disguise.

She stammered a few more seconds before he leaned in and whispered. "Haven't thought of a boy's name yet, eh?"

Her hand flew to her chest. "Boy's name? I–I have no idea what—"

"It's okay," he softly interrupted. "I'd wager I'm the only one who notices because I'm the only one close enough to see your pretty face."

The attendant placed a plate and a cup in front of Cassie before grabbing an apple from a basket and setting it next to the food. Despite how hungry she was, she couldn't make herself pick up the sandwich. Fear had knotted her stomach, and all she could think of was being dragged back to San Francisco to face a horrifying future.

"Go on." Drew patted her shoulder. "Eat."

"But—"

"Eat." He plucked the red apple from the counter. Pulling a knife from his coat pocket, he popped open the blade and proceeded to peel the fruit. "Go on, now. Eat."

The sandwich was cold and stale, but it still filled her grumbling belly. She took a sip of the lukewarm tea and grimaced.

Drew chuckled and asked the attendant for sugar. The man plopped a cracked sugar bowl on the counter. She added more than she should have but enough that she could bear the taste of the bitter tea.

"Where you bound?" He sliced her apple, setting the pieces on the plate before folding his knife and tucking it back in his pocket.

She plucked a slice and chewed it, not sure whether to answer. At least having food in her mouth gave her an excuse not to immediately reply.

"I won't bite you," he soothed. "I'm just…concerned. Little girls shouldn't travel alone out here. Too many people willing to take advantage."

She straightened up so fast, her spine almost snapped. "I am *not* a little girl, sir."

He shrugged at her indignation. "Hard to see exactly *what* you are through those filthy clothes. You don't talk like an uneducated person, either. Is the food good?"

Cassie murmured a fibbed *yes* and took another bite of the sandwich. Didn't matter that it had all the flavor of her own pathetic cooking or that the ingredients were far from fresh. Hunger was hunger, and she hadn't eaten anything except a piece of bread and some jerky in almost two days. She didn't even mind that Drew seemed intent upon delving into her situation. There was no way he'd ever connect the person sitting beside him with her true origins.

The attendant set a scribbled bill next to her plate, and before she could grab it, Drew snatched it away.

"I can pay for my own food, sir."

The time the smile was more of a smirk. "Of that, I have no doubt. Oblige me this one time. Why don't you pick up the rest of your food, and we can sit over in one of the booths and talk?"

"That would *not* be a good idea."

"Oh, I think it would. Trust me, we could use a little more privacy." He gaze shifted to the attendant, who was clearly listening in on the conversation as he turned his head to the left and leaned closer.

"B–but—" Her sputtering protest was stopped by Drew grabbing her plate and getting to his feet.

"Follow me." He led his way to the farthest booth, put her food down, and scooted onto one of the bench seats.

Cassie picked up her tea and followed, not only because the rest of her meager meal was now sitting in front of Drew, but her curiosity was killing her. She set her cup down and took the opposite bench.

"I have to say, seeing you here and dressed like...*that* was quite a surprise, Miss Shay. Do you want to explain why you're on a train, in boy's clothing?"

She froze in fear, her hands gripping the table until her knuckles blanched. "M–my name is not Shay."

He gave his eyes an exaggerated roll. "Oh, please. Don't take me for a fool."

The ruse ended. "How could you know?"

"You don't remember me. I'm not surprised. You must have had hundreds of guests at your estate that day."

"Remember? We've been introduced before?"

"Your twenty-first birthday party. I was one of the entertainers."

Searching her memory, Cassie focused on Drew's face. The understanding came on her in a rush. "*Henry the Fifth*—the Saint Crispin's Day speech!"

"So you *do* remember."

"You were brilliant."

She watched him smile, really looking at his face for the first time. He appeared different than when he'd performed at her birthday party. Perhaps now that the heavy stage make-up was washed away, she could see who he truly was, not the character he'd been portraying that day.

His blue eyes held a world of intelligence that he was applying to her, judging from the slight smirk on his full lips. Drew's blond hair was a bit longer than most men of fashion wore, brushing each shoulder, but she attributed that to him being an actor. Artsy types never followed style dictates.

A dark coat covered his muscular frame, the same type of jacket sailors wore. But the masculine clothes seemed too rugged for Drew. He was...pretty—the only word to describe a man who had such refined features. Long eyelashes. Slender fingers with manicured nails. An elegant, thin nose. She envied how red and full his lips were, cringing at how dirty and unfeminine she must appear with her ragged clothes and smudged face.

"Are you ready to tell me why you're here?" he asked.

Another bite of the apple kept her from replying. She knew nothing about him except he was an actor. In her tenuous situation, trust needed to be guarded—if given at all.

"I know." He put his elbows on the table and propped his chin on his hands. "You're a runaway."

Her cheeks flushed hot, and she knew she was revealing far too much in that simple reaction.

"What I need to know is…what exactly are you running away *from*?"

"Sir, I assure you—"

Drew waved her off with a flick of his wrist before setting his chin back on his hands. "Your assurance won't go far with me, cutie. I need to figure out for myself exactly what you're doing and whether I can earn your family's benevolence by hauling your pretty little *derriere* right back to San Francisco."

Cassie gasped. "You wouldn't!"

"No?" He sat back and folded his arms over his chest. "Why exactly wouldn't I? If your uncle or grandfather ever got wind that I found you—traveling all alone and dressed as a boy, mind you—and didn't help get you home… Why, my name would be mud."

Her heart in her throat, she reached across the table.

His hand shot out to hold hers, showing there was some compassion in his soul. Surely a man who could move her to tears with his recitation of one of Shakespeare's greatest soliloquies would understand if she gave him a smidgen of the truth.

"I shall beg if I have to, but, sir, I do not wish to return to San Francisco. Please allow me to maintain my ruse."

His fingers squeezed hers. "Then tell me why I should keep your secret."

"I am to be married to a horrible, horrible man. I had to leave to escape that fate."

"Why would your family ever make you marry someone so…as you say…horrible? The dowry you possess should offer you the choice of any husband you wish." Blue eyes searched hers, but Drew's hand stayed firmly locked around her fingers.

Trying to give him all the sincerity he needed and praying he believed her, Cassie confessed some of her story. "My family is forcing this marriage on me. This man has some hold over them. He pressed for this marriage, and my grandfather and uncle wouldn't deny him."

"Why do you consider him a bad choice?" His eyes narrowed. "Unless… Does he beat you?"

The question she'd feared the most because it reached right to the heart of the matter. Her mother had always told her a wife's lot in life was to bear all her husband heaped upon her—his sexual advances—repugnant though they were—his desire to bed other women, even his need to raise a hand in discipline.

Cassie never believed such nonsense.

When she'd been a child, her father's way of punishing her mother had been to slap her until she could barely stand upright, then he'd lock them both in a closet for hours and hours. She always thought her mother's fear of closed spaces had been born in that punishment. Cassie had learned to soothe her mother through her fears by telling her stories and stretching her own imagination.

A man who loved and cherished a woman shouldn't hit her or lock her away, and Cassie had barely known her father. She didn't mourn his passing.

Robert had struck her—only once when she dared to interrupt an interlude he was having with one of the maids.

Cassie's response when he'd slapped her face so hard her ears rang had been to throw herself against him and raise her knee to his groin with enough force he'd doubled over and coughed hard enough she was amazed he hadn't passed out.

Once her grandfather was told, she was beaten—but not by Robert. By her uncle with his cane. It had taken weeks for the bruises on her face, shoulders and back to heal. Although she'd been spanked by her father and uncle when she'd been a child, she'd never been beaten before.

She wasn't about to stay in San Francisco and marry Robert, knowing she faced a lifetime of such brutality.

"Miss Shay?" Drew prompted, rubbing his thumb over her palm.

"Yes."

"Yes, he beat you?"

She nodded.

He sat there considering her for several long moments. "It appears I have no choice."

"No choice?"

"You need my help." He heaved a lengthy sigh. "'Frailty, thy name is woman.'"

Cassie tossed him an annoyed frown. "'Men are sometimes master of their fates.' And women masters of theirs, Mr. Pearson. You are not the only one who can quote Shakespeare. Or shall we switch to the Bible? 'Be strong and of good courage, do not fear nor be afraid of them.' Deuteronomy—chapter thirty-one, verse six, I believe."

"'Do not neglect to do good and to share what you have…' Hebrews—chapter thirteen, verse sixteen. While I love a good literary duel, we are back to my original dilemma. You need my help and my silence, so I must champion your cause."

A shadow cast over their joined hands, and a voice filled with barely restrained fury cut through the air. "What you *must do* is let go of her before I knock out every one of those shiny white teeth."

"Ty!" Cassie dropped Drew's hand and reached out to lay hers on Ty's forearm. His hands were fisted against his slim hips, and his eyes had narrowed to angry slits. "Are you hungry?"

Hungry? Ty couldn't even think about anything but his anger, although a smile twitched at the corner of his lips at the pluck Cassie seemed to have in bushels. "I skipped right over hungry when I woke up and found you'd left our bed."

She blushed to the roots of her hair. "Ty!" she squealed before she lowered her voice. "What will Drew think of you speaking to a lady in such a manner?"

"A lady?" He arched a disapproving eyebrow. "Don't rightly give a damn what *Drew* thinks." He lifted his hand to tug her cap down lower. "Didn't figure a man sharing a berth with his younger brother would raise too many eyebrows."

The man sitting opposite her—this Drew, as she called him—snorted a laugh, so it was clear her disguise hadn't fooled him at all.

Trying to size up the man, Ty had to swallow the jealousy that covered him like a cloak.

The man returned the intense scrutiny.

Drew was everything a woman had to consider handsome—hell, he was as pretty as some women. Cassie must have seen something in Drew she liked, or else she wouldn't have been chatting with him so sweetly.

And holding his hand.

Damn, how he'd wanted to put his fist right through the pretty boy's face.

"Mr. Bishop, this is Drew Pearson." Cassie nodded at the man opposite her. "Mr. Pearson, this is Ty Bishop."

Drew's lips set into a frown. "Is this the man we spoke of, Miss Shay?"

"God almighty, he knows your name?" Ty tried to keep his voice below the shout that wanted to erupt. "You can't run 'round telling everyone who you are. That pitiful disguise is bad enough. Why, a blind man would know you ain't a boy!"

"It truly is a bad disguise, isn't it?" Drew actually smiled at Ty.

Ty still wanted to punch his lights out, but one side of his mouth rose in a grin. "Yeah, it's mighty sad."

Cassie sat up a little straighter, raising a defiant chin. "I thought it was a perfectly wonderful disguise."

"You were wrong." Turning to Drew he said, "You'll keep her secret." A command, not a question.

"I'll make that promise," he replied, "just as soon as one of you answers my question, although I'm leaning toward believing you are not her—as she says—horrible fiancé."

"Her *fiancé*?" This time he did shout, and the few diners in the car turned to stare at them.

Ty threw himself down on the bench next to Cassie, forcing her to move over to give his bulk room. Their thighs pressed tightly together, and every time she tried to move away, he only spread his legs a little wider to force contact. It was past time she got used to his touch.

She finally finished trying to pull away and actually pinched his hip when he pushed against her one more time.

That earned her a smile until he remembered Drew's words. "What in the hell is he talking about, Cassie?"

Drew was the one to answer. "From what she's told me—which isn't much, mind you—she's running away from San Francisco so she doesn't have to marry a man her family chose for her. A man, I might add, who beats her."

"I'll kill him," Ty blurted out before he could stop himself. "No man who's worth a damn hits a woman."

For some reason, his words made her press closer to him. "While I appreciate your chivalrous response—"

"My what?" Maybe if he read as much as his adopted father, Adam Morgan, he would understand more of the big words that seemed to constantly roll off Cassie's tongue.

Again, Drew filled in the information. "Chivalrous—it means gallant, courteous, brave."

"Yes," she said. "Ty is all those things."

Her words seemed a bit too dreamy. And damn, if that didn't please him.

"You never said *why* you were running away," Ty scolded, giving her hat another tug.

"*You* never asked. You simply followed me whether I desired an escort or not."

He couldn't remember spending time with any woman that made him smile half as often as only a few minutes with Cassie could. "Saucy vixen, ain't ya?"

A laugh drifted from across the table. "Might I be brazen enough to ask something?"

Ty gave Drew a curt nod.

"Since you're not the person she ran *from*, are you the person she ran *to*? Are you two…close?"

She sputtered in protest. "Mr. Pearson! Why, I–I didn't…I am not…carrying on with Mr. Bishop."

Leaning back, Drew drummed his fingers on the top of the table. "If you really are intent upon me keeping this secret of yours, you both need to satisfy me as to whether Miss Shay will be better off in your company, Mr. Bishop, or better off being returned to her family—her very rich and powerful family. The same one that could hunt me down like a rabid dog should they know I helped shelter her, especially since I'm assisting her in staying with a man whose intentions might not be…respectable."

Ty leaned forward and set his jaw. "I could end your problem right now,"

"And, pray tell, how could you do that?"

"I could just shoot you, grab Cassie, and get the hell off this train."

Her outraged gasp echoed through the dining car, again drawing stares.

Since he'd already decided to get off the train at Missoula, he dismissed the other people, figuring once they were on horseback again, no one would have any idea of where they were heading—especially since he was well-trained in how to keep someone from picking up their trail.

"You will do no such thing," she insisted, tugging on his arm.

Drew just grinned at him. "Whether you realize it or not, Mr. Bishop—"

"For the love of God, can we please stop with the *miss* and *mister* manure?" Ty asked, groaning. He was a Montana guy, always would be. The polite way city folk talked grated on his ears like a rooster crowing before sunrise.

"Fine, *Ty*," Drew replied. "Whether you realize it or not, you more than answered my concerns."

"How exactly did I do that?"

"You're protective of Miss…of *Cassie*. You clearly have feelings for her, so I need not worry about her being harmed in your company."

Before Ty could deny any tender feelings for Cassie, the conductor walked into the dining car. "Next stop Missoula! Five minutes to Missoula Mills!" He hurried through the car to exit through the far door.

"My stop," Drew said. "Where are the two of you heading?"

As Cassie opened her mouth, probably to reply, Ty reached out to grab her hand and gave it a cautionary squeeze.

She looked up at him with those incredible hazel eyes.

He gave his head a quick shake.

"Might I make a suggestion?" Drew pushed his way out of the booth to stand at the end of the table and stare down at them. "My parents live in Missoula. You both look a bit worn out. I can offer you a room—" A smile spread across his face. "—or *rooms*. You can get hot baths, warm meals, and good night's sleep. You can always catch tomorrow's train if you're traveling farther on this line."

Ty shook his head at the same time Cassie nodded. "We ain't stayin' with his folks, Cassie."

"Why on earth not?"

"We don't know anything about them."

"Then we shall just have to get to know them while we are their houseguests. I can have a bath, Ty. A *bath*." Her smile all but stole the breath from his lungs.

He suddenly knew he could never deny her anything.

Ty looked back to Drew. "You sure your folks won't mind? Can't let no one know 'bout who Cassie really is."

"I would warn them to keep silent. They are quite adept at keeping secrets."

A loaded response if he'd ever heard one.

"Please, Ty?" Cassie gave his hand a squeeze. "A hot bath." Her sigh hung in the air.

Drew put the last nail in the coffin of Ty's resistance when he looked at her and said, "My younger brother will have some clean clothes for you, and Ty can have some of mine. We're near to the same size."

Ty gave Drew a nod and pulled Cassie up off the bench. "You go get the rest of our things. We can put the horses in a livery and follow Drew to his parents' place."

The train slowed, the jerky movements causing her to lose her footing and stumble against him. His arms wrapped around her to hold her steady while her hands landed against his chest. The feel of her pelvis pressed so closely against his was nothing short of agony.

When he'd awakened, he'd been dreaming of her, stroking her lithe body while he kissed her. The dream had been so real, he'd blindly reached out, wanting to touch her, but she was gone.

After calming his panic, he went in search of her. Finding her so cozy with another man had sparked a fury that nearly blinded him.

How in the devil had she managed to capture his attention so completely? Hell, he was even dreaming about her.

At least tonight, he would have chaperones aplenty. But once they started the two-day ride to White Pines, he and Cassie would be alone. Riding all day. Camping at night. Not another soul in sight.

How was he supposed to keep his hands off her?

Chapter Six

Cassie pulled her pathetic jacket a little tighter, trying to keep the biting wind whipping around her from blowing it open again. She hadn't considered its lack of warmth, only chose it to serve the purpose of disguising herself as a boy. Dismissing the late autumn cold, she tried to focus instead on the happiness that seemed to radiate from Drew like a halo. Ty, on the other hand, remained stoic, as she'd quickly learned was his way.

"My mother will be so pleased," Drew said, a bit breathless as he hurried up the street. His eyes sparkled like an eager child on Christmas morning. "I promised her I'd be back last year. And Father—I've missed Father. I should have returned before now, but…"

"But what?" Cassie asked, hoping conversation would help keep her mind off the numbing cold. She longed for her fur-lined cloak and favorite wool mittens before scolding herself that silly luxuries weren't worth the torture of being tied to a brutal, adulterous man for a husband.

Better to suffer a chill and find a more rewarding life for herself.

"My oldest brother and I parted on bad terms. A quarrel with no resolution. I stayed away to keep peace in the family. But I've missed my parents dearly. I shouldn't have avoided them."

"Why did you quarrel with your brother?" It might not be any of her business, but his voice sounded so forlorn. She'd had few people to share her problems with other than Old Tim, and she hated to think her new friend had no one to confide in.

Drew never answered, instead stopping at a whitewashed house and staring.

"This your place?" Ty inclined his head to the home.

With a hard swallow and a nod, Drew stepped up onto the porch to knock on the door before stepping back down only a pace away from Cassie and Ty.

A few moments passed, and she began to fear no one was home. The promise of a hot bath and a warm bed might not be fulfilled. Worse, they'd have no place to sleep and then where would they go? Tendrils of fear began to weave through her limbs, intensifying the cold.

As if reading her thoughts, Ty stepped up behind her and whispered, "Saw a general store a few streets back. We can buy some bedding and some food. We can camp just outside town. I'll make sure you're warm, Cassie girl."

Cassie girl.

An endearment?

He'd used the term before, but she'd assumed it was a mere slip of the tongue.

An endearment.

Her insides warmed even as she shivered from the stray flakes of snow that began to dance around them.

"No, no," Drew replied over his shoulder. "There's no problem. My family will welcome us. I'm sure of it."

Grunting in response, Ty stepped back, his gaze searching the house as if seeking a threat. His right hand kept drifting to his hip.

After a few of those movements, she realized he was reaching for a gun he clearly missed—the one her uncle had stolen. She tried to follow Ty's scrutiny and saw the drapes in a second-story window pulled aside. A red-headed woman—perhaps in her early twenties—peered down at them. Before Cassie could wonder at one of Drew's relatives having such fiery hair, the door opened.

"Well, well. The prodigal son returns." A man with the same light hair and eyes as Drew leaned his shoulder against the doorframe and folded his arms over his broad chest. His fine suit spoke of wealth.

Huddled behind him was a plump woman dressed in an opulent green gown who Cassie assumed was Drew's mother. Her hair was more gray than brown, and she clasped her hands together as tears rolled down her cheeks.

"Aaron." Drew met the man's eyes with his own. "It's good to see you again, brother." He looked past him to the woman. "Mother, are you well?"

When she moved forward, Aaron's arm shot out to block her before sweeping her back several paces. "She is quite well—at least she was until *you* darkened our doorstep. We were sitting down to a fine meal, and now we must face the distasteful task of asking you to leave."

So much for a warm welcome…

The hatred in Aaron's tone and hard eyes forced Cassie to move closer to Drew and take his hand in hers, somehow knowing he needed the connection.

"How dare you flaunt your sins in front of us!" Aaron's face grew ruddy and splotchy as he stared at their joined hands. "Release that boy!"

Good God. Aaron thought Drew had used her in the way a man used a woman.

Her face could hold no surprise because she'd already guessed Drew's preference. Among the wealthy of San Francisco were men who favored other men. No one spoke of it openly, but the more affluence they had, the less they were shunned by society. She never saw them as anything other than people.

Fury at the man's judgmental self-righteousness bubbled up inside her until her words came spilling out. "We've committed no sin. Are you casting stones, sir?"

Drew tugged at her hand. She glanced up to see him give his head a small shake.

Eyes narrowed in anger, he turned back to his brother. "Where is Father?"

The smirk on Aaron's face made her long to slap him.

"Father is dead," Aaron replied.

Drew took a stumbling step forward. "No… *No!* When?"

"As if you possibly cared. You brought him nothing but shame."

Drew's hands clenched into fists. "*When,* damn you!"

"Two months ago. This home now belongs to me, and you are no longer welcome here." His cruel eyes fixed on Cassie, making a shudder rip through her. "Neither is your…*friend.* God's hooks, you're finding them younger and younger, Andrew. Surely you haven't extended your indulgences to mating with children as well as men?"

Thankfully, Ty held his silence. She wanted to turn to see his face, to discover what his real reaction was to Aaron's condemnation, hoping she didn't see the same hatred in Ty's eyes she viewed in Aaron's. If only Drew would look at her, he'd realize she thought no less of him now.

"I'm sorry, Mother." Drew's his eyes brimmed with tears. "I wish I had been here when Father died. I wish… I'm so sorry, Mother."

"Oh, Andrew…" She bit back a cry by putting a lace handkerchief to her mouth.

"Go!" Aaron shouted with a wave of his arm. "You will *never* be welcome here again. You're a disgrace!"

"Mother?" Drew's word was a plea that almost made Cassie weep for the hurt he must be going through. She would never give a man like Aaron the satisfaction of knowing he'd inflicted a wound. "You would turn away your own son?" Drew asked.

More tears spilled over the woman's lashes. "Aaron, please. He's your brother. Surely we should let him stay with us tonight—"

"No!" Aaron pushed his mother back. With a sob, she disappeared into the house. Turning back to Drew, he said, "Leave! Don't ever darken my door again!" The door slammed with a resounding bang that should have shattered the nearest window.

Drew stood there, staring at his family home for several long minutes. Since he hadn't dropped her hand, Cassie didn't pull away.

Ty had stepped up behind her, and his palms settled on her shoulders. She wondered what he thought of the revelations about Drew. Her own heart ached for her new friend, wondering how horrible it would feel to be rejected so completely by family.

But she already understood—her relatives had chosen Robert Putnam over her or her happiness. Perhaps that was why she and Drew had connected so quickly.

"We need to go," Ty said softly. "We can get a few miles 'tween us and this city before we make camp for the night."

"Drew?" Cassie squeezed his hand. "Are you ready to go?"

"Go?" He looked down at her, his eyes glazed and lost.

"We're ready to move on." She laid a hand on his arm. "We can buy some food and bedding and make a camp for the night."

Tilting his head, he stared at her a few long moments. "Why would you want a man like me to go with you?"

Fixing a smile on her face, she replied with as much conviction as she could muster. "Because you're my friend."

"After everything you just heard, you still call me 'friend'?"

She tried to keep the smile on her, blinking to hold back the tears stinging her eyes. "'A friend should bear his friend's infirmities.'"

"The Bard was indeed wise." A sad chuckle fell from Drew's lips. "'I desire you in friendship, and I will one way or other make you amends.'"

"Time to go," Ty said, his voice gruff as he tugged Cassie's shoulders.

"Am I free to accompany you?" Drew asked, releasing his grasp on Cassie and staring at Ty.

Ty shrugged. "Suit yourself."

It wasn't the invitation she'd hoped for, but at least he didn't give Drew the same cruel reaction as his family. When she found a moment alone with Ty, she'd try to explain to him why she'd made the choice to keep Drew close—at least she would if she could figure out her own motivations.

Kindness?

Christian charity?

A kindred spirit who knew what it felt like to be rejected by family?

For now, she was simply grateful for Ty's acceptance. She dropped Drew's hand and turned to face Ty. Pushing herself up on tiptoes, she kissed his beard-stubbled cheek.

He grunted in response, grabbed her hand, and started to drag her away.

"Coming?" she called to Drew over her shoulder.

Drew stared at the house while Ty kept moving up the block. Worried Drew had changed his mind, she almost planted her feet, but he finally turned and followed.

They'd traveled less than a block when shouts caught her attention.

"Master Andrew! Wait! Master Andrew!"

"What on earth…?" Cassie muttered.

The young woman, the redhead who'd been peeking at them from the second-story window of the Pearson home, ran down the street, a carpetbag in her hand.

Drew stopped and stared at her. "That's Brigit—my mother's personal maid."

"What's she want?" Ty asked.

"Haven't a clue."

Breathless, Brigit skidded to a stop in front of Drew. She shoved the bag at him. "Yer mother sent these for you and yer…friends." Her thick Irish accent made it almost impossible for Cassie to catch all her words. "I'm to tell you to take the gray gelding yer brother Ashton has at the livery. It be yers now."

Opening the bag, Drew looked inside before nodding.

"What is it?" Cassie asked.

"Clothing. Enough, I imagine, for all of us."

Brigit reached inside her cloak and pulled out a small leather pouch that she pushed at Drew. "She sent this as well. I'm ta tell you she wishes she had more to give you."

"What happened to my father, Brigit?"

"The cancer took him." She put a hand on the fist he had clenched around the bag. "'Twas quick. He suffered little."

The sound of clinking coins seemed as loud as church bell chimes as he struggled to untie and open the bag. Tears had formed in his eyes, and he swallowed hard when he peered inside. "I shouldn't take this."

"G'on with ya," Brigit said with a hesitant smile and a flip of her hand. "Yer mother wanted you to have it."

She whirled around, obviously intent on leaving, but he grabbed her shoulder.

"Please give Mother my thanks…and my love," he said.

"I will." Brigit reached up to pat his hand before hurrying away.

"At least I can help now." He tied the bag closed and tucked it in his coat pocket. "I have a horse and some money to buy us some supplies."

"You'll be traveling with us." Cassie was being bossy, but she figured that was what Drew needed at that moment—someone to tell him what to do until he could figure things out for himself.

"I don't even know where you're going," he replied.

"White Pines." Ty's quick answer surprised and pleased her because he revealed his willingness to allow Drew to join their little journey.

"Might as well. I've got nowhere else to go. Once a vagabond actor..." His smile wasn't genuine, but she understood. He glanced to Ty. "Don't suppose there's a theater in your fair town, is there?"

"Building one now. Ain't got much call for actors yet, though. You can get work on a farm or a ranch," Ty replied.

"A farm or a ranch?" Drew's chuckle sounded sadly like a sob. "I suppose it's good for a man to have choices in life."

"Then let's go shopping," she suggested. "We can buy some food, a few blankets, everything we need."

"There's just three things I need," Ty said.

"And what would those be?" Cassie asked.

"First, a hat. Second, a gun."

She tilted her head and considered the grin on his handsome face. "And, pray tell, what would be the third?"

His eyes twinkled. "To get you home with me, where you'll be safe."

Chapter Seven

Ty cut a wedge of cheese and handed it to Cassie.

They'd managed to find a good place to camp for the night, but there hadn't been time to snare a rabbit. He should have bought some bacon, but then he also would've had to purchase cooking utensils. Better to go with simple things.

She deserved better than cheese and bread. If they rode hard tomorrow, he'd make camp early to do a spot of hunting. One more night after tonight, then he'd have her in White Pines where she could get that hot bath and comfy bed Drew had promised.

Drew.

Ty hadn't planned on him tagging along. After the humiliation the man suffered at the hands of his family, they couldn't leave him behind. Then again, families had a way of disappointing a person.

Ty's father had shoved him in an orphanage when his mother died because he felt he simply had too many mouths to feed. Looking back, that abandonment had been the best thing to happen to him because he met Jake Curtis at that Denver home for children.

"I need to wash." Cassie stood and groaned as she arched her back to stretch. "I smell like a stable."

"I'm so sorry, Cass." Drew poked at their small fire with a stick. "I promised you a hot bath." He glanced over to the blankets she'd laid out for the night. "And a soft bed."

She smiled at him, the forgiveness clear in her beautiful eyes. "I am quite content with your company instead."

"May I escort you to the brook?" Drew asked.

"I'll take her," Ty snapped.

While some of the jealousy he'd felt over Cassie's closeness to Drew had vanished with his brother's revelations, Ty still resented the connection the two clearly shared from the moment they met.

"Might I please borrow some clean clothes?" She nodded at the carpetbag sitting next to Drew's bedding. While they'd purchased a few essentials like food and blankets, they hadn't spent coin on clothes since Drew's mother had sent some.

"Of course." While Drew dug around in the bag, she plucked the bar of soap from the supplies she'd purchased. He handed her a folded pile of clothing. "These must be my brother Asher's. They're too small to be mine."

Ty hated asking for a fresh change for himself, figuring he could just go on stinking until he got home. Hell, he'd been on many a cattle drive where the cowboys smelled worse than the stock by the time they reached a railhead.

Drew handed another pile to him. "These are mine."

"I ain't taking your stuff."

"Nonsense. I owe you more than a change of pants for letting me follow you and Cassie on this little odyssey."

"This what?" Damn, if he'd only had more of an education, he might understand all the things that Cassie and Drew liked to say, but he'd keep on asking them to explain so he didn't feel left out.

Coming to stand at his side, she was the one to reply. "He means a strange and daunting trip. I shall bathe first, then when I return, you may take the soap and see to your own needs."

"You ain't going nowhere without me. Too many animals prowling 'round at night." That and his fear that somehow, someplace the Shay's bloodhounds would find her and steal her away from him.

"I couldn't possibly bathe with you watching."

"I'll turn my back." Ty wrapped his hand around her upper arm and started toward the trees. He'd found a good-sized stream earlier—the perfect place for a wash. "You can watch all you want while I take mine."

Cassie's mouth opened and closed, but she was clearly too shocked to say a word. Heavens, he loved to get her riled up. She was such a joy to watch.

"You two enjoy your baths," Drew drawled.

Ty lost sight of their camp as he weaved a path through the pines.

She jerked her arm away. "You don't have to drag me, sir. I can walk under my own power."

He simply grunted and hiked toward the stream. After only a few minutes, the clearing came into sight. The brook wasn't too deep, but the water was moving at a pretty good clip.

"At least I know you can swim," he quipped.

"That you do. Now if you'd be so kind as to stand over by those trees and turn your back, I can get this filth off me."

Ty marched the distance back to the woods, glancing over his shoulder a couple of times to be sure he was close enough to get to her should she need any help.

Cassie quickly shed her coat, but when her gaze caught his the last time he peeked, she threw a glare at him so hot he was amazed sparks didn't shoot from her eyes. "A gentleman would not look!"

"Ain't a gentleman." Facing the trees, he crossed his arms over his chest and sighed in resignation.

He had no doubt her bath would be quick. This time of year, the water had to be close to ice. Surely she was smart enough to just splash the water on her body rather than wade into—

Her enraged screech pierced the air.

Whirling in response, he reached for his Colt, his heart pounding a rough.

The weapon never left his holster because there was no danger. Cassie's bellow came from where she now stood thigh-deep in the brook, wearing nothing but the beauty God had graced her with.

A groan slipped from his lips. The woman was perfectly shaped. High, firm breasts with nipples that had tightened to hard buds. A narrow waist. Beautifully rounded hips. Her hand had dropped to shield her femininity, but not before he got a glimpse of a V of brown curls.

"Mr. Bishop!"

With a smirk, he tugged on the brim of his hat. "Miss Shay. You called?"

Hardly believing the audacity of the man, Cassie sputtered in protest, trying to cover herself and knowing she was doing a terrible job of it. How dare he not turn back around! Her unladylike scream had prompted him to face her, but once he realized she wasn't in need of assistance, he should have given her privacy again. A gentleman would have.

Ah, but—as Ty rightly claimed— he was no gentleman.

"Turn around!" she ordered.

His hand cupped his ear. "Pardon? A mite hard to hear you from over there."

The laughter in his voice and the leer on his face pushed her temper hot enough she forgot about the bone-chilling cold. To hell with her nudity!

She picked up a rock and hurled it at him. As always, her aim was true. Had he not sidestepped the stone, she would have knocked the new hat from his arrogant head.

"Take your bath, Cassie girl." With a chuckle, he tugged on the brim of his hat again and gave her his back.

Driven by embarrassment, Cassie knelt in the freezing water and quickly soaped her body. The scent of roses surrounded her, but she couldn't enjoy it. By the time she rinsed the suds from her body and hair and tossed the soap on the grass, she could barely feel her fingers. As she tried to stand up, her foot slipped on a slick rock, causing a cramp to shoot up her calf. She fell back into the brook. Sputtering, she struggled to keep her head above the rapidly moving water, but her arms wouldn't obey the commands of her mind.

Before she could draw a breath to call out for help, Ty scooped her up in his arms. He carried her to the shore, grabbed the drying cloth she'd brought, and covered her. "Where's the cramp?"

How he knew her affliction was beyond her, but pain stopped her from contemplating anything but how to ease the knot in her muscle. Tears streamed down her face, and her teeth chattered so hard she couldn't answer him. Her calf felt as if someone had stabbed her. She groped at her leg, whimpering and wishing her hands would stop trembling so she could rub out the God-awful hurt.

Ty brushed her hands away and used the heel of his warm hand to force the knot out. Cassie tried not to whine, but the pain was truly getting the better of her, and his assistance hurt almost as much as the cramp. She buried her face against his neck and tried to stop crying.

With gentle rubs, he slowly relaxed the muscle, and she mercifully felt the agony ease. His warmth was stealing away her chill, and she was reluctant to have him move away.

"Better?" His voice was low and tender.

She nodded against his skin.

"You need to get dressed."

"How did you know I had a cramp?"

"Happens in icy water." He stood up, still holding her in his arms.

"So you won't bathe? You smell like hell, Mr. Bishop."

He nuzzled her neck. "You smell like heaven, Miss Shay."

How in God's name could she get him to put her down without baring her body to him again? All she had covering her was a thin drying cloth. The moment he released her, she'd—

She didn't have the chance to worry a moment more. He put her on her feet, turned on his heel, and walked back to the brook.

Picking up the soap, he sniffed it. "Roses? I have to smell like *roses?*"

"I'm sorry. I hadn't thought you might wish to use it."

A disgusted snort floated across the way. His back to her, he put his hat aside and started unbuckling his new gunbelt while he toed off his boots.

Taking the hint, Cassie faced away from him and worked on drying her shivering body. Dragging on the clean clothing, she fought the chill and waited for the sounds of Ty shouting at the iciness of the water. He never did, and when she realized things were too quiet, her concern made her glance back to the brook.

His back was to her. Thank heavens, because she couldn't have torn her eyes away if she'd wanted to.

The man was a mountain of muscle. Defined shoulders. Narrow hips. And the most devilishly delectable dimples just above his rounded backside.

Suddenly, she didn't feel so cold, and decidedly wicked thoughts crowded her mind.

Scolding herself as a wanton, she tried to regain control of her imagination. She didn't succeed.

Never in her life had she looked at a man and felt such a desire to know all there was about what happened between a man and a woman. Then again, Ty was the first naked man she'd ever seen. Her mother had given her little guidance—most of what she'd learned about mating came from Old Tim's awkward explanation. He'd felt someone needed to educate her about the ways of the world, but she still felt ignorant—something she despised.

Losing herself in her admiration of Ty Bishop's strong body, she was taken by surprise when he turned around. "Why, Cassie girl. Didn't think you'd be one to peek."

Her face was on fire, but she stared anyway. His chest was covered with a light coating of hair that thinned to a line, fanning his navel before spreading out around his—

Good God, what was wrong with her?

Her eyes went back to his face, and the grin she saw there pushed aside her mortification, replacing it with a need to knock his arrogance down a notch. A little bravado allowed her to give him as good as he'd given her.

She cupped her hand to her ear. "I am truly sorry, but I'm having difficulty hearing you from so very far away."

His laughter made her smile, and his gaze held hers until she turned away.

She threaded her fingers through her hair to try to work out some of the tangles and then wove it into a long braid. Once she was able to let it loose again, it would be too curly to manage. But the braid was efficient and would help her maintain her ruse should they encounter other people on their trek.

"Ready?" Ty said, having crept up behind her.

Cassie jumped in surprise. "You move like a ghost."

"Thank you kindly."

"It wasn't a compliment. You scared the life out of me." Grabbing the pile of dirty clothes, she held out her other hand. "The soap, if you please."

"Left it by the brook. Why?"

Just as Old Tim had taught her, she would be as self-reliant as possible. "I need to wash out the rest of our clothing. We can hang them from the trees to dry tonight while we sleep."

***

Drew was still solemn when Cassie followed Ty back to their campsite.

She could try to coax him out of his melancholy, but the type of wound his brother had inflicted wouldn't heal easily. Only time would help—time, friendship, and understanding.

A yawn slipped out, and all she wanted to do was crawl into her four-poster bed, drag her down quilt over her exhausted body, and sleep for hours and hours. Instead, she lay down on the bedding she'd spread on the hard ground and covered herself with a wool blanket.

Drew stretched on the opposite side of the small fire, his back to her.

"Sleep well, Drew," she called to him.

"You as well."

Sleep was quickly overtaking her, but Cassie was jarred awake when Ty flopped down beside her. "You should not sleep so close to me, Mr. Bishop. It isn't proper."

"Passed proper days ago, and I told you to call me Ty. Promised to keep you warm tonight, remember?" Wrapping an arm around her waist, he drew her closer, pressing his front to her back. Then he dragged her blanket over both of them. "Go to sleep, Cassie girl."

She was simply too tired to argue with him. Her last thought before sleep claimed her was that he was, indeed, keeping her very warm.

***

"So let me see if I understand this correctly..." Cassie shifted in her saddle to relieve the incessant pressure on her sore backside. "You went to live with Adam Morgan even though you and Jake tried to rob the man?"

Ty nodded. "Sounds odd, don't it? He said since we didn't have anywhere else to go, we might as well go back to Montana with him. Adam's been like a father to me and Jake. He's a good man, taught me right from wrong. God knows where I'd be if—" He swallowed the rest of his words.

Trotting her mare up closer, she tossed him a smile to turn his sad thoughts. "Do you like being a real cowboy?"

"A *real* cowboy?" He snorted. "Never thought 'bout it."

"But being a cowboy is so...*romantic*. In the books I've read, they talk about how wild and exciting the cowboy life can be."

Good Lord, I sound like a ninny.

"Books? About cowboys?" Drew interrupted. "Why, Cass, are you saying you read *dime novels?*" He clucked his tongue. "And here I thought you were a *lady.*"

His wink made her cheeks flush hot. She opened and closed her mouth, not sure how to reply. Ty's chuckle only made her cheeks warmer.

"I'm just teasing," Drew said.

Desperately wanting to steer the conversation a new direction, Cassie ferreted more information. "Do you plan to work on the ranch for the rest of your life? The Triple Springs, is it?"

"*Twin* Springs," Ty corrected. Then he shrugged. "Don't rightly know what the future holds. Adam gave me some acres to call my own. Might just build a cabin and stay there 'til I'm old 'n gray."

A cabin. A simple cabin with a garden and a cat and a man to call her own—all she'd ever wanted, and it seemed Ty wanted it as well. Perhaps they were more alike than she'd come to believe.

A contented sigh slipped out. Mercifully, both her traveling companions ignored it.

The contentment faded as she thought about reaching White Pines. "Adam and Grace Morgan will not welcome me."

"Can't lie and say they'll be happy to have a Shay comin' back to town," Ty replied. "Shays ain't my favorite, neither."

"Pray tell what harm—" She clapped her mouth shut before the ridiculous question slipped out.

As if he would let it pass. "Other than try to drown me? How about having me beaten near to death?"

"My family had you beaten?"

"Stephen Shay was tryin' to get to Grace. Had me beaten in Denver to make it look like a robbery so he could be the one to save me—gave him an excuse to follow me back to White Pines. The man hounded Grace her whole damn life."

Cassie wished he'd at least whitewashed the facts a little to spare her feelings. "Will they hate me?"

"Can't rightly say. Your family put Grace through hell."

"Grace. Jake's mother?"

He nodded. "You saving Jake's life will be in your favor. The fact you ran away from them can't hurt. Not sure what they'll think about you being Stephen's niece."

Niece?

Where had he come by *that* misinformation?

She almost corrected him before realizing the folly.

Her father was the man who'd raped Grace Morgan—when she was barely more than a child, according to what Cassie had overheard. She was already facing condemnation simply for who she was even though she hadn't met anyone in White Pines except Jake. Perhaps by hiding her father's identity and letting them believe one of her uncles was her father, she would at least be given a chance to fit in. The only relationship they were sure of was that Derrick was her uncle. She had five others.

Jake was her half-brother. She'd had a hard time coming to terms with that. Her father had railed at her mother, blaming her over and over for not giving him a son. Yet, he'd had one all along—one who was clearly close to Cassie's own age. And that son had been created when he'd raped a woman barely past her first flux.

She'd never loved the man.

Now, Cassie hated him.

What would it have been like to have a brother, to not be a lonely only child?

How would Jake react when he discovered she was his sister?

How would his mother react?

She turned the topic. "How did Grace come to marry Adam Morgan?"

"I was wondering the same thing," Drew chimed in.

Cassie had almost forgotten he was riding with them.

"Came lookin' for Jake," Ty replied.

Cassie's curiosity was still unquenched. "Why would Grace put Jake in an orphanage?"

"Didn't. Gave him to the Curtis family to adopt. They got killed, and Jake ended up with me in Denver. Grace never even knew 'til he was already grown up."

Although she was dying to ask about Ty's family, she didn't. It was difficult enough for him to talk about *Jake's* past. No wonder, considering how much the men had suffered. Reading between the lines was easy enough—Ty and Jake had known starvation. "Grace came to find Jake and met Adam. Yes?"

Another nod.

"She told Jake about his father's family," she added. "That he was a Shay."

"He's a Curtis. Always will be." Ty's jaw clenched. "Jake got an invitation to San Francisco from your uncle. Then he almost killed us both." He gave his horse a kick to hurry ahead, effectively ending the conversation.

She had no doubt everyone in White Pines would despise her. They would never welcome her in their fair town.

No, she would be forced to move on, and that meant she'd be leaving Ty Bishop behind.

Chapter Eight

For the second morning in a row, Cassie woke up on top of Ty—her face pressed to his neck, her legs resting between his in an indecent position.

Fire flared to life inside her, settling low between her thighs. Sweet Lord, but the man was turning her into some wanton creature who could do little to control her desire whenever he was near.

Now she needed to politely and gently extract herself from the embarrassing situation before Ty woke and—

"I'm startin' to like the way you wake me up," he said in a husky whisper.

Yesterday, she'd scrambled off him and in her haste, slammed her leg into what was obviously a tender area. His curse had echoed through the woods, making her more careful this morning.

Trying to roll away, she was stopped when the arms he'd wrapped around her waist clasped tighter. "Careful," he cautioned.

"I remember." But he wouldn't release her. "Shouldn't you loosen your hold, if you wish me to move?"

Instead of answering her, his hand grabbed her braid and gently tugged her down until his lips touched hers.

Cassie had waited for this, wanting to experience his kiss again. Having Ty hold her through the long cold night was wonderful, making her feel almost cherished. She could make believe that he truly cared for her—that he held her close because he had feelings for her and not simply because he worried whether she was warm enough or because he felt he owed her his protection for rescuing him.

Her greatest fear was that he could never forget who she was—a member of the Shay clan—or that her uncle tried to murder him. Even worse, once they reached White Pines, her true relationship to Jake was sure to come out because she wouldn't lie to protect herself if one of them guessed the truth. Not that she would *volunteer* the information...

Her father had been a terrible man, not only to her and her mother but to Jake's mother as well. Once the truth was revealed, Ty would hate her.

Everyone would hate her.

The kiss quickly changed from sweet and gentle to warm and consuming when Ty's tongue slipped past her lips to mate with hers. Cassie had quickly learned how much joy could be found in such an intimate kiss, and she'd craved it—dreamt of it—since the last time he'd kissed her. With a moan, she tried to mimic his actions, hesitantly letting her tongue chase his as it retreated. He gently held it with his teeth and then gave it a tender pull. Everything inside her sprang to life.

His hands settled on her hips, and he pressed his hips up immodestly against her center. Heat burned low in her belly, her most private area feeling heavy and damp. From what she'd seen of Ty's body as he'd bathed in the brook, what had hung limp between his thighs had now changed size. Considerably.

Fear seized her imagination as she thought of the horrible things her mother had said about what a man could do to a woman. Cassie scrambled away, her knee connecting with his groin again.

Ty hissed, rolling to his side and pulling up his knees. The curse that fell from his lips was one of the words she'd been told *never* to use.

"I'm so sorry, Ty... I didn't mean..." Knowing nothing she could say would make him feel better, she slipped away to tend to her needs, hoping he'd forgive her for always being so clumsy.

Ty took several deep breaths, waiting for the pain in his balls to ease. She'd make a eunuch of him yet—one way or another. It had been a mistake to sleep next to her, but he'd worried about whether she was warm during the cold autumn nights.

That lie didn't even hold up for a few precious seconds. He'd lain side by side with her because he desired her. Something about Cassie Shay had enchanted him from the moment he'd seen her, and whatever spell she'd woven around him seemed to grow stronger with each passing day. He tried to convince himself he only felt responsible for her because she'd saved his life. He argued with himself that he was being a gentleman by protecting her from her ogre of a fiancé and her disgusting family. He even explained his desire as nothing more than a simple lusting.

None of those tacks worked for a damned minute.

No, Cassie was more to him than a woman in need of help or a quick roll in the hay. Tender feelings—the type he'd seen in Jake whenever he was around his wife Emily or in Adam whenever Grace was near—had ignited deep inside.

In some ways, he resented that she'd affected him so strongly. His life was fine as it was. Turning it upside down would only bring strife.

What he intended to do about Cassie, he wasn't sure. All he knew was that he couldn't let her go. Not now.

Not ever.

"Better?" Drew said from across the dead fire. "That had to hurt like hell."

Ty scowled and sat up. The disapproving frown Drew had thrown his way when he'd first slept next to Cassie spoke volumes for what he thought about the arrangement. No doubt Drew also felt the need to protect her after she'd supported him when his family had tossed him out.

"That woman's a menace," Ty replied.

"That woman's a temptation. What I need to know is...how much is she tempting *you?*"

The sharp pain in his groin had faded to a dull ache. No, it was Drew's question that caused him discomfort now.

Ty chose not to answer.

"I feel responsible for her," Drew pressed on. "I plan to watch out for her well-being."

"She ain't your responsibility," Ty snapped, hating feeling like some kind of cornered animal.

What he did with Cassie Shay was none of Drew's business, and he hated the man pressuring him about things he hadn't even figured out himself.

"She's the type of woman a man marries, not one he tumbles."

"I ain't tumbled her."

"*Yet.* They'll come looking for her, you know. Once they figure out where she's run away to, the Shays will be knocking on your door. And they won't be happy."

He'd thought of that too—he just hadn't figured out the proper solution to keep Cassie safe yet. Perhaps Drew would make a good ally, as would Ty's family and friends when he finally got her to White Pines. "I reckoned."

"And?"

"And *what?*"

"What will you do when they show up?"

Ty shrugged. "I guess we'll just have to cross that bridge when we come to it."

"What bridge?" Cassie's sweet voice called as she emerged from the shelter of the pines.

Throwing a cautionary glare to Drew, Ty turned to frown at her. He'd grown tired of her having to wear men's clothing, and he longed to see her in a dress or a skirt, something that showed her for the beautiful woman she was.

"We need to get moving."

***

White Pines was even more beautiful than she'd expected.

Straight out of one of her books, the town represented all the romantic notions Cassie held of the Wild West. Two-story buildings lined the streets. A wooden walkway ran the length of the town on both sides of the main road, protecting people from walking through dirt and mud. Horses stood waiting at hitching posts.

Enchanting.

A saloon. A boarding house. A church in the distance. Even a small theater that was in the middle of being constructed. Everything about the town fit her imaginings, and she sighed in satisfaction. She wouldn't have to find a way to steal away to the Dakotas after all because there was no way that territory could hold a candle to White Pines, Montana.

She'd come home.

"Ty!" a slender brunette called from the door of the marshal's office. "You're back!"

An enormous smile lit Ty's face.

Cassie had to swallow hard to keep her jealousy at bay. The woman was beautiful with a long, dark braid that hung nearly to her hips. A heart-shaped face framed blue eyes as clear as a crystal stream. She was short, almost as tiny as Cassie herself.

"Ty! You're home!" the woman called again, waving her arm.

"Victoria!" He nudged Duke with his heels to speed the last of their journey.

When he reached the woman, he jumped down from the saddle, embraced her, and swung her in a big circle.

Drew rode up next to Cassie, close enough their knees brushed, and reached for her hand. She gladly accepted his fingers closing around hers, needing to pull from his strength. After a bolstering squeeze, he released her.

She'd never allowed herself to consider that Ty might have a woman waiting for him when he got back to his town. Not that she'd bothered to ask—whether from fear or assumption.

That oversight had come home to roost.

A tall man with brown hair stepped from the marshal's office, a tin star pinned to the right side of his vest. "Ty! Welcome home."

Ty shook the man's hand. "Glad to be back, Matthew. Jake turned up yet?"

"We got a message from him yesterday," the marshal replied. "Should be here later today. Wish you'd have let us know you were safe." His amber eyes settled on Drew and then on Cassie before he frowned.

"I brought some friends with me." Ty nodded toward them.

Friends. Why did his choice of words make Cassie feel as if she would weep?

Probably because she'd led him on, brazenly kissing him. Heavens, she'd awakened on top of the man—*twice!* He surely thought she was a woman of loose morals, not one he would ever consider courting. She might have enjoyed his kisses—like the one they'd shared this morning that all but melted her bones.

But he clearly believed nothing special occurred. His kisses had meant everything to her, yet they'd meant nothing to him.

Cassie bowed her head, trying to find the inner strength to graciously greet the people who obviously loved Ty and face them as his *friend.*

Drew's hand settled over hers where it rested on the saddle horn. "Be patient, Cass. Let's meet these people, find out everything before you get upset. That woman might not be his—"

"I am *not* upset," she snapped before letting him say a word that would pierce like a knife to the heart.

His fingers brushed over her cheek, and she realized tears had already spilled over her lashes. "'Be joyful in hope, patient in affliction...'"

She loved how her friend could so easily divert her sadness. "Romans, chapter twelve, verse...twelve?"

"Correct, as always. I know how you feel about Ty."

She tried to dismiss him with a flip of her wrist, but Drew grabbed her hand midair.

"I'm here if you need me. No matter what." Leaning in, he pressed a kiss to her cheek.

"Thank you, Drew."

An exaggerated clearing of a man's throat drew her attention. Ty had dragged the woman over to her, and the marshal had followed close on their heels.

Cassie's cheeks burned when she realized they'd seen Drew's quick kiss and probably misinterpreted it.

Frowning up at her, Ty crooked his finger.

She bent down and was taken by surprise when he snatched the cap from her head and her braid tumbled out.

"Ty!"

Now the marshal and the woman *both* frowned.

"Ty?" the man said. "What's going on here?"

"Told ya. Brought a couple of friends back with me." Nodding at the marshal, Ty said to Cassie and Drew, "This is Matthew Riley. He's the law in White Pines." He smiled at the brunette. "That's Victoria Riley, Matthew's wife."

"And your sister," Victoria added. "Well, not his *real* sister." She turned to Cassie and Drew. "He's already got plenty of those, but we grew up together."

Cassie would have breathed a sigh of relief at the news that Ty didn't claim Victoria if she hadn't been keenly aware of the intense scrutiny directed at her. Since Ty didn't seem inclined to introduce her, she feared for a moment he'd decided to hide her family name. Wondering if she also needed to try to conceal her identity, she looked back to him for guidance.

With a heavy sigh, he took the lead. "That's Drew Pearson, and this...*this* is Cassie Shay."

"Shay?" Matthew roared. "She's a *Shay*?"

Ty nodded as he reached up to help her from her horse. His big hands settled on her waist as he lifted her effortlessly to the ground.

She sidled up next to him, hating the condemnation flowing to her from the marshal.

"Yes, Mr. Riley," she replied, angry at herself that her voice trembled. "I'm Cassandra Shay."

Matthew snatched the hat from his head and slapped it against his thigh. "What in the hell are you doing, Ty?"

"She saved my life," he replied, seemingly calm and collected. He wrapped a protective arm around her shoulders and hauled her up even closer against his side. "Saved Jake's life, too."

"What happened?" Victoria asked, her eyes never leaving Cassie.

"We didn't get quite the welcome we'd hoped for. Derrick Shay and his little lapdog tried to kill us."

"Kill you?" Matthew smacked his hat back on his head. "I warned when that bastard Derrick invited Jake to come to San Francisco."

"How 'bout we save the whole story for when Jake gets here and we can tell everyone at the same time?" Ty glanced back over his shoulder. "Cassie and Drew can stay out at the Twin Springs—"

"No!" Cassie shouted before she could stop herself. Taking a quick breath to try to calm her racing nerves, she added, "I mean, no, thank you. I'm grateful for the offer. I just...couldn't possibly impose."

Ty glared down at her. "Cassie... There ain't anywhere—"

"I can't stay there, either, Ty," Drew said as he dismounted. "Your father surely wouldn't want you extending an invitation to us without his permission."

"It's my home too," Ty insisted. "Adam won't—"

"Ty..." Victoria laid a hand on Ty's free arm. "Think about Grace for a minute."

A responding scowl told Cassie all she needed to know. She would sleep in the street before she'd force a woman her father had wronged so badly to give her shelter. "I saw a boarding house..."

"That's a marvelous idea, Cass." Drew tossed her a smile. "We can take rooms there—"

Ty was shaking his head before Drew could even finish. "Used most your money on supplies."

"I have money," Cassie asserted.

"*Of course*, you do." Matthew snorted. "You're a *Shay*."

Straightening her spine, Cassie met the marshal's hateful gaze as Drew came to stand at her other side. It was painfully obvious Matthew had already decided what he thought of her just by the condemning tone of his voice.

"Matthew…" A growl rose from Ty's throat.

Matthew's dark eyes narrowed as he pushed the brim of his hat back with his knuckle. "Have you forgotten what Stephen Shay did to Grace? To me? To *you*, for Christ's sake!"

"I ain't forgotten."

"Then why in the hell would you bring his…what? Do you even know how she's related to Stephen?"

"She's his niece," Ty replied, looking down at her.

The moment of truth had arrived. She's promised herself she wouldn't lie, not after everything her father had put these good people through—after everything he'd put her mother through. No, best to lay the truth out on the table now.

She opened her mouth to speak.

Drew's hand suddenly encased hers, and he squeezed her fingers. *Hard.*

Glancing back at him, Cassie knit her brows at why he'd want her to keep silent. Since her father hadn't been active in San Francisco society, she wasn't sure whether Drew knew her father's identity or not. From the way his hand was cutting off the circulation in hers, Drew not only knew, he didn't want her to confess.

But why?

"She's Derrick's niece too," Ty added.

Cassie gave Drew a curt nod and dropped his hand. "Derrick is my uncle, but my grandfather is my guardian. Both of my parents are dead."

It wasn't a lie—it simply wasn't the whole truth.

So why did it feel so bad to say the words?

"You're one of the New York Shays?" Matthew still frowned at her.

She didn't confirm or deny, holding her tongue until she could get Drew alone and ask why he'd steered her down this path.

"Cassie, why are you dressed like a boy?" Victoria asked.

"'Cause we had to get her outta San Francisco without her family following," Ty replied before Cassie could figure out how to answer.

"You mean you *kidnapped* her?" Matthew's question came out a roar. "They'll come here to get her back."

"Didn't kidnap no one," Ty replied. "Just helped her escape."

"*Escape* her family," Matthew added. "What in hell possessed you to bring the wrath of the Shays down on us all? Jesus have mercy, haven't they hurt us enough? She'll make things worse—*much* worse!"

It was all suddenly too much. Their hatred. Her own fear. The hurt that she'd finally found a place she could call home but would have to quickly be moving on.

Her gaze flew to her friend's. "Drew?"

"Let's go, Cass," he replied. "We'll go get a couple of rooms 'til we can decide where to go from here."

Ty almost shouted at her to stop when Cassie pulled away from him to follow Drew, but he was torn between her and his family.

Matthew and Victoria glared at her as Drew handed her Duchess's reins and then started to lead his own horse toward the boarding house down the street.

Cassie turned back once to glance at Ty over her shoulder.

The pain in her eyes hit him like a blow to the gut. "Don't go!" he hollered.

She shook her head and glanced away.

With all the anger bubbling through him, Ty turned back to Victoria and Matthew. "What kind of welcome was *that?*"

"Welcome? You expected me to *welcome* a damn Shay?" Matthew's voice was loud enough Cassie and Drew had to have heard. "Not now, not *ever*."

"Ty..." Victoria laid her hand on his shoulder.

He had to fight the urge to jerk away from her touch. He'd known her most of his life, and he'd never seen her be anything but generous and caring. "She's not like them."

"She's one of them," Victoria replied.

"You know...when Grace came here sayin' she was Jake's sister, you all gave her the benefit of the doubt. But I bring Cassie to you and—"

"It's not the same at all," Matthew insisted.

"*But* we all gave Grace a chance. Cassie's trying to find a better life, just like most everyone who comes out here."

Matthew set his hands against his hips as he worked his jaw—his way of saying he wouldn't budge.

Victoria, on the other hand, seemed lost in thought.

Maybe that was a good sign.

All Ty could think about was getting to Cassie and smoothing over the lack of welcome she'd received from the people he'd told her would accept her. Perhaps he'd had a little too much faith in his family and friends, or perhaps he'd underestimated how much pain Stephen Shay had caused Matthew and Grace.

Either way, Cassie was the one who suffered.

Drew was giving her the support and comfort Ty wanted to provide, causing jealousy that sat on his chest like a heavy weight.

"Let her get settled, Ty," Victoria said. "We need to talk to Daddy and Grace and see what they think is best to do with her."

"Do with her?" Ty asked, his tone angrier than he'd intended. "She's not a stray puppy, Victoria. You can't give her to someone else to take care of. I brought her here. I need to watch after her."

Matthew's frown didn't fade. "Her friend—Drew, was it?—seems to be taking good care of her. Let him." His jaw worked again until he said, "A Shay. Damn it, Ty. What in the hell were you thinking?"

"I was thinking she saved my life. I was thinking she saved Jake's, too. And I was thinking you all would treat her a helluva lot better than you did."

Mounting Duke, Ty rode away before he said something he'd regret. As he passed the boarding house, he had to fight the urge to stop and check on Cassie. Her anger needed time to cool, and if he went charging in there, he might really mess things up, especially since he didn't know if she wanted to keep pretending to be a boy.

No, he'd wait until morning. For now, he'd go back to the Twin Springs and talk to Adam and Grace to see if they could help him fix this mess.

Chapter Nine

"Lie down, Cass. You need to get some rest," Drew called from across their small room.

She stared out the second-story window, hugging herself and rubbing her upper arms. Yes, she was tired. The day had been draining, both physically and mentally.

But rest?

Impossible.

People still bustled along the busy street, mostly men heading to the Four Aces—the local saloon. The moon cast enough light she could clearly see their faces. Not sure why she checked each one, she simply kept looking.

Oh, who was she trying to fool?

She searched those faces to try to find Ty Bishop among them. How she'd allowed her attachment to the man to become so strong so quickly remained a mystery, but attached she was—and probably would be for a long, long time to come.

Then she suddenly saw Ty sauntering toward the saloon with his typically cocky gait. Her gaze followed him across the road to where he clapped his hand against the shoulder of another man waiting on the boardwalk. *Jake.* He'd returned to White Pines as well. Ty would be relieved his friend was home safely. She could almost feel him relax as the two of them spoke.

Her heart wanted him to somehow realize that she watched him, to look up and see her and know he'd made a huge mistake in walking away with no fond farewell. If he was truly her love, he should feel her gaze upon him and should come running and beg her forgiveness for being such a callow cad. A soul mate would sense her—no matter the distance between them.

As the men turned and entered the bar, Ty never looked back.

"I love you, Ty Bishop." Her whispered words slipped out.

"Cass..." Drew patted their small bed. "Come and sleep. We'll start fresh tomorrow."

The town would surely be scandalized if they discovered that she and Drew taken a room together. She didn't give a damn. Her old life was over. All the silly rules that went along with that life were over too. She needed a friend right now. Since Drew hadn't consulted her when he'd made the arrangements with the boarding house owner, he must have known how much the day had cost her and decided to remain close. Besides, she'd still been dressed as a boy when Drew had spoken to the shopkeeper. The skinny man probably thought they were brothers.

Arms wrapped around her waist from behind, hugging her close. "He hurt you."

A small mocking laugh slipped out. "More than he shall ever know."

"Ah... So that's it, then. You love the cowboy."

Cassie nodded, seeing no reason to deny it to Drew—the only person who seemed to care about her. His hug was comforting, but it wasn't what she needed.

Only Ty could truly mend her hurt.

Pushing out of his embrace, she went over to pick up her bundle of cash from where she'd set it on the dresser. "At least we have some funds left."

"We need to figure out where we go from here," Drew added.

She didn't ask why he said "we." She knew. They'd become their own family—outcasts who were unwanted and unwelcome to the people who meant the most to them.

"The Dakotas," she replied. "Exactly as I planned from the beginning. We'll build a farm there. A house. A barn. A garden."

He shook his head and went back to sit on the edge of the bed. "It's too late, Cass."

"Too late?"

"We can't get that far and find—let alone *build*—a place to stay in time for winter. Winters here aren't like San Francisco. You've never seen the kind of snowstorms we get out here. Real blizzards."

"How exciting. I would love to see a real blizzard."

His laughter made her bristle, reminding her too much of her grandfather and uncle whenever she mentioned she wanted to go to college or to travel the world and see its wonders.

"Trust me," he said. "You haven't missed anything—except maybe a bad case of frostbite."

"Then where shall we go?"

"We stay here."

Her mouth fell open as she blinked in confusion. "Here? Stay *here*? Are you jesting?"

"I assure you, I'm quite serious," Drew replied. "We'll find a place to stay tomorrow. A house or a cabin we can call our own close to town."

"Why?"

"We both need to tend our wounds. To heal. We'll figure the rest of the future out come spring."

Wounds. Heavens yes, she had wounds, but they were all on her heart. As were Drew's.

Perhaps he was right—injuries like that needed time to repair every bit as much as physical hurts.

Staring at her roll of money, Cassie frowned. "If we stay in White Pines, this will have to last us a long time, Drew."

He patted the bed, so she put the money back on the dresser and went to sit next to him.

"It will last until we find ways to make more," he said. "Did you see the theater they're adding to the saloon? We can work there, Cass."

"What could I possibly do there? You're the actor."

"Ah, but you know Shakespeare too. We can *both* act. Can you sing as well?"

The man had lost his mind. "I–I couldn't possibly…"

His lips touched her forehead. "Sure you could. Let's start fresh tomorrow, start asking around to find out where we can call home for a while."

One question gnawed at her, and she would get no rest until she found out Drew's reasoning. "Why didn't you let me tell Ty my father's name? You let him believe I wasn't Stephen Shay's daughter."

"After that greeting? No, angel, that's knowledge best kept to yourself. At least for now."

She dropped her gaze. "I promised myself that I wouldn't lie to Ty."

"You didn't *lie*. You just…withheld information."

"A lie by any other name…"

"Would still keep the peace. They'll find out. One day. Just not *today*." He stood up, pulled Cassie to her feet and dragged back the quilt. "Come to bed."

Letting Drew pull her down with him, she stretched out at his side. He threw an arm over her waist and yawned.

How odd to be so close to a man's body and feel nothing but the comfort of friendship. Of course he felt nothing but friendship for her, either. Her family would still be scandalized at their conduct.

That delicious thought helped Cassie find her first smile since she'd left Ty.

She shifted a little to get her bunched up shirt straightened, wishing she had one of her soft cotton nightdresses instead of the clothes Drew loaned her. She wanted—no, *needed*—to feel like a woman again.

"You win," she finally said. "We shall stay. But I will buy myself some dresses. If I must stay in this place, I will stay as me, not as some…boy."

Drew chuckled. "I'm sure you will dazzle him, cutie."

"I am not speaking of Ty."

"Oh, no. *Of course*, you're not."

She drifted to sleep, thinking about the time she would see Ty again and planning on how she'd blister his ears for leaving her so abruptly before she threw herself into his arms and kissed him.

***

"…and that's how we finally got back home." Ty took a long pull on his beer.

"Sounds like quite an adventure." Jake sipped his drink.

Ty nodded. "Figured you had an adventure of your own."

"Nothing but a boring train ride and a couple of days on the back of my horse."

"Should have sent Cassie with you. She sure made the trip…*interestin'*." Besides, had she traveled with Jake, she wouldn't be attached at the hip to Drew Pearson.

How easy it had been for the two of them to leave Ty standing there, trying to convince Matthew and Victoria that he hadn't betrayed them or Grace by bringing Cassie to White Pines. For a moment, he fretted that Drew's family had been wrong about his preferences—that Drew liked women, especially Cassie, just fine.

Still, Drew wouldn't have taken the kind of public humiliation his family had put him through if he didn't live the life they'd condemned him for. Ty's own jealousy was the only thing that made him fear the bond between Cassie and Drew. At least she was still close at hand. Now he needed to find a way to keep her in White Pines.

"No way in hell you'd have let her go." Jake grinned. "You wanted her with you. Wanna explain what's going through that head of yours?"

"What'cha mean?"

"Who do you think you're foolin'? You like that girl, Ty."

He shrugged in response. It was hard enough admitting his feelings to himself—he wasn't nearly ready to admit those feelings to anyone else. *Even Jake.*

Jake's lips pulled into a tight line, and he stared for long moments. A heavy sigh slipped out. "She's a Shay. Can you *try* to make that matter?"

"She's not like them. She's kind. Got a heart."

No wonder she wanted to get away from her family. How difficult would it have been for a woman with so sweet a nature to grow up around such cruelty? Yet she'd come out untarnished. Pure of heart. Full of life.

Perfect.

Jake drank his beer and stared at Ty before he spoke again. "Won't matter to Grace."

"Didn't matter to Matthew and Victoria, neither. Wish you coulda seen her face when Matthew found out her name."

"Victoria's name?" Jake drawled.

Ty shot his friend a frown, not appreciating the humor. "Was like she got...hit or something."

"Stephen Shay hurt Grace more than he hurt Matthew. Can't imagine Cassie's feelings won't get stomped if she and Grace meet up. You know, it just might be best if you let her go."

"Can't."

"Can't?" Jake shook his head. "Won't."

"Fine. *Won't.*"

Grabbing his mug, Ty swigged down some beer. He wasn't much of a drinker, but with the nonsense he'd gone through the last few days, he should be drinking whiskey instead. Maybe getting good and drunk would help him forget for a while.

"Ty, we've been friends since...well, forever."

With a resigned sigh, he put his beer aside and prepared for another scolding.

Victoria had already performed that duty, giving him an earful and letting him know how disappointed she was in him for not caring what bringing Cassie here would do to Grace. Granted, he only knew a little of the nightmare Grace had suffered at Stephen Shay's hand, but the man was dead and buried. Cassie was only his niece, and she'd obviously had little contact, being as she grew up in New York. Probably explained a lot about why she was so unspoiled.

A man like Stephen Shay raising her?

She'd be nothing but another rich bitch—the kind that used to sneer at him and Jake when they were children begging for food.

"You need to let her go, friend," Jake insisted. "We got her outta there. We paid our debt."

"She saved your life, *friend.* Or did you forget?"

"I remember just fine, but we did like we promised—we helped her escape from her family. Let her go her own way now, while you go yours."

Go my own way?

Hell, Ty didn't have a clue which way he *wanted* to go let alone was *supposed* to go. He'd held that parcel of Twin Springs land for years since

Adam had given him the deed, but he'd never made plans for it. He'd never thought about a day beyond the one he was living. He never worried about the future.

'Til he met Cassandra Shay.

Ty thought about the future now. A lot. He'd dreamed of a cabin he'd built on his land—a cabin for the two of them—but that dream was being soundly destroyed by his friends and family.

And he hadn't even faced Adam and Grace yet.

Jake was right. Holding tight to Cassie would cost Ty dearly.

What he needed to decide was if he was willing to pay that price.

***

"This will do." Cassie held the calico dress to her front, grateful the store had one already sewn. "And I shall take the other two as well. I also need petticoats and…" She looked around the General Store to be sure no men were in earshot. "…underthings. I have no camisole or–or bloomers."

"Lord, child." The shopkeeper's wife took the dress from her and draped it over her arm with the other dresses Cassie had chosen. "You really were left with nothing, weren't ya?"

Drew came up behind her. "She's quite lucky to have escaped with her life."

Cassie would have grinned at his exaggeration, but at least he backed up her fib. "I will need a pair of shoes and some stockings as well."

"Imagine that." The older woman placed the items on the long, wooden counter. "Stagecoach bandits taking everything you owned. What a world we live in!" She headed to a back room, still muttering to herself.

"Did you stop to consider that your story doesn't account for why you're dressed as a man now?" Drew asked with a chuckle.

"I told her they wanted my expensive dress and forced me to strip and wear some of their cast-off clothing," she replied with a smirk. "I'm quite used to thinking on my feet."

Her family had taught her that lesson from an early age. A well-fabricated lie often kept her from punishment and allowed her to run free most of the time. She lied to get away from her mother's misery, her grandfather's scrutiny, and to spend time with the only person who truly loved her—Old Tim.

At least Drew was her friend, so she wasn't all alone in the world now that Ty…

Now that Ty has left me behind.

"I've been talking to Gideon Young over there…" Drew nodded to a tall, raven-haired man. The man nodded back. "There's an abandoned cabin on his land. It's only a short ride from town. A man and his wife lived in it for a year or so 'til they decided Montana wasn't what they'd bargained for and headed back East. Gideon says he and his brother can't keep the place up, so we can stay there for a while to decide if we like it or not. Even has a small barn."

"I still hoped we would leave White Pines."

"You can't leave, Cass. Not 'til things are settled between you and Ty."

"Oh, I do believe they were settled quite fine yesterday."

Drew leaned a hip against the counter. "*Nothing* got settled yesterday. He greeted his family. We walked away. Give the man a chance."

A chance to do what? Break her heart again? "What does Mr. Young want in way of payment for the cabin?"

"Right now, nothing except for us to set it to right again. Seems it's a bit of a...mess. He has some lumber we can use and—"

She shook her head. "I know nothing about building."

"You're in luck. I've built everything from castles to forests."

"How do you *build* a forest?"

"*Sets*, Cass. I'm an actor. Who do you think builds the sets?"

He had her there. "We don't have much money."

"Gideon says there's a little furniture still there that we can use, and it'll be a great place to stay and regroup. Gideon claims there's even a small vegetable garden we might forage some food from. Next spring we can plant—"

"Spring? You still think we'll be here come *spring?*"

"I do." He stood back to his full height and placed his hands on her shoulders. "It's late autumn, angel. We couldn't head out anywhere now. Have to wait out the winter, then we can make some long-term choices. We talked this out last night. Remember?"

A resigned sigh slipped out before the full weight of his words descended. "Drew, *you* should be moving on. I cannot allow you to feel...obligated—"

"Look down the street. There's a theater being built as we speak, so I'll have work. That solves our money problems. Besides, I *am* obligated. You stood by my side...especially after what my brother said." He hung his head as his hand fell away. "You're the one who should be moving on. Without me."

She took his hand in hers. "Together. We will do this *together*. Please tell Mr. Young we would be glad to accept his offer."

The shopkeeper's wife returned with several undergarments and a pair of shoes which she laid on the counter next to the dresses. "Will that be all?"

"No." Cassie smiled at Drew. "We shall need some cleaning supplies as well."

Chapter Ten

Cassie glanced up from the well and smiled despite herself. "'Twould seem gossip travels as fast in small towns as it does in San Francisco."

Drew pulled the saw from the slat of wood he'd been cutting. "What do you mean? Is Gideon back with more wood?"

She shook her head and pointed at their guest, who was fast approaching on his horse. "Mr. Bishop has already come for a visitation."

Drew's laughter floated in the air as he picked up the cut piece of timber. "Then I shall leave you two to your privacy." He headed back into the cabin, still chuckling.

Setting aside the bucket full of water, she wiped her hands on her filthy pants. The better part of the day had been spent cleaning the windows and walls of the large two-room cabin that was now her home. The last hour she'd been on her knees, scrubbing the floor. She still wore boy's clothes to save her new dresses wear and tear, but she suddenly wished she'd donned the calico instead. Better to have a new dress dirtied than for Ty to think of her as masculine. Just once, she wished he would see her as a real woman—that he would treat her like a real woman.

Ty practically threw himself off Duke's back. "Have you lost your mind?"

"I beg your pardon?" Picking up the heavy bucket, she let it dangle from her fingers.

His hand shot out, snatching the bucket away from her. "What in the hell's going through that pretty little head of yours?"

Figuring it would help her aching back to have him carry the water inside, she resisted the urge to grab the bucket back. Perhaps he *did* see her as a woman and wanted to be gallant.

"I have no idea what you are referring to, Mr. Bishop." She headed toward the cabin, hoping he would follow.

"Oh, for the love of... Stop that sh— Um...manure." Ty's height forced him to duck to get under the doorframe. His gaze wandered the modest cabin, and his scowl grew fiercer.

She smiled up at him, hoping to appear innocent of taunting him, even though that was exactly what she was doing. "Stop what manure?"

"Stop calling me Mr. Bishop. You only do that when you're angry."

Her smile grew. Ty knew her better than she thought. "Fine. *Ty.* What makes you think I have—as you say—lost my mind?"

"Nothing else could explain you decidin' to stay here instead of in town. A woman out here on her own—"

"Oh, but you've been misinformed. I'm not alone. Drew is—"

Ty set the bucket down hard enough water sloshed over the sides. "Drew! Don't that just figure."

His angry eyes fixed on where the topic of their discussion was aligning his board onto the wall he was constructing to create bedrooms.

"Hello there, Ty," Drew called in a sing-song voice. "You've come to see our new place?"

"You ain't got no more sense than her, do you?"

She knew what he was thinking, that the place was a mess. He was right.

But she also knew that when Drew and Gideon were done making repairs and she was finished giving the place a thorough cleaning, it would be a nice little home.

Picking up a scrub brush, Cassie crouched next to the bucket. After dipping the brush in the water, she ran the bristles over the harsh soap, got back on her hands and knees, and started cleaning the floor where she'd left off.

"Cassie!" Ty's shout echoed off the cabin walls.

Sitting back on her heels, she knit her brows. "What?"

"You can't live here! Especially not with—" his eyes stayed fixed on Drew, "—*him*. Ain't proper."

"To hell with proper," she replied.

Ty's mouth dropped open. "To hell with... Ladies don't say *hell*."

"*This* lady does." She went back to scrubbing the floor. "If you plan to stay, you could at least lend Drew a hand. We should get the walls built before we get the beds."

"Beds?"

"Yes, Ty. *Beds.* Two of them." If she didn't know better, she would have assumed he was jealous. "What brings you out here?"

"Came to see what trouble you'd gone and gotten yourself into this time."

Her gasp brought a smile to his lips. "*This* time? I am not one to court mischief, sir."

"Could've fooled me." His gaze wandered the cabin. "Place is bigger than I thought."

Amazed he saw the potential as well, Cassie gave him a smile. "It is a nice size. Drew is building walls so we can each have a room. Now we must find a place to buy some furniture. Perhaps there are some craftsmen in White Pines?"

Ty nodded as his eyes came back to gaze at her. "Can help you with that."

"We also need some linens, a chair or two. Things for the kitchen." A sigh slipped out as she considered all she and Drew would need to buy to make the cabin a true home. "One step at a time, however." She chuckled. "I suppose it's one *dollar* at a time. Drew and I will surely have to find a way to earn some money soon to get all that we need. Do you know who owns the theater?"

Ty didn't reply.

Cassie glanced up from where she'd begun to scrub the floor again and found him lost in thought. "Do you know who owns the new theater, Ty?"

"I gotta go."

On that, he turned and strode out of the cabin, ducking under the door frame on his way out.

"Ty!" Dropping the brush, she scrambled to her feet and followed. She caught up with him as he got on Duke's back. "What's wrong?"

"Just remembered someplace I gotta be." He reined Duke to the left.

"Wait!"

Pulling back on the reins, Ty looked down at her. "What did'ya want, Cassie girl?"

Time. What she wanted was more time with him and some brilliant stroke of inspiration so she could figure out a way to get him to stay. Drew's company was nice, but she'd missed Ty more than he could possibly know. No sooner had he arrived than he was running right back out the door.

Cassie wrung her hands. "Um...perhaps...you'd like..."

What? What could she propose? Lemonade? A piece of pie? As if she had anything to offer him as enticement to stay...

Her mind came up blank and her pride stung. "Oh, bother. Never mind. Go on. Ride away. Just see if I care."

Whirling on her heel, she headed back to the house. As her foot crossed the threshold, she felt a strong arm slip around her waist and tug. Her back was plastered against Ty's strong chest.

He clucked his tongue before kissing the ticklish place behind her ear. "That quick temper of yours will get you in trouble some day." His voice was filled with laughter.

"I never possessed a quick temper until I met you."

A good girl would pull away from the near embrace, but she didn't feel much like a good girl—never did when she was with Ty. Being in his embrace was too wonderful to force herself to move.

Ty turned her in his arms. Pushing back the brim of his hat with his knuckle, he leaned in closer. Thinking he meant to kiss her again, she closed her eyes and stretched up on tiptoes. Instead of his warm lips pressing against hers, a rough cloth rubbed her cheek. Her eyes flew open to find him gently wiping her face with a handkerchief. She tried not to let him see her disappointment.

"Did you scrub the dirt off the floor and put it on your face?" he asked with a heart-stopping grin.

She shrugged and fought back the tears that threatened as she once more faced the stark fact that her feelings for him ran deep but weren't returned. Humiliation made her cheeks burn.

"I gotta go," he murmured. A long finger lifted her chin until she looked into his eyes. His penetrating gaze refused to release her.

Try as she might, Cassie couldn't make herself move. "So you said. Farewell, then."

Suddenly, he didn't seem to be in such a hurry, slowly dropping his head as his lips drew closer and closer to hers. His warm breath rushed over her face, sending a shiver racing the length of her body.

She closed her eyes again, waiting with held breath for his kiss.

"Farewell, Cassie girl."

By the time she opened her eyes, Ty was already mounting Duke.

Cassie clenched her hands into fists.

Ty watched her closely, enjoying every emotion she so freely displayed on her dirt-smudged face. By the time she started sputtering at him, she'd clearly settled on angry.

"Go on, then, Mr. Bishop. Just go." She punctuated the last word with a haughty flip of her wrist.

She'd wanted him to kiss her—that came as a welcome surprise. Damn, but he wished now that he'd gone right ahead and planted one on her. Problem was his family was wary of her, and the thought of them being unkind made him decide to give Cassie some breathing room.

The moment he'd ridden back to town and discovered she'd left the boarding house, he'd realized just how ridiculous it was to ever think he could leave her alone. A few questions to the town gossips had quickly revealed her destination, and his worry over her made him ride hard to get to her new home.

The empty cabin on Gideon Young's spread—not exactly the type of home Ty had pictured for Cassie Shay. He'd seen her real home. How in God's name would she ever be happy moving from the Shay estate to a two-room, run-down cabin? She deserved so much better. Not that he was the man to offer her that.

For now, he'd do what he could to see that she was safe and comfortable.

"I'm going, Cassie girl. But I'll be back. Soon."

***

The sun was just beginning to drop on the horizon when Ty returned to Cassie's cabin. Pulling the brake on the wagon he'd driven, he climbed down and started to unload the supplies.

A loud squeak announced the opening of the cabin door. "Well, well." Drew leaned his shoulder against the frame. "What have we here?"

Ty grunted and hauled another chair over the side of the wagon.

"Cass?" Drew called over his shoulder. "Did you forget to tell me it was your birthday?"

"Birthday?" Her voice rang from inside the cabin. "Why in heaven's name would you think it's my birthday?"

"Because someone's come to visit," Drew replied. "And he's bearing gifts."

Instead of responding to Drew's ridiculous comments, Ty nodded at the wagon. "So you gonna stand there all day crackin' wise, or are you gonna help me get this stuff inside 'fore it gets dark?"

With a laugh, Drew came over to the wagon, hefted a bag of flour over his shoulder, and headed into the cabin.

Cassie stepped outside to allow him to enter. "Ty! What on earth...?"

Ignoring her question, he picked up one of the chairs and carried it into the house as she followed. He placed the chair in front of the small pot-bellied stove and turned to go fetch the other.

He ran right into Cassie, who had set her hands against her hips. "What's going on?"

"Got you a few things I thought you'd need."

Since Adam had always given him room and board yet still paid him a salary for his work on the Twin Springs, Ty had squirreled away quite a nice little nest egg. Up until today, he'd never had a reason to spend it. The mere thought of Cassie passing even a single night without something she needed irritated him like finding a farmer stringing barbed wire across good pasture land.

"I can see *that*," she drawled. "What I don't understand is *why*."

He simply shrugged and side-stepped her.

She hurried after him. "I don't understand."

Ty grabbed the second chair and followed Drew, who was carrying an armload of linens, back into the cabin. As he set the chair down, the sounds of another wagon pulling up reached him. "Looks like the rest of it's here."

"The rest of it?" Cassie asked as she followed him outside. "The rest of *what?*"

"Matthew. Victoria," Ty said with a nod. "You remember Cassie and Drew."

"Of course," Victoria called as Matthew stepped down from his wagon and reached for her. "Good to see you both again."

Cassie could only stand and gape at what was happening around her. The wagon Matthew had been driving contained two headboards and bedding in addition to a crate with four chickens. Never would she have expected Victoria to extend a polite greeting, let alone bring things for her and Drew to use in their new home.

"I–I don't understand."

Victoria came to stand in front of Cassie. "We wanted to help... and to apologize."

"Apologize?"

Taking Cassie's hand, Victoria cradled it in her own. "Matthew and I were just so shocked yesterday. We owe you an apology for the less-than-hospitable greeting. We're here to make amends." She tugged until Cassie followed her over to the wagon. "We've brought you some things to help you settle in the cabin. Ty told us you had next to nothing."

Their generosity rendered Cassie speechless. She blinked back tears and glanced over to Ty. He held her gaze for a long moment before giving her a curt nod and grabbing a sack of potatoes, which he carried into the cabin.

While the first two wagons had been a surprise, the third thoroughly threw Cassie for a loop. From the distance, she saw two people swaying with the movement of the wagon over the rutted road and wondered who else could possibly be coming to call. As they drew closer and she realized they were more mature than the rest of the people running in and out of her new home, the answer came to her in a rush.

The time had arrived for her to face Grace and Adam Morgan.

Chapter Eleven

The wagon ground to a stop, and Ty stepped over to help Grace to the ground. "Thanks for comin'," he said as Grace kissed his cheek.

"For you, Ty," she replied.

Cassie pressed herself against Ty's side.

He reached down to clasp her hand and wasn't surprised to discover she was trembling. "It'll be okay, Cassie girl," he whispered.

She squeezed his hand in reply.

"Grace, this is Cassie."

The two women stared at each other for what seemed like far too long. He almost cleared his throat to break the silence when Grace spoke.

"Ty has told us so much about you."

Her words were clipped and held a depth of meaning, but then again, she wasn't known for being outspoken. She wasn't exactly frowning...but the welcoming smile he'd grown to know and love hadn't appeared. He feared Grace would never get past Cassie's last name to get to know the real woman.

Adam came to stand at Grace's side, and he wrapped his arm around his wife's shoulders.

"Cassie," Ty said. "This is Adam Morgan—the man who raised me."

She bent her knees slightly and bowed her head. "A pleasure, Mr. Morgan." She did the same for Grace. "Mrs. Morgan."

"Cassie..." Ty hated that his voice held a note of scolding, but she was slipping back into her impeccable society manners—probably as a way to shield herself from the tension of meeting Adam and Grace. He didn't want her to hide that feisty spirit he'd grown to love—to let it disappear again—fearing the more she buried it, the harder it would be to dig it out again. "You can call 'em by their Christian names."

"They have not given me leave to be informal."

"Well, then," Adam said, his voice booming and friendly. "Consider this our blessing." His hand shot out to her.

Cassie met it with her own, and the two shook hands. "Thank you, Adam."

Grace didn't extend her hand, but she did say, "Call me Grace. Please."

"Thank you, Grace. I'm very pleased to meet you both. Ty speaks of you fondly."

"As he does you," Adam replied. "Brought you some things for the house."

Cassie dropped her gaze to the ground. "You're far too generous. I couldn't possibly accept—"

"Nonsense," Adam said. "Ty told us how little you had. Only neighborly to share a few things with you." He took her hand again and led her to the back of the wagon.

Grace looked up at Ty. "She's not what I expected."

"How so?"

"She doesn't seem...spoiled." Her eyes wandered to the cabin. "I just can't imagine a *Shay* agreeing to live in a place like this."

"She's not like them, not from what I've seen. Told you what she did for Jake and me."

She nodded, but her teeth tugged on her bottom lip. "I'm still worried, Ty."

"About?"

A heavy sigh fell from her lips as she crossed her arms around her waist. "They'll send someone to find her. You know that, right? She can't run away and pretend she isn't what she is."

"A Shay."

Another nod. "Stephen might be gone, but that doesn't mean his family isn't dangerous to us all—especially to Jake and to you."

And perhaps Grace as well. Ty hadn't thought of that. The family still blamed her for Stephen's death, and if they hunted Cassie all the way to White Pines, they would surely want to exact some revenge on Grace. Not that anyone could reason with the Shays and try to get them to see how truly insane Stephen had been—how he'd chased Grace all over the country to try to catch her. *That* truth was conveniently ignored.

"We'll just all have to be on our guards then," he said.

Her lips thinned as she frowned. Then she turned on her heel and headed to the back of the wagon.

Adam handed her a large wicker basket.

"Seeing as we haven't had a chance to set up the kitchen, I brought us all a meal," she announced.

"Oh, Grace," Cassie said, "how kind you are. I fear cooking is not one of my skills."

Grace carried the basket to the cabin door. "Then I shall have to teach you."

Ty took Cassie's hand and led her into the cabin as Adam followed. "Where's Drew?"

"He has gone to dine with Gideon and his brother."

The word *good* almost slipped out before Ty stopped himself. His jealousy was unreasonable, but it refused to be pushed aside.

As his eyes adjusted to the dim light in the cabin, he was pleased to see the wall Drew had been constructing was completed. Although there were no doors yet, Cassie and Drew would each have their own bedroom. After being tortured with images of her sharing a room with him at the boarding house, Ty would sleep much better knowing her bed was going to be as lonely as his own.

Thankfully, the beds he'd purchased were small enough to fit in the tiny rooms. It would take some work to get everything set up before true darkness settled. At least there were some lamps and kerosene in the supplies he'd purchased.

Grace shook out the blanket Adam had brought inside and sat down next to her basket. One by one, she pulled out containers of food. "Let's eat."

"I'm so dirty." Cassie took a step back from the blanket. "Perhaps I should go wash and change first."

"Your hands are clean," Adam replied. "We've got a layer of dust from riding here. No one cares, Cassie."

She glanced down at her outfit. "I have new dresses. I could change."

"Nonsense." Grace patted the empty spot next to her. "You must be starving. Come and eat."

"Thank you." Cassie let Ty help her down, a muffled groan slipping out as she settled herself.

He grinned at her. "Sore?"

She nodded as Grace handed her a plate.

"The place is so clean." Grace pulled a towel off a large bowl full of boiled potatoes. She passed the bowl to Cassie. "I can't imagine how much work it was to get rid of the dust and dirt."

"Been empty almost a year," Ty added. "Find any critters?"

Cassie smiled. "A family of squirrels had decided the stove was to their liking. They didn't take it too well when I removed their nest."

"We'll have to be sure and clear away anything they left behind in the stovepipe." Adam passed a plate of fried chicken to Ty. "Can do that tomorrow, son."

Ty nodded, took the chicken, and dropped several pieces on his plate before handing it to Cassie. "Still lots to do here. After supper, we can finish unloading."

***

Cassie kept waving despite the dark now concealing the wagon, fearing the Morgans would think her ungrateful.

They seemed nice enough and had obviously gone out of their way to help settle her and Drew in their new home. They'd generously given her items— several that still needed to be unpacked—for the kitchen as well as a few pieces of furniture.

But below that gratitude rested a bit of unease. Grace was a very pretty woman—brown hair pulled into a tight bun and brown eyes that appeared wise—yet she didn't smile at Cassie. Not once. Ty received Grace's smiles, as did Adam. Even Drew was gifted with a grin or two. Yet each time Grace's gaze settled on Cassie, a frown touched her lips. Not that Cassie could blame her. The Shays, especially her father, had given Grace a great deal of misery through the years.

Adam was less reticent. His blue eyes were every bit as wise as Grace's, and his brown hair held enough gray to make Cassie think of him as a father-figure. He was quick with a smile and a kind word, and she'd instantly liked him—probably because she'd always wanted someone to treat her like a *real* father would. Instead, she'd been born to a man who treated his wife and daughter as if they were nothing but possessions.

Ty wrapped his arm around her shoulder, and she allowed herself the luxury of leaning closer. Drew and Gideon stood by the barn, talking softly. Their new landlord had quickly struck up a friendship with Drew, and it seemed that wherever Cassie saw one, the other was by his side.

"I should be going," Ty said softly as he squeezed her tighter against him.

"It is getting late. I cannot thank you enough for everything, Ty."

His shrug jostled her.

Gideon and Drew came striding over to the cabin.

"Cassie… I think I'll go out to Gideon's house for a while," Drew said.

"Got some more wood there he can fetch back," Gideon added.

Cassie wasn't entirely sure why, but the men obviously wanted some time alone. "Well, then. We would be thankful to have some more wood. Perhaps Drew can fashion a way for me to hang my dresses so they will not wrinkle."

Ty's smile always made something inside her melt. "If I hadn't seen you wear one back in Frisco," he said, "I'd be thinkin' you didn't own any dresses, Cassie girl."

She longed to show him exactly how wrong he was. Not that she was vain, but she knew he might be surprised at her appearance in proper clothing. Her hand brushed her cheeks as she wondered how much dirt covered her face.

Ty's hand followed hers as his thumb rubbed across her cheekbone. "You need a bath."

"That would be heavenly, but I fear one thing we do not have is a tub."

"I have something that might work," Gideon offered. "'Specially since you're such a little bit of a thing." His wink softened his statement. "Drew can bring it back, or I'll send Caleb over with it."

Since Cassie had yet to meet Gideon's brother, she thought it a splendid idea. "Please send Caleb. I've yet to thank him for allowing us to use this cabin as our home."

"I can go get it for you," Ty offered, his voice a bit gruff. "No need to be sending for Caleb."

Drew arched an eyebrow. "Why not? It wouldn't be out of his way, but you'd be heading the other direction. Maybe he and Cassie might find they have something in common."

"They don't." With a frown, Ty turned Cassie to face him. "You don't go near Caleb Young. Did you hear me, Cassie? You'll stay away from him."

"Why on earth would I want to stay away from Caleb?"

Although he had plenty of sound reasons he didn't wish them to meet, Ty couldn't think of a single one he could admit to Cassie. The women of the town found the dark-haired man so handsome they practically swooned at his feet.

There was no way Ty would let someone like that near his Cassie.

"Um...well...he's... Damn it, Cassie. Just stay away from him."

"Your moods, sir, are like the wind." Whirling around, she pulled out of his embrace and headed into the cabin.

"Drew," Ty snapped before turning to follow her, "bring back the tub."

As he entered the cabin, Drew and Gideon headed toward Gideon's wagon. He stomped into the cabin and slammed the door.

"Ty! I was under the impression you were going home." Her frown was as fierce as a winter wind. "I do not appreciate you ordering me about. If I want to meet Caleb Young—or any other man for that matter—I will. You have no right—"

"I'm sorry."

"Pardon?"

"I said I'm sorry. You're right. I shouldn't boss you 'round. I just...I didn't..." Hell, he couldn't say what he was really thinking without looking like some barely-weaned puppy chasing after his mother.

Don't meet Caleb because you might think he's a handsome bastard.

That smacked of jealousy—exactly like his resentment of her spending so much time with Drew and Gideon. *Any* man that took her attentions away was a threat.

Could the tender feelings he'd always thought he'd never feel be taking root in his heart?

The cabin walls suddenly seemed to be closing in on him. "I gotta go."

He jerked the door open, practically ran outside, and jumped on Duke's back.

Cassie stood in the door and brushed away a tear. "You didn't say goodbye."

Chapter Twelve

Cassie handed the cast-iron skillet to Grace.

Grace put it on the bottom shelf before rising back to full height. "Once we get the kitchen set up, I'll come and teach you to cook. Victoria and Emily would like to come as well."

Emily—*Jake's wife*.

Cassie had been looking forward to meeting her. The notion of having all those women in her new home was a bit daunting, but also exciting. She'd never fit in well with San Francisco society ladies. The women there always seemed a bit shallow and petty—worrying about frivolous things like whether their hair was coiffed properly or their dresses had wrinkles.

She'd preferred to spend time in the stables with Old Tim and the horses. They would ride for hours, or he would teach her something new. How to shoot a gun. How to trap a rabbit. How to build a fire. How to hide in the woods. All those activities gave her far more enjoyment than sitting in a stuffy solarium, drinking too sweet tea, and eating soggy finger sandwiches while gossiping about people she barely knew and cared nothing for.

"Drew needs to cut the firewood into smaller pieces. Some are too big for the stove." Grace placed one more log on the fire then shut the door on the little black stove. "Ty knows how. He should show Drew."

"I shall be sure to tell him, but I chopped most of those pieces myself. I will take more care next time." Smoothing her hands down her skirt, she smiled at Grace. "I cannot thank you enough for everything you and Adam have done for Drew and me."

"We did it for Ty," Grace said almost absentmindedly before she grabbed a saucepan from the wooden crate.

Her words burned like fire licking Cassie's skin. Despite their generosity, the Morgans were never going to be able to forget who she was. How could she ever win Ty if his family couldn't learn to accept her?

They'd been polite. They'd been kind. But the emotional distance they kept from her was as obvious as a red satin dress at a funeral.

They didn't want her in White Pines, and they didn't want her with Ty. Their tolerance of her had been at his insistence or because they simply wanted to please him.

"Has he seen your new dress?" Grace set another pan down next to the last of the dishes.

"Not yet. I had hoped to see him—" Cassie dragged her teeth against her bottom lip.

Grace's smile showed she knew what Cassie had been about to reveal. "Soon, Cassie. Ty will be here *soon*. He had to ride the fence line and then help Adam in the barn. I'm sure once his chores are done, he'll be heading right over here."

"Really?" The insecurity was plain in her voice, but where Ty was concerned, Cassie had trouble concealing her feelings.

"Really. I should be heading back home now. Benjamin will be driving his father daft."

"How old is your son?"

"Almost three." Her face shone like sunlight as she talked about her child. "He asks the most curious questions. Wants to know why the grass is green, why the sun has to set, why birds can fly when he can't. His favorite word is why. Keeps Adam and me on our toes just to find answers to placate him." A proud smile crossed Grace's face. "He can already read."

With a chuckle, Cassie let a quote slip. "'The low vice, curiosity!'"

Grace tilted her head. "Byron or Tennyson?"

Her cheeks flushing hot, Cassie replied, "Byron. I fear that I have a habit of quoting great writers. I would imagine it is a tiring trait for people to tolerate. My mother grew quite weary of it."

"'Better a witty fool than a foolish wit,'" Grace replied with a lopsided smile. "My brother and I share the same vice."

For the first time since she'd met Grace, Cassie felt the spark of a connection. "*Twelfth Night.* One of my favorites."

"Mine as well."

Before she could enjoy the newfound common ground, the door burst open. The women whirled to face two men, both dressed in dirty clothing and carrying guns.

Cassie reacted with little thought, kicking the gun out of the first man's hand before whirling to slam her arm against the other man's wrist. Pain shot from elbow to fingers, but she pressed her advantage and drove her knee into the first man's groin.

He backhanded her hard across the cheek, knocking her to the floor before he dropped to his knees, shielding his injured area with his hands.

Brushing aside the painful throbbing in her face, Cassie scrambled to help Grace where she struggled on the ground with the first man.

Grace reached for the second gun, but the injured intruder dropped forward and got his hands on it first.

"Stop!" He rolled over and pointed the gun at Cassie. "Stop or I'll kill her!"

Grace muttered a curse as she backed away from the man she'd fought and rose to her knees.

Cassie kept an eye on the threatening gun as she scooted closer to Grace. They helped each other to their feet. "What do you want?" she asked.

Still groaning and rubbing his injured groin, the man ignored the question and turned to his friend. "Bud?"

He nodded at Grace as he wiped his bleeding cheek with his sleeve. "That bitch scratched my face, Jimmy."

"Yeah, well the other damn bitch busted my balls."

"I insist you tell me what you want." Cassie was grateful her voice didn't quiver despite her fear.

"*You.*" Jimmy flashed her a menacing glare. "We're takin' you back to your grandpappy."

"The devil with that." Cassie crossed her arms sternly over her breasts. Her face and arm seemed to throb in rhythm with her pounding heart, but she refused to show them how much she hurt.

Jimmy's aim switched to Grace. "You're comin' with us, or she dies."

"You won't take her," Grace insisted, trying to step in front of Cassie.

Struggling to mask her surprise, Cassie put her hand on Grace's arm and tried to pull her back. "No, Grace..."

"Grace?" A low chuckle rose from the bandit's chest. "Well, hell. You're Grace Riley, ain't ya?"

"Grace *Morgan*," she corrected, raising her chin defiantly.

Jimmy grinned, revealing several rotted teeth. "You saved me a trip. We're here for you, too, little lady."

If her grandfather wanted Grace, it could only be to hurt her. Cassie couldn't allow that. "Leave her be, and I'll go with you without a fuss."

"No." Grace reached for Cassie's hand. "We're *both* staying put. If these men know what's good for them, they'll get out of here before my husband arrives. And my brother—*the marshal*."

The fat man laughed in her face. "You ain't scaring me none. Got a lot of money resting on gettin' you two to Californie. You're both goin' even if we have to knock you out and throw you over the rumps of our horses."

He stepped closer to Cassie, flipping her loose hair with the barrel of his gun. "A shame we cain't...get to know each other better." He licked his lips, making bile rise in the back of her throat. "You're a mighty purty li'l girl. Heard you got a weddin' waitin' soon as we get you back. Your grandpappy says Mr. Putnam needs an heir." He fluffed her hair again until she jerked her head back. "If he weren't payin' so well, I'd have an itch to put my cuckoo in his nest a'fore I return you."

Cassie spit in his face, which earned her another slap across the cheek that knocked her into Grace's arms.

Grace cradled her against her shoulder. "You won't touch this girl again," she ordered, her voice full of fury.

"Cain't rightly touch neither of you, not the way I wanna. Strict orders. Can knock you 'round though if I gotta. A bruise or two won't cost me none. Git your coats on. We're leavin'."

***

The ride had been rough. Trying to balance on a horse with her hands tied behind her took most of Cassie's concentration, especially since she sat behind Grace in the same saddle.

Grace shifted her weight often, and the women had quickly learned how to lean on each other when they needed to so they could keep their seats. Because the area was unfamiliar, she couldn't even form any kind of mental map to follow back if they managed to escape Jimmy and Bud. But if she saw any opportunity, she'd grab it—and Cassie knew how to keep them hidden until help came.

Guilt weighed on her, making her stomach lurch. Grace wouldn't be in this mess it she hadn't been helping Cassie. Once again, a Shay had put the woman in harm's way. No wonder Matthew had greeted her with such anger. Cassie would do anything she could to rescue Grace from having to endure any more misery from her wretched family.

Using her training from Old Tim, she watched her captors closely for any sign of weakness, any drop in their defenses so she could take advantage and help Grace slip away.

Only the two men who'd kidnapped them held them captive—an advantage because that made the odds even. Cassie wasn't sure if Grace could handle herself in a scrap, and she didn't wish to put her to a test. Not every woman had the kind of training in protecting herself that Cassie had, although Grace hadn't hesitated to grab for the dropped gun back at the cabin. If push came to shove, however, she would give Grace the opportunity to escape—even if it meant Jimmy and Bud dragged Cassie back to San Francisco.

She'd find a way to escape. Again.

Somehow...

"Stoppin' here for the night," Bud announced. "Get somethin' to eat and some sleep."

Neither woman replied to that edict.

The men dismounted, roughly hauling both women from their horse. Before too long, they were settled in front of a fire, their hands now bound in front of them and their ankles tied. At least they had their coats, but Grace had to be as cold as Cassie was.

Reaching over, she took Grace's tied hands into her own and gently rubbed. "The fire will help."

Grace raised her gaze to Cassie's and gave her a weak smile. "I'm used to worse. Grew up running chuck wagons on cattle drives."

"Cattle drives?"

"My brother and I worked cattle drives until we finally came to White Pines. Before I met Adam."

"Why?"

Grace seemed lost in thought before she finally replied. "I needed to keep a low profile. Your uncle Stephen had a sort of...obsession. He had me followed for many years."

The story didn't come as a surprise, although Cassie's heart ached for her mother. She'd always known his father had other women, but she'd assumed they were harlots or whores—not women like Grace.

How many other good women had he hurt in his life?

"I'm so sorry, Grace."

"Wasn't your fault."

"Who followed you?"

"Detectives. Bounty hunters like these. Stephen himself. Matthew and I learned to recognize them quickly and flee when we had to."

"Cowboys, detectives, *and* bounty hunters. You truly *have* seen the best behavior of men," Cassie said with a crooked smile.

At least the captors were allowing them to speak freely. Perhaps between her wits and Grace's obvious intelligence they could devise a way to escape.

"I would say your family was the one to introduce me to the worst that people can do or be," Grace replied with a fierce frown before her features softened. "I'm sorry, Cassie. That was cruel of me."

"No, no. I don't wish for an apology, especially for my family. I know what they are capable of. Why do you think I ran away?"

"Why *did* you run?"

"Because I was to be married to a man who cast his lot with my uncle Derrick—a man who obviously sees nothing wrong with hiring bounty hunters to drag me back to where I don't wish to be." A small, rueful laugh escaped. "A shame they could not marry each other. I am quite sure Robert and Uncle Derrick would be very happy together."

At least Grace smiled at the ridiculous remark before she reached up to brush her fingertips over Cassie's cheek. "You have a bruise. It will likely turn into a black eye as well."

She tried to give Grace a smile that said it didn't matter, although even the woman's light touch caused pain.

One of their captors dumped some jerky and bread in each of the women's laps. They ate in silence, and Grace kept as close a watch over the men as Cassie did.

"Surely, they cannot be here alone, just the two of them," Cassie whispered as she nibbled at the stale, brown bread.

"They're alone." Grace kept her voice as low as Cassie's. "I've dealt with bounty hunters before. They're too greedy to split the profit too many ways. No, they're alone. I'm sure of it."

"Drew should have returned to our cabin by now. He'll find help."

"Adam will come for me." Grace's voice held so much conviction and love it sent a wave of envy through Cassie. "As Ty will come for you."

Cassie wanted to believe that—to know Ty would be so angry at these men taking her away that he came charging in like Lancelot to Guinevere's defense. A silly romantic notion, but the hunger for him ate at her, as did her fear that he would do exactly that—come charging in and get himself hurt trying to rescue her.

Damn you, Grandfather.

The man had cost so many people so much. As had her uncle and Robert. And, of course, her own father.

Cassie's gaze settled on Grace again. The woman was a tower of strength, never doubting that her husband would come to her aid. To have faith like that in someone had to be a wonderful and fulfilling thing, something that would make life perfect. Grace was loved, and she knew that love was enduring.

With a shake of her head, Cassie tried to push aside her envy and focus on the present. Wistfulness would get her nowhere except standing before an altar next to Robert Putnam.

"Should we make a plan?" she whispered.

"My plan is to wait until one of them leaves long enough for us to untie each other and attack the other man. Then we do what we can to subdue him so we can slip away."

"Do you know the way back?"

Grace hesitated before replying. "Well enough to get us away from here. Adam and Ty will do the rest."

"And Drew."

Her dark eyes settled on Cassie. "Yes, I'm sure Drew will be with them. What do you feel for him, Cassie? You live together, after all."

"We only live in the same home because we have no one else who—"

"What about Ty?"

Cassie released a sigh. "Ty. He's an entirely different kettle of fish. I still don't know what we share." *If we share anything at all...*

"Do you love Drew?"

"Yes, I do."

"That makes no sense. How can you love two men?"

Grace's question told her a lot about Ty's character—he hadn't revealed Drew's secret. It also told her that her feelings for Ty were far too transparent, even to people who didn't know her well.

She chose to let the observation about her love for Ty Bishop pass without clarification. "I love Drew as a *friend*."

"Yet you live in the same home. People talk."

"Hang the gossip. I have been proper my whole life. To hell with propriety!" She lowered her voice when she realized how loud she'd become. "Drew and I need each other right now." How could she explain it to Grace in a way the woman would understand? "He protects me."

"Ty would protect you."

One of their captors stomped over to them and handed them a canteen. "Drink."

Since he shoved it toward Grace, she took it first, taking a long drink before handing the canteen to Cassie.

The water felt wonderful to her parched throat, but before she had a chance to drink her fill, the man snatched it back.

"Sleep now. We start ridin' at sunrise." He headed back to the small fire and kicked dirt on it to drown it.

"It's cold tonight. We need the fire," Cassie insisted

Grace put her bound hands over Cassie's. "Don't show them any weakness."

Drawing strength from Grace, she nodded.

Their time would come.

***

Ty signaled to Adam that there were only two men before he scooted back into the underbrush. Everything inside him ached with the need to charge into the campsite, guns blazing. Blood lust like he'd never felt raced through him. He wanted to kill both the filthy men with his bare hands.

And he wanted them to *suffer*.

Robert Putnam had to be behind the kidnapping, probably in cahoots with Derrick Shay since Grace had been taken as well. Both women appeared well, but it was dark and hard to see much. A good thing for the men, because if he'd seen that they'd hurt Cassie, they'd both have bullets through their brains.

He reached Adam, and the two men worked their way back to Drew, Gideon, and the horses. Since they weren't sure about how many threats they faced, Jake and Matthew had remained in White Pines to protect the other women and the children. Adam and Ty reluctantly took Drew because he refused to be left behind. It seemed wherever Drew went, Gideon followed. Since Ty had grown up hunting with Adam and Jake, he knew how quietly he and Adam could move. Drew and Gideon were unknowns.

"How many?" Drew asked once they reached him.

"Two," Ty replied.

"And the women?" Gideon asked.

"Fine. Tied up, but it don't look like they've been hurt."

Adam set his jaw. "We need to think this through."

Ty was grateful for his presence because his own anger made it difficult for him to think logically. Allowing his emotions to take charge might get Cassie and Grace hurt.

"Drew, Gideon," Adam said, "We'll wait 'til one of them slips away to piss. Ty will move to take the one left behind while I get to the women. While Ty takes down that man, you grab the other when he comes back."

They nodded in reply.

"I don't want any killing unless we have no choice. Let's just get them disarmed and give them a message to send back to the Shays."

Clenching his hands into fists, Ty tried to rein in his temper. "They'll just keep comin' if we don't—"

Adam was already shaking his head before Ty even finished the thought. "No killing. We're not putting Matthew in the position to have to arrest us. Getting the women back is most important. We'll let the men know that this is the only time anyone walks away from trying to get to Grace or Cassie."

Ty finally conceded with a nod. "Next time, they're carried away in a pine box."

Chapter Thirteen

Grace nudged Cassie with her shoulder. "Bud's gone."

Lifting her head and blinking the sleep from her eyes, she looked to where Grace pointed. "How long?"

"Not sure, but look at Jimmy."

The man had fallen asleep leaning against a tree.

They'd never have a better opportunity to try to escape. Cassie reached for her ankles and started working on the knots as Grace did the same.

"We won't have much time. Bud might just be going to relieve himself," Grace said as her fingers tugged at the rough ropes binding her.

"I pray he gets lost." Cassie's fingers were so cold, it was next to impossible to get them to obey her wishes. "Those men surely know how to tie knots."

"I wish I had my knife," Grace said. "I usually carry it for protection, but I left it behind today."

"Protection?"

"Force of habit. After Stephen raped—" Grace released a heavy sigh. "I'm sorry, Cassie. I keep forgetting he was your uncle."

With a shake of her head, Cassie shifted her hands to Grace's ropes, hoping she'd have more success. "My fingers refuse to work."

"Mine as well. It's too cold."

About to grab Grace's hands in her own and see if they could rub some warmth back into them, Cassie froze at the movement in the trees.

Grace obviously heard it as well because her gaze shifted to the woods. "Jimmy left on the other side of the campsite," she whispered.

"Then who—"

Her question died when Ty suddenly dashed from the trees to wrestle Bud to the ground.

She wanted to cry out in joy until she felt the hand on her shoulder. Her head whipped around to find Adam kneeling behind her and Grace.

"There's one more." Grace raised her bound hands to touch her husband's face.

"Ty knocked him out cold already." Adam's voice was gruff, and he suddenly brushed Grace's hands away and gathered her into his arms. "You okay, darlin'?"

"I'm fine."

Had she wanted to say anything more, she wouldn't have been able to because Adam's mouth covered Grace's for a long and fairly passionate kiss.

Cassie shifted her gaze, worried for Ty's safety. He had Jimmy on his back, straddling him as he hit the man again and again with his fists. "Ty! Stop!"

But he didn't.

Her heart slammed against her ribcage as she tugged on Adam's arm. "Adam! Please! He'll kill him!"

He released his wife, stepped around the women, and ran to grab Ty by the neck of his coat. Despite his efforts, it took him a moment to drag Ty away from Jimmy.

Ty's breath was heavy, leaving his mouth in bursts of white clouds. He rolled his shoulders and walked over to where Cassie sat on the ground. Dropping to his knees, he picked up her hands. "You all right, Cassie girl?"

There was blood on his knuckles, but she couldn't tell if it was his or from where he'd beaten Jimmy. "I should be asking you that question. Look at your hands."

He stopped long enough to swipe his knuckles against his pants before returning to untying her. With a frustrated growl, he finally lifted his pant leg, pulled a knife from his boot, and sliced through the ropes.

Cassie flexed her fingers to try to return her circulation while Ty removed the binding on her ankles. Rising to his full height, he grabbed her arm and pulled her to her feet. About to thank him, she suddenly found herself tugged into his arms as his mouth slammed down on hers.

The kiss caused everything around her to fade away, the world reduced to the feel on his warm tongue gliding across hers, the taste of him, and the heat of his embrace. His hand cupped her neck, holding her still as he kept up his assault on her senses.

She looped her arms around his neck and pressed her breasts against his chest.

His growl told her he enjoyed her boldness. Surely, he couldn't kiss her like this and not feel *something* for her.

The loud clearing of someone's throat brought her slowly back to reality. Her cheeks hot, she stared at the ground as Ty eased away from her. She couldn't seem to let go of him until he gently grasped her arms and pulled them from around his neck.

By the time she gathered her wits and glanced up, she found Adam grinning and Grace looking at anything but her and Ty.

Adam was the first to speak. "We need to get you back home."

Cassie nodded before glancing over to Jimmy. Adam had evidently used the time she and Ty had been busy kissing to pick Jimmy up off the ground and bind his hands. Now, he sat on the ground, leaning back against a tree.

Before she could ask what had happened to Bud, Gideon broke through the shelter of the trees, dragging a bound Bud, who stumbled to keep up. Drew followed close behind and pushed Bud to sit next to Jimmy before hurrying over to Cassie.

He embraced her, lifting her clean off her feet. "You're safe. I was so worried."

Ty seized her waist, pulled her out of Drew's arm, and held her against his side. He didn't say anything, but the grip was tight enough she gave his hand a gentle tap to ease up, which he did.

"What do we do with those men?" she asked.

"We send them back to your family with a message," Adam replied.

"Message? What kind of message?"

Ty shot a glare at the men. "That they leave you the hell alone now."

How wonderful it would be if things were only that simple. Cassie knew better. Her family wouldn't be deterred simply because a couple of their hirelings weren't successful in their mission.

No, her grandfather and her uncle would only see this failure as a challenge.

She leaned in closer to Ty, pleased when he wrapped a protective arm around her shoulder.

Drew walked over to stand next to Gideon in front of the bounty hunters. "So do we kill them or what?" he shouted, louder than necessary.

"No!" Cassie left the shelter of Ty's embrace and hurried over to Drew. The rest of their group followed.

"You will *not* kill them," she ordered. "Just send them away."

Adam took the lead. "You're lucky men," he said to Bud and Jimmy. "The little lady here doesn't want your hides nailed to the closest tree. We're gonna let you go, but only because we have a message for your boss."

"A message?" Bud asked through his puffy lips.

Cassie winced when she saw how much abuse Ty had inflicted on the man. One of his eyes was swollen shut, and blood trickled from the corners of his mouth. "My family needs to know that I shall never go back. Tell my grandfather I have left San Francisco and that I have no intention of returning. *Ever.*"

"He ain't lettin' you go that easy, missy," Jimmy said. "We ain't takin' you back, but your family'll send more next time. Someone not as nice as Bud and me. No, the Shays will send somebody who'll hurt you and your friends."

"Leave her alone," Grace scolded. "She's made her choice, and it's to stay in Montana."

The horrible man snorted. "You think it's that simple, do ya?"

Grace's frown shifted from the odious man to Cassie. She didn't have to say the words for Cassie to understand what she was thinking. Nothing was ever that simple with her family. Shays would not be denied.

Cassie gave Grace a brusque nod and tried to think of some message she could send that would let her grandfather and uncle know she would never marry Robert.

The right words wouldn't come.

"You think they'll just let you go, missy? Next time, there'll be more than what your menfolk can handle. Why don't you give in now? We'll take you back—"

"I won't go back!" She looked around, wishing Ty would say something, that he would convince the bounty hunters to never come after her again.

"You won't have to," Drew said, his voice barely a whisper. "I won't let them take you back, Cass." He stepped around her to face Bud and Jimmy. "She won't be going back to California." His voice grew louder and louder. "Because she's my wife now. She's no longer Cassandra Shay. She's Mrs. Andrew Pearson. Tell her family *that!*"

Cassie's mouth dropped open, and everything inside her wanted to scream that it wasn't true—that she'd fallen for Ty Bishop. That if she was going to be anyone's wife, she wanted to be Ty's. But she held her tongue. If her grandfather's men saw even a note of dissent, they'd pick up on it and share that with her family. Let them believe she'd taken Drew as her husband. Perhaps that news would do what Drew hoped it would and get them off her trail so she could live her own life.

Ty stopped breathing, hardly believing what he was hearing. Everything inside him screamed to pull Cassie to his side and claim her. The thought of Drew naming her as his wife turned his insides into lumps of fury and jealousy although Drew didn't consider Cassie as anything but a friend. The reason he'd made his announcement was to save her more kidnapping attempts by the Shays' lackeys—but even knowing it was best that they thought her already married, he had to resist the urge to shout a denial.

His gaze caught Cassie's, and he shot her a fierce frown that he hoped let her know this was far from over.

Her chin rose a bit, and her spine straightened. That defiant reaction made him relax. She would get through this, then they could talk about some very serious decisions that needed to be made. Sure, Drew's idea to pretend he'd married Cassie might solve the problem now, but that didn't mean the Shay's pursuit of Cassie would end.

Only a true marriage would stop them.

***

Cassie shifted in Ty's lap, trying to find a more comfortable position. He'd insisted she ride with him, and she loved the comfort she found in his arms. The warmth. The security. She felt almost cherished.

"Stop that." His hand settled on her hips and held her still. "Quit squirming."

"I am sorry. I just…" *Just what? Want to get as close as I can?*

She could smell him, masculine and earthy. She could feel his hard body. All her strength was employed in keeping from throwing herself against him and kissing him the way he'd kissed her back when he'd rescued her.

"Just what?" he whispered close to her ear. "Just want to ride with Drew? He is your *husband* now."

A gasp slipped from her lips as she turned to face ahead so she didn't have to look in his eyes. "He is *not* my husband."

"That's what he told those bounty hunters."

"A lie. A fib. Something to try to get my family to let me live in peace."

Ty snorted. "Sounded real enough to me."

How could she tell him she would never marry Drew because her heart seemed to have settled on him?

Warm lips pressed to her ear. "Are you tellin' me you wouldn't marry Drew?"

Cassie shivered from the heat his touch sent racing through her. "I wouldn't marry Drew." Her voice sounded breathless, the last word nothing but a squeak as Ty's tongue traced the shell of her ear.

"Good. I'd hate to think I was courtin' a married woman."

She whirled around to gape at him. "Courting? You wish to *court* me?"

"We're home, Cassie girl."

White Pines.

Home.

The town truly was her home now.

Because wherever Ty was, that would always be home.

Chapter Fourteen

Cassie sat down as Drew and Ty paced around the Four Aces.

The place was empty of customers because it was closed until the wall between the nearly-completed theater and the saloon could be knocked out.

Grace and Adam sat next to her at one of the round tables as Gideon stood with his back pressed against the wall and his arms folded over his broad chest.

She couldn't stand the silence a moment longer. "I appreciate how worried you all are, but I assure you I'm fine."

Ty stopped on the opposite side of the table and slapped both his palms against the surface, causing everyone at the table to jump. "Fine? You were kidnapped!"

"Well, yes, but—"

"You think I'm gonna let *that* happen again?"

"Well, no, but—"

"Then we need to think of a way to keep you safe." Ty put his hands on his hips. "Somethin' to keep 'em away from you."

Drew came to stand at Ty's side. "I believe I have the perfect solution."

"There. You see?" Although she had no idea what her friend was talking about, she hoped he would bail her out of this predicament. She hated that everyone felt responsible for her, but she hated even more than she'd let the threat of harm draw so close to Ty and his family. "Drew has the perfect solution."

Shooting Drew a glare, Ty swept his vest aside and put his hands on his hips. "And what exactly is your brilliant solution?"

Drew didn't seem at all intimidated. "The same one I had back in the clearing, of course. I'm going to marry Cassie."

Gideon pushed away from the wall and strode to Drew's side. "That was just a ruse—a way to keep 'em off her trail. You didn't mean to really do it. You ain't marrying her."

With a decisive nod, Drew said, "I *am*. It's the only solution."

She didn't even have the chance to deny him before Ty slammed a fist down on the table. "No! You ain't marrying Cassie."

"Why in the hell not?" Drew's scowl was every bit as fierce as Ty's. "Her family will just keep coming back. I can give them a reason not to. If I marry her—"

"You ain't marrying her!"

Ty stared at her. She could swear she saw pain in his eyes, which made little sense being as the man should be grateful to have her welfare placed in another's hands. She'd been nothing but a burden from the moment she'd helped him and Jake from that miserable cave.

"I *have* to," Drew replied. "There's no other solution. After everything she's done for me, I owe her this much."

Gideon threw Drew a glare, turned to narrow his eyes at Cassie, and then grabbed his coat. He stomped out of the bar.

The half-doors swung in his wake, their insistent squeaks grating her frayed nerves as she shivered from the hatred Gideon had directed her way. All of this turmoil was her fault, and it was up to her to find a way out of the mess.

But how?

"Ty," Grace said in a voice so quiet it was almost missed. "Perhaps this is a good idea. Perhaps Drew is right, that he should marry Cassie."

"How can you say that?" Ty demanded.

Cassie waited to hear her reason, even though she thought she already understood. If she would marry Drew, she would no longer be a part of Ty's life. He would be free—as would his loved ones—of any association with the Shay family.

"Because," Grace replied, "we all know her family will never let her go."

"I'll protect her," Ty insisted. "I won't let her family take her."

"Until they kill you." Wiping away a tear, Grace took a shaky breath and pressed on. "You don't know the Shays like I do, Ty. You don't know what they're capable of. Let Drew marry her. He can take her somewhere far away. He can give them a reason to leave her be. She'd be safe. You'd be safe. We would *all* be safe."

"Gracie…" Adam's voice was soft and low as he placed his hand over hers where it rested on the table. "Stephen's dead now. He can't hurt you anymore."

"Then why was I taken too?" Grace pulled her hand back. "The Shays want to punish me for killing him. This will *never* end. If they keep coming to fetch Cassie back, they'll hunt me as well. If she's gone…perhaps they won't think finding me is worth the effort."

"I'll protect you." Adam wrapped his arm around his wife's shoulders.

"You'll protect Grace, but Cassie needs me to keep *her* safe," Ty insisted. "I ain't afraid of her family."

Grace turned to Cassie. "Forgive me, Cassie. But I see no other way. You should marry Drew."

Until the moment she'd spoken, Cassie had always held some small hope that one day Ty's family would learn to accept her—that at the very least, they'd tolerate her being a part of Ty's life. God forbid any of them someday find out she was Stephen's daughter.

That fact, they would surely never forgive.

Her heart felt like a fine piece of crystal that had been hurled against a wall. No matter what she felt for Ty, no matter how she'd already handed him her heart, she could never have a future with him. Nor could she keep putting someone as kind and generous as Grace Morgan in danger.

She had no choice.

"I shall marry Drew," Cassie whispered, nearly choking on the words as she did all she could to keep the tears stinging her eyes at bay.

For a long moment, no one spoke. Her heart pounded a rough cadence, the sound echoing in her ears.

When she couldn't stand the stilted silence a moment longer, she said a little louder, "I shall marry Drew. That will solve all our problems."

"No!" Ty stalked around the table before standing at her side and glaring down at her with hard and angry eyes. "You ain't marrying Drew."

All she wanted to do was throw herself into his embrace and have him tell her he would take care of her. Instead, she wrapped her arms around her middle, not trusting herself to speak.

"It's settled then." Drew came to stand at her other side. "We can head down to the church tomorrow and—"

"Back off!" Ty reached across her to give Drew a shove back.

Cassie found her voice. "Leave him alone. He only means to help me."

"You can't marry him. You...*can't*." His shout had fallen to a whisper.

"I must. It is for the best." Why did the words hurt so much?

He grabbed her hand, pulled her to her feet, and dragged her toward the front swinging doors, not even bothering to grab either of their coats. His legs were so much longer than hers that she had to run to keep up.

"Where are you taking me?" She glanced back over her shoulder to see the confused frowns on every face they left behind.

"We need to talk."

"About what?" she asked as he dragged her into the theatre.

The place was a mess of partially constructed walls, sawdust, and tools. She tripped over a few pieces of cut lumber that the builders had left behind on the floor. "This has all been settled, Ty."

Ty gripped her shoulders and turned her to force her back against the wall. "You ain't marrying Drew."

His words forced the tears she'd been holding back to finally spill over her lashes. "You cannot tell me what to do. I must protect you. I must protect your family."

"Cassie..."

She swiped away the moisture from her cheeks with the back of her hand. "No. No, I shall marry Drew. I can continue my plans to go to the Dakotas. My family—"

"Will still come for you." He snatched his hat from his head and slapped it against his thigh. "Damn it, Cassie... Drew ain't the kind of man a girl marries. He can't be a husband to you. He can't... He won't... Damn it, Cassie!" His words fairly tripped over one another. "Think about it. Ain't you wantin' a family of your own? Ain't you wantin' kids?"

"Of course I want children."

"Drew can't give you kids."

Cassie hadn't wanted the truth thrown in her face. All she could think of was protecting Ty. From her somehow hurting him. From her family bringing him harm. From a future where he would grow to resent her for tying him down when he wasn't ready. "He could. Drew could be a father. He *could* give me children."

"He *won't*. Ain't you seen him and Gideon together? They...like each other. Drew won't be a husband to you, Cassie girl. He won't give you kids."

She knew that. At least her *mind* knew that. Her *heart* was too battered and bruised to do more than ache at the possibility of being locked in a marriage where she would never know love beyond that of companionship.

Ty was right.

But she couldn't let him know it.

With a shake of her head, she tried to move.

He braced his hands on either side of her shoulders and pressed his body hard against hers.

"Let me go," Cassie begged. "Why won't you let me go?"

"I can't."

"You *can*. This is for the best. Why should it even matter to you? Why can't you leave me alone?"

"This is why." His mouth covered hers as his arms wrapped around her waist, pulling her tightly against him.

Cassie struggled to push Ty away, her hands pressing against his chest as she twisted to get him to break his hold. She might as well have been trying to move a mountain. His only response was to slip his tongue between her lips and stroke the roof of her mouth.

The heat between them flared as bright as any fire, and she surrendered. Her palms slid up his chest until her struggles became caresses. She stretched her arms around his neck. Her tongue sought his, advancing and parrying in the erotic exchange. All the man had to do was kiss her, and she could think of nothing but kissing him back.

Ty's hands moved down her back, stroking and caressing until they settled on her backside. He pulled her up hard against him, and she could feel his hard length pressed against her. Rubbing herself against his arousal, she swallowed his growl and smiled against his lips.

When he finally ended the kiss, she was panting for breath and entirely unsure of what to say. She framed his face with her hands, loving the rough feel of the emerging whiskers against her palms. "Oh, Ty... What are we to do?"

"You ain't marrying Drew."

Everything came tumbling back with his arrogant statement. They were right where they started, and even if he was able to scatter her thoughts with nothing more than a heated kiss, her problems still remained. "I see no other solution."

"I do."

Cassie arched an eyebrow. "Pray tell, what solution do you propose?"

"Marry *me* instead."

Her heart skipped a beat. Surely she'd heard him incorrectly. "Marry *you?*"

Ty hated the incredulous sound of her question, as though becoming his wife would have been unthinkable. In his estimation, Cassie being married to any other man on the face of God's green Earth was absurd. Picturing her in another man's arms—even Drew's—was enough to make him want to hit something. Hard.

Somehow he had to convince her that he would make her a good husband, even though he wasn't entirely sure what a good husband was supposed to do.

Adam and Jake would just have to teach him.

"Yes, ma'am. Marry *me*. I can be your husband. I can give you children."

A blush spread across Cassie's cheeks and down her neck. "You would expect...intimacy?"

At least she didn't sound appalled at the prospect. If the way she kissed him was any indication, there was a heap of passion in Cassie Shay, and he wanted to explore it. "Hell, yes. You think I wouldn't want to bed my own wife?"

"You want...to bed me?"

His hand rose to cover her breast, and he gently stroked until her nipple hardened into a peak.

"Yes," he said, drawing the word out with a hiss. He savored the way she arched into his touch. "I want to bed you. I want to be your husband in *every* way."

Now that the words were out of his mouth, he no longer felt trapped. All along, he'd been fighting the feelings he had for her. Suddenly free from restraint—knowing she would belong to him—he realized he'd settled on her for a wife the moment he first saw her.

"I mean it, Cassie girl. Marry me."

"Do you love me, Ty?"

Ty dropped his hand back to his side.

Do I love her?

He wasn't even sure what love was. His whole life, he'd been taking care of himself. Sure, he had Jake. And then Adam had become a father figure for him.

But *love?*

Love was supposed to be something so strong and so enduring it could weather any storm. At least that was what Grace always told him. She'd read him stories where the knight always rescued the fair maiden so they could live happily ever after and face any trial life tossed at them—so long as they were together.

Ty had never felt that kind of attachment to anyone. Anything that came his way he handled solo. He'd been on his own since his kin dumped him at the orphanage at an age so young, he couldn't honestly remember what living with his family had been like. Sure, he exchanged letters and visits with a couple of his siblings.

But did he *love* them?

Ty wasn't sure he even knew *how* to love.

How was he supposed to answer Cassie's question? Women, he'd learned, were a mite touchy where tender feelings were concerned. They always seemed to have some romantic notions that he never truly understood. He didn't believe she'd appreciate his honesty about the subject—not that he'd had much experience wooing the weaker sex. If he gave her the truth, she would never agree to marry him. And while he didn't understand love, he did know he felt *something* for her—something that went beyond simple lust. Something that made him believe he could spend the rest of his life at her side and be content.

It wasn't love.

But it was enough.

"Cassie girl... We ain't known each other nearly long enough to know if—"

Her hands shot out, pushing him back. He tripped over a piece of wood and sprawled on his ass.

She hurried away, shaking her head.

"Wait! Cassie, please!" Scrambling to his feet, he chased after her, catching her at the entrance to the Four Aces. He grabbed her shoulders and turned her to face him. "Why'd you run away?"

"I cannot marry you." Cassie's voice was shaky, and a few tears traced paths down her cheeks.

"Why not?"

"You don't love me."

"Cassie..."

She shook her head. "I cannot marry a man who doesn't love me."

He scoffed at her. "You were going to marry Drew. He doesn't love you, either."

"He does. He loves me—as a friend."

"I love you...as a friend."

She angrily scrubbed her tears away, her hurt switching to anger so quickly, Ty's head was spinning. "I don't wish for you to love me as a friend!"

"You ain't making any sense. You'd marry Drew because he's a friend, but you won't marry me for the same damn reason?" As God was his witness, he would never understand women—especially *this* woman.

She tried to push his hands away again, so he held tight. "Let me go. I'm not marrying you. I'm not marrying anyone!"

His patience was at an end. "What are you talking about?"

"I don't *have* to marry anyone. Now let me go."

Ty obeyed, mostly because he knew when she was this upset he'd never get an answer that made any sense. He trailed her inside the saloon.

"Cass, did you decide?" Drew asked. His gaze settled on her face and he frowned. "What's wrong?"

"Nothing," she replied. "I have come to a decision."

"What exactly have you decided?" Grace asked, her eyes rising to meet Ty's.

"I shall not marry now."

"But Cassie—" Drew began before Cassie interrupted with an abrupt slash of her hand.

"My family believes me to be already wed. I do not have to follow through." When Drew opened his mouth, she fisted her hands. "I will *not* be forced to make such an important decision on a whim. I fled to escape one forced marriage. I refuse to be pushed into another. I am very tired, and I believe I shall go home now."

On that pronouncement, she grabbed her coat from the back of the chair, turned on her heel, and stalked out of the saloon.

Adam stood up and grabbed Ty's arm when he tried to hurry after her.

Drew exited, most likely to follow her back to the cabin.

"What the hell, Adam?" Ty stared at the restraining hand. "I need to talk to Cassie."

"Let her go. We need to talk," Adam replied as his wife nodded.

"About?"

"A lot of things..."

Since Drew was chasing after Cassie, he knew she'd get home safely, so he decided to indulge Adam. Jerking a chair away from the table, he flopped into it. "Talk."

Adam and Grace shared a long look, the kind Ty had learned was a way they could communicate without words. On Grace's curt nod, Adam turned to Ty. "Do you love Cassie?"

Ty was getting damned sick and tired of *that* question. Nor was he particularly willing to share all he felt with anyone else—even Adam and Grace. "I ain't known her long enough to know."

"Then why?" Grace asked. "Why should it matter if she marries Drew?"

Swiping the hat from his head, Ty dropped it on the table. He ran his hand over his face as he tried to figure out a way to explain things without revealing Drew's secret. After watching the man get tossed into the street by his family, he didn't think it would be wise to gossip about him, especially in a town as judgmental as White Pines could be.

"It just…does," he replied. "I asked her to marry me instead."

"Oh, Ty…" She sighed. "That would be like signing your own death warrant. Drew has already placed himself in danger with his ruse. Should you marry her… I'd fear for you."

"Do you think you owe her for saving your life?" Adam asked.

"Of course I do. But…it ain't that. There's just somethin' about her…"

I sound like an idiot.

"She turned you down," Grace said. "She wouldn't marry you."

He nodded, still feeling the pinch of hurt over Cassie's refusal of his proposal. "At least she ain't marrying Drew, neither." He had time now to try to woo her. There was no way he was letting her slip away now that he'd made up his mind.

She belonged with him—that's all there was to it.

"I'm gonna marry her."

"But she didn't agree?" Grace asked.

His temper bubbled over. "Why do you hate her so damn much?"

"I don't *hate* her! She's a wonderful person. But…she's a Shay."

"She's not like them," he insisted.

"I know that." She took a deep, shuddering breath. "Her family is the problem. Don't you see? They'll never let her go. Just like Stephen would never let me go. They'll keep coming back for her. If you marry her, they'll kill you." She put her hand on his arm. "Please, Ty. *Please* think about that before you do anything rash."

Since he didn't consider marrying Cassie to be rash, he nodded. This subject was obviously too upsetting for Grace to think clearly. Once he and Cassie tied the knot and Grace—and everyone else—realized nothing bad would happen, then they'd learn to accept her as his wife.

Only one obstacle remained.

Cassie would have to agree to marry him.

"I'm taking you home, Gracie." Adam rose and held his hand out to his wife. "You coming back to the ranch?" he asked Ty.

With a nod, Ty grabbed his hat and put it back on his head. Plucking his jacket from the chair, he jammed his arms inside it and headed out of the Four Aces. As he threw himself onto Duke's back, he formed a plan.

One month.

He would give Cassie one month to change her mind. And in that month, he would do everything he could to convince her that he'd make a good husband.

Chapter Fifteen

"I cannot believe how big it is," Cassie said as she stood center stage.

"No bigger than most theaters," Drew replied. "Remember, when that wall came down, we became one building instead of two." Pointing to the tables spread through the saloon, he smiled. "Your job will be to get your voice to project to the farthest table. And remember—there will also be noise from the crowd."

"Noise? But surely people will not be rude enough to speak during a performance."

His laugh was loud enough to echo through the cavernous room. "Oh, angel. I forget how sheltered you've been. They'll talk. They'll spit tobacco. They'll clink their glasses. They'll even heckle us or point their guns at us if they don't think we're doing a good job. It will be a din."

"I cannot do this, Drew." When he'd asked her to perform Shakespeare for the introductory show at the Four Aces' new theater, she'd thought it a grand adventure—especially when he'd proposed that they do some scenes from her favorite play, *Romeo and Juliet.*

Now that she was standing on the stage and realizing how many people would be watching them, she feared she wouldn't be able to follow through. "I was wrong. You need to find someone else to play Juliet."

"You *can,* and you *will.*"

"But—"

"You're simply having a bit of stage fright. It shall pass."

"I shall lose my supper."

His laughter brought a hesitant smile to her face. "My first performance, I emptied my stomach into a bucket just off stage. Everyone gets stage fright, Cass. You're strong. You can do this." He turned her to face him. "Now, we practice." He took a piece of chalk and strode closer to the edge of the stage before crouching to mark an X on the floor. "Stand here when you say those last lines we practiced."

Hurrying over, Cassie placed her feet on the chalked lines. "How am I to remember all this?"

"All what?" he asked with a lopsided smile.

"All...everything. My lines, my—"

"You already know the lines. You've quoted *Romeo and Juliet* more times than I can count."

"*My* lines," she continued, "and where to stand, and what to do with my hands. Are you certain I am the right person for this part? Surely, there is another woman who would love to play Juliet."

Drew put his hands on her shoulders and pressed a kiss to her forehead. "You're young and beautiful—the perfect Juliet."

"Is there a particular reason you've got your hands on her every damn time I see you?" Ty's voice boomed through the empty saloon.

She jumped in surprise, clipping Drew's chin with the top of her head.

An easy smile crossed Drew's face. "Simply giving her a little reassurance. Surely you've noticed she needs a bit of encouragement and nurturing from time to time." He turned back to her. "I need to work on the set for a while.

We'll finish blocking later."

The sound of his feet slapping against the stage faded after he disappeared behind the curtain.

Ty strode over to the stage. As he stared up at her, he snatched the hat from his head. "What's blocking?"

"And good afternoon to you too, Mr. Bishop."

He rolled his eyes as he climbed up on the stage. "For God's sake, don't start with that Mr. Bishop sh—"

"Ty!"

"—*stuff* again."

She couldn't help but smile at the disgruntled frown on his handsome face. "I was merely reminding you to use proper manners."

Crooking his finger, he called her closer.

Cassie was helpless to resist.

When she stood in front of him, she tossed him a sweet smile even though she expected a scolding. Hands grasped behind her back, she rocked on her feet, waiting to hear what he'd say.

His words came as a shock. "Good afternoon, Cassie girl."

Ty was clearly trying hard to be polite. The last week, it seemed like the rough cowboy she'd known—the one who always liked to boss her around—had learned something from her. Cassie hadn't decided if she liked this new side of his personality or wished that he would never change.

Since the kidnapping, something between them had been...*different*. He didn't come to see her nearly as often as he had when she'd first arrived in White Pines. When he did, he never made a move to touch her. She missed his kisses more than she would ever let on, not wanting him to know how deeply he'd ensnared her heart.

Perhaps he was sorry now that he'd tendered a marriage proposal. That thought made her sad, because ever since the words had fallen from his lips, all Cassie could think about was how much she wished she had accepted his offer—although she also wished his desire to marry her had come from true affection rather than a simply masculine wish to protect her.

Suddenly nervous to be in Ty's presence, she knelt down to grab her copy of *Romeo and Juliet*. "H–how is your family?"

His response was his typical shrug.

"Grace and Adam are well, I pray."

She'd made a point of asking after them every time she saw Ty, hoping he would let them know she was concerned about their welfare and wishing they'd one day forgive her for the ordeal she'd put them through. With her luck, Ty probably forgot to pass on her well wishes and greetings. The man seemed to think grunts and nods were all he needed to use to make conversation.

She took a seat at one of the tables as he did the same. "Will you be coming to see our play?"

With another shrug, he dropped his hat on the table.

Cassie had to swallow her hurt feelings at his nonchalant reaction, not that she expected anyone to be waiting in line to see Shakespeare performed at some small theater in Montana. But she'd hoped Ty would want to watch her and that he might appreciate the message of the story since it seemed their families were as determined to keep her and Ty apart as the Capulets and Montagues were to separate their star-crossed lovers.

"What's it about?" Ty asked.

"*Romeo and Juliet?* You've never heard of it?"

"Nope."

She tried to hand him her book, but he held up his palm.

"You may read my copy, Ty."

"I ain't readin' your book."

Scooting her chair closer, she opened to the page of the scene she and Drew had been rehearsing. "Will you at least help me run my lines? I'm so frightened that I'll forget the words."

Ty pushed the book away. "Can't."

She tried not to pout, but his reaction hurt. "Why not?"

"You don't need my help. You got Drew to do that...nonsense."

"But I *do* need your help. Oh, Ty...I'm so awfully nervous." She slid *Romeo and Juliet* back toward him again. "Won't you please read Romeo's part to help me? You can correct me should I miss a word."

Shoving his chair back, he grabbed his hat from the table and slapped it back on his head. "I gotta go."

"Go? But you've only just arrived...and I–I haven't seen you in two days." Her cheeks flushed hot, but Cassie couldn't stop herself from revealing her hurt. "Have you been busy?" *Too busy to even come see me?*

The near panic in her voice hit Ty hard. Although Cassie clearly struggled not to show her disappointment that he might leave, she failed miserably. And damn, if that didn't please him. Having been around people who said one thing and did another when he was so young, her honesty and openness were a pleasant contrast.

She'd missed him—maybe even as much as he'd missed her. Two days away from her had been agony, but three mares had decided to drop foals, one after another thanks to the full moon.

"*Very* busy," he finally replied.

"And what have you been busy doing?" She traced the edges of the worn book with her fingertips.

"Delivering foals."

Her smile lit up the entire saloon. "How wonderful! How many?"

"Two colts, one filly."

"Well, then, you truly *were* busy." She got to her feet. "No wonder you cannot find the time to run lines with me."

That wasn't the true reason, but Ty wasn't about to embarrass himself by being honest with her. A woman of Cassie's breeding and education, she'd never understand what his life had been like, growing up in an orphanage and on the street.

"So...you'll be leaving now?" she asked softly, her fingers returning to the book.

He didn't want to go. He'd missed her so much, he ached inside. When each foal had been born, all he wanted to do was see how she would react to watching the spindle-legged babies take their first hesitant steps—to share those experiences with her.

He forgot his embarrassment. "No. Don't have to go quite yet."

Her head tilted as she considered him with those sparkling hazel eyes before flipping open the book again. "Then I would be so grateful to have your help."

"I can't."

"I see... You're afraid I will tease you should you not perform the words as an actor would. Please don't think that. I simply need the first few words of each of Romeo's lines so that I may respond as Juliet."

Ty almost smacked the damn book to the floor, having to resist the urge to tear it apart as she placed it in his hands. Cassie had it all wrong, but how could he possibly tell her the truth without losing all her respect? "Cassie girl..."

She sighed, long and loud. "This is frivolous to you, I know."

"What the hell is frivolous?"

"Silly. Unnecessary."

"That it is."

Her gasp near to knocked him over. "You think I'm silly and unnecessary?"

He knew then and there that he would never understand how the woman's mind worked. "I didn't say that. I said *this*—" he nodded at the book, "—is silly and unnecessary."

"I need your help. Please?" A slender finger pointed to the middle of the page. "We can start here."

She'd left him no choice. He stared at the jumble of letters and tried to do what Jake had taught him by sounding out each of the letters. "Th...then...m...moo..vee.. Oops. Move...n...no...not —Then move not... Wah...why...why..lee... Wylie?"

Cassie's brows were knit, and she watched him so closely he could feel his face flush warm. Shit, he was actually blushing.

"Not Wylie. *While*," she corrected.

Angry and frustrated, Ty slammed the book shut and dropped it on the table. He shook his head—not even bothering to wish her a farewell—and strode out of the Four Aces.

She'll never want to see me again. I'm so far below her, I'm not worthy to lick her shoes.

Before he could berate himself any further, a firm hand on his shoulder spun him around. He found himself face to face with an enraged Cassie Shay.

"How *dare* you!" Her fists were clenched against her sides. "How *dare* you walk away from me!"

"I–I thought you wouldn't want to be around me now."

"And you thought this because?"

"I can't read." Grabbing his hat, he slammed it to the ground, venting his embarrassment and anger. "There! Are you happy now? I said it. I can't read. I'm not like all the other guys you've known. I'm not like Drew. I'm just some stupid cowboy who—"

"How *dare* you!" She was shouting at him again, but he had no idea what she was raving about.

"How dare I *what?* Lie to you?" He shook his head. "I never told you I could read."

A tear spilled over onto her cheek, and he couldn't help himself. He raised his finger to wipe it away.

Her arm shot out, blocking him before she scrubbed her face with the backs of her hands. "How dare you think I would be so judgmental? You don't know me at all, Ty Bishop, if you believe I would be so shallow as to tease you because you have difficulty reading."

An acerbic laugh slipped out. "Difficulty? You mean because I'm too stupid—"

Her dainty foot stomped on the wooden boardwalk. "If you say that word one more time, I shall be forced to slap you. You are *not* stupid. You are smart and resilient and strong and—"

"Everyone can read, 'cept me."

"Old Tim couldn't read. Not when I first met him. He'd never had the opportunity to go to school. I taught him. And he sure as...as...*hell* was not stupid." Damn if her cheeks didn't flame a brighter red at using a curse word.

Then he suddenly understood. Her angry tears. The compassion in her eyes. She wasn't upset that he couldn't read—she was upset that he'd assumed she'd condemn him because he lacked that skill. He also understood something else.

Cassandra Shay cared for him. Everything from her angry tears to the way she berated him screamed the fact.

He reached for her, but she took a step back. Ty wouldn't allow her to pull away. His hands wrapped around her upper arms and he tugged her closer. Knowing this wasn't the place or time, he still couldn't stop himself from kissing her. Her eyes grew wide as he lowered his head to hers, giving her time to pull away should she wish to. Then her eyes closed and she rose up to meet him in the middle.

The world could have stopped spinning at that moment and he wouldn't have cared. The feel of her lips against his was about as close to heaven as he thought he would ever get—until Cassie boldly slid her tongue inside his mouth. With a low growl, he wrapped his arms around her, lifting her clean off her feet and kissing her the way he wanted to—deep and long and lovingly.

Her mewls were music to his ears, and she stretched her arms around his neck to hold him closer. Desire rose up inside him, making him burn for her. All he wanted to do was drag her to the closest bed and make love to her until neither of them could move.

Ty didn't want to acknowledge the hand insistently tapping his shoulder until he realized just how many people were paying witness to their affectionate display. He sighed against Cassie's lips and slowly set her on her feet, expecting Drew to be the interruption. When he glanced over his shoulder, he was surprised to find a grinning Gideon Young.

"Um...sorry to interrupt you," he said, clearing his throat loudly. Ty almost laughed at the red tinting Gideon's cheeks. "Drew and I are heading out to my place. He wanted to know if Cassie wanted to come and have lunch with us and Caleb."

"No, thank you, Mr. Young," Cassie replied. "I shall walk back to the cabin get something to eat." Despite her earlier boldness, she was back to being proper. Her cheeks were every bit as red as Gideon's, and Ty chuckled when she avoided eye contact.

Just to fluster her a little more, he leaned down and pressed a quick kiss to her lips. "I can take you home on Duke. I could use a spot of lunch myself." That, and she wouldn't be around Caleb Young.

"I would enjoy that, Mr. Bishop."

"Well then... I'll see you later." Gideon marched away.

Ty let her fetch her coat and then took her hand to lead her to where Duke was tied in front of the Four Aces. "Never had your cookin'." He lifted her onto the horse's back.

"I dare say you will be impressed."

"I'll just bet I will." Throwing himself into the saddle, he settled Cassie in front of him, threaded his arms around her waist to grab the reins, and backed Duke away from the hitching post. "Hold on, Cassie girl." He prodded the horse into a canter.

Several people waved as they passed down Main Street. Cassie waved back, something Ty hadn't expected.

He'd worried that someone who enjoyed the finer things in life would feel lost in a small Montana town. But she not only lived, she thrived. People accepted her, and she blended in as though she'd been born in the territory.

Perhaps Cassie was finding her place in White Pines after all.

Chapter Sixteen

"Ty!" Cassie exclaimed. She practically bounced in the saddle before she squeezed him tighter around his waist. "It's snowing!"

He hadn't really noticed until then. October always brought snow to Montana, and since it was expected, he hadn't given it much thought. "So it is. Light, though. Won't measure up to more than a few inches. Just wait a week or two. Then you'll see some *real* snow."

"I've never seen this much snow before. Why, it's already blanketing all the grass and flowers!" She let go of his waist and grabbed for the flakes as they fell from the sky.

"You've never seen snow?"

"It doesn't snow often in San Francisco and never enough to cover the ground. Isn't it beautiful?"

"'Spose. I guess I've seen too much of it. Ain't quite as pretty when you're trying to walk through waist-deep drifts to get to the barn and feed the animals." He reined Duke to a stop when they reached Cassie's cabin.

After he dismounted, Ty lifted her by the waist and set her from his horse's back onto the grass, which was quickly becoming blanketed with a thin layer of snow.

She paced around, her head bowed as she watched the pattern of footprints she left in the dusting of snow. Her laughter reached something inside him, bringing a smile to his lips.

By the time he led Duke to the barn, removed the saddle, and left the horse with Cassie's new goat—the one Gideon had given her—she was lying in a thin patch of snow, flapping her arms and legs.

A childhood memory popped into his head, one of the few good recollections he had. He and his sister, Sara, had been enjoying one of winter's first snowfalls by laughing, tossing snowballs at each other, and making snow angels. After all the bad things that happened to him when his father had dumped him in that orphanage, he'd almost forgotten that his entire childhood wasn't bad. He'd been close to his siblings, Sara in particular since she was only a year younger.

Something about being around Cassie was opening up a side of him he'd lost track of somewhere. He'd learned to anticipate the worst in people, always expecting to be bitten by any hand that fed him. He never felt that way around Cassie—probably because she gave of herself freely without expecting anything in return. Amazing she would be so unspoiled, considering the way her own kin had treated her.

Ty wanted to shelter her from anything that could taint her heart the way the world had tainted his. He wanted to keep the evil of her family from ever touching her again. The only way he knew how to do that was by marrying her, but she'd turned down his proposal because he hadn't offered up some romantic nonsense about love.

Love was for women—he needed a more practical solution.

He could lie to her and tell her that he loved her, but that would turn him into one of the cheats he wanted to protect her from.

He could just come out and *order* her to marry him—that way he'd be letting her know who wore the pants in their relationship. But he could never force her, not after what the Shays had been trying to do by demanding she marry Robert Putnam.

A third choice brought a smile to his lips and made his body tighten in anticipation.

Ty would give her his child. Once he got Cassie pregnant, she'd have no valid reason to turn down his proposal. It wasn't as if he was trapping her. She'd responded to his touches, his kisses. And he wanted her as his wife and would treat her well.

They could live on the ranch in a house he'd already planned in his mind. While it might not be as fancy as what she'd known in San Francisco, it would be comfortable. He'd convince her that he would honor every vow he took, and if God was truly merciful, perhaps Ty would even grow to love her one day— probably when he was old and gray and bouncing a grandbaby on each knee. He'd make a good father, and he'd make sure he put his children before everything else.

For once, he'd be part of a real family.

When she stood up and brushed the wet snow from her arms and skirt, he went to her side to help. His self-control was strained close to snapping as his hands deliberately brushed her backside to remove some clinging snow.

She tossed him a coy smile over her shoulder.

He winked in return.

"I promised you some lunch," Cassie said.

"That you did, Cassie girl."

"It's getting so cold out here."

"That it is."

Funny, but when she turned to face him and set her hands against his waist, she wasn't acting as if the cold bothered her. In his estimation, the world had grown decidedly warmer.

Her smile was bewitching as she fluttered her lashes and pursed her lips.

The woman wanted to be kissed?

Well, then…he'd oblige her.

His mouth swooped down to capture hers, and he didn't wait for her to open her lips. He forced his tongue into her mouth. A whimper rose from her throat as her tongue returned his caress. They broke apart long enough to catch a few gulping breaths before surrendering to another soulful kiss.

Ty reached his limit of self-control—passed it when she hesitantly moved her hips forward to press against his groin. Without breaking the kiss, he scooped her up in his arms and carried her to the cabin.

Fumbling with the lock, he finally let them in. He stepped inside, kicking the door shut behind him. As he cradled Cassie, he leaned back against the door and continued to ravage her mouth.

Perhaps seducing her wouldn't be as difficult as he'd expected. Her virginal attitude should have required some forceful coaxing—perhaps even a bit of begging—but she eagerly returned his kiss as she tugged his hat off and tossed it aside. Then she laced her fingers through his hair, effectively holding him right where he wanted to be—with his mouth against hers.

When Ty found the strength to ease back, they were both panting for breath, making small white puffs rise around them. Cassie shifted as if she wanted to be put back on her feet, but he wasn't ready to turn her loose.

"Quit wiggling," he scolded.

"Am I not too heavy to hold?"

He snorted. "Hardly weigh anything at all. Need to get some meat on those bones, Cassie girl."

Her responding huff raised another white cloud. "I wanted down to start a fire. It's so cold. We shall both freeze if I don't."

"I can do that." Not that he wanted to take the time. Besides, once they were beneath the quilt together—naked—they would generate *plenty* of heat. He considered telling her just that simply to see her reaction.

Holding her against him, he debated on whether to let her have her way and build a fire or simply carry her to her room. His body screamed for her, throbbing in anticipation of feeling her tight, wet heat surrounding him after he plunged into her. His mind told him to resist—that his plan to make love to her and get her pregnant could backfire—making her hate him for tricking her.

Funny, but the scolding voice sounded a lot like Adam's as it echoed in his head.

"Ty?" She placed her cold hands against his cheeks.

"Your hands are like ice, woman. Why ain't you wearing gloves?"

"I didn't know it was going to snow. Besides, I have no gloves."

"Victoria will knit you some."

"I would love to learn to knit," she said. "Would she perhaps instruct me?"

When he shrugged, he almost dropped her.

Tightening his grip, he held her as a war waged between his cock and his conscience. Cassie didn't help when she slipped her hands inside his coat and rubbed her palms against his chest.

"Stop that," he scolded.

"I must borrow some of your heat."

What she was doing was trying to drive him out of his mind. "Cassie…"

"Stop growling at me. You sound as mean as an old bear."

"You're from San Francisco. You ain't never heard an old bear."

"I know they growl, just like you're growling at me. Why are you so prickly all of a sudden?" Her hands flitted over his chest, making him suck in a breath.

Should he simply tell her? God help him, he wanted to. He wanted to tell her—in vivid detail—*exactly* what was making him growl. He wanted to tell her how much he wanted to kiss her breasts, to run his hands over every inch of her soft skin, to bury himself so deep inside her they became one flesh.

Tempering his words, he said, "It's the way you're touchin' me."

"I told you, I am merely borrowing your heat."

"You're making me *plenty* hot."

"How could I make you hot when you claim my hands are like— Oh…" Cassie tucked her face against the side of neck, hiding from him.

Ty chuckled at her innocent response until she started to pull her hands back. "Don't. Leave 'em there. I like it when you touch me."

"I like touching you." Her fingers spread to fan out over his chest and up his shoulders. "You're so different than I am. Hard. Hot."

He had to keep from laughing right in her face. "Oh, I'm *hot* and *hard* all right. Cassie, if you keep touching me like that, I'm going to—" Biting back the words, he shook his head.

"Going to what, Ty? Kiss me again? I–I want you to. I do like the way you kiss."

A groan slipped from his lips.

"You don't like kissing me?" She jerked her hands back and struggled in his arms.

"Quit wiggling. Yes, I like kissing you. You don't understand what you do to me at all, do you?"

"Yes, I do. I make you mad. Every time I am in your company, I raise your anger, judging from the way you constantly snap at me."

"No, you raise something else entirely."

Her indignant gasp brushed over his face. "You must put me down now."

"I must, must I?" He was done trying to figure out her thought process. The time had come to let the woman know what kind of temptress she was.

Striding over to her bedroom door, he nudged it open with his shoulder and carried her inside. He shut it with his foot. The afternoon light spilled through the small window, giving the room an orange glow.

"Ty? What in heaven's name—"

His lips covered hers, simply to keep her quiet for a moment. He let her body slide down his while he kissed her long and deep. She tasted so sweet, and every time he kissed her, he lost a little more control. Her coat was quickly brushed from her shoulders. His fell behind him. He started to remove his gun belt.

"Ty?" She looked up at him, her eyes as wide as saucers.

He laid the Colt on the only other furniture in the tiny room—a small wash table. Then he let her know exactly what he was thinking. "I want you, Cassie."

Her gaze shifted from his face to the bed. As her cheeks tinted red, her eyes found his again. "You cannot mean—"

"Oh, but I *do* mean." Ty toed off his boots, all the time holding her gaze.

She swallowed hard and breathed rapidly, as though there wasn't enough air.

"It'll be okay, sweetheart."

"It will?" Cassie only took one step toward the door before he grabbed her shoulders and turned her back. Although she sputtered in protest, he kissed her again, unleashing the hunger deep inside him for the first time.

He needed her acceptance, and he meant to have it. The kiss was one of total possession—and total commitment. His mouth slanted over hers, his tongue thrusting between her lips—a kiss that demanded her response.

And respond she did, her tongue as wild as his as she looped her arms around his neck and moved her hips against him, revealing some of her own urgency. He splayed his hands over her backside, loving the way it curved into his palms. Then he lifted her hard against the erection straining his pants.

He caught her gasp with another hot kiss, rubbing himself against her, needing her to want him as desperately as he wanted her.

When he finally broke the kiss, she sighed against his lips.

Disappointed, Ty let go of her and backed away, taking her response as regret.

Cassie's bewildered expression stole his breath. "Oh, no. You are *not* going to leave me feeling like...like...*this* again and do nothing to ease my torment."

"Torment?"

"Pain. Agony. Hurt."

"I *know* what torment is," he snapped. "I just... What do you mean? Ease your torment?"

Contemplative, she nibbled on her bottom lip as she wrung her hands. "I... I... You make me so... It feels like..."

Then he understood. "Hot? Are you *hot* for me, Cassie girl?"

With a curt nod, she took a step back, causing the back of her legs to hit the bed. A quick glance over her shoulder sent more color to her cheeks.

He'd been wrong. She wasn't ready. Not yet.

Ty stooped to grab his coat, but she hurried to him and laid her hand on his shoulder. "Don't."

His gaze captured hers. "What?"

"Don't put your coat back on."

Slowly rising, he shook his head. "I should go."

"Don't go." She threaded her arms around his waist. "Kiss me, Ty. Please kiss me."

He shook his head. "I can't, sweetheart. I can't keep kissing you. I want...I *need*...more." Hell, he had to be the most frustrated man in all of Montana.

Tilting her head, she cupped his cheek in her palm. "What do you need?"

"I need to make love to you. Holding back is...painful."

"Then don't hold back."

"Cassie... You've never...um... Hell, you're a virgin."

Her smile was as bright as sunlight. "'And Romeo, not death, take my maidenhead.'" Her fingers worked on the buttons of his shirt.

While he might not have understood the words, he knew what her body was telling him. "Are you sure?" He stared into her eyes. "If you...if *we*...do this, there's no going back. Are you sure?"

"I am sure." Her hands trembled as she unbuttoned her blouse.

He shrugged out of his vest and whipped his shirt over his head, not even bothering to finish unbuttoning it. Then his tanned hands gently brushed hers aside to take over the enticing chore of undressing her.

She looked away, nibbling furiously on her bottom lip.

Cautioning himself to go easy, Ty couldn't suppress a sigh at her unease. He wasn't sure what to say to soothe her. He always got tongue-tied whenever he needed to find the right words. This time, showing would probably be a hell of a lot more effective than telling.

The last buttons were concealed beneath the waistband of her heavy skirt, so he tugged her shirt loose. After unfastening those last obstacles, he stroked his palms up her flat stomach, across her full breasts, to her shoulders, where he pushed her shirt from her body.

Her camisole was whisper-thin, revealing more than it covered. The tease was exquisite as he took in the shadow of her nipples, loving how they hardened to strain against the snow white fabric. He let his hands return to her breasts, stroking the peaks with his thumbs.

Cassie had dropped her arms to fist her hands against her sides, but she leaned into his touch. Her eyes were squeezed shut and her cheeks were bright with color.

Damn but he was proud of her for trying to conquer her fear. He'd find the control he needed to go slow—to be sure and bring her pleasure in her first bedding—even if it killed him.

Dropping to his knees, Ty put his hands on her hips and pulled her close. Her clean scent filled his senses, the smell of roses that he knew he'd never tire of. He pressed kisses to her linen-shrouded belly, loving the heat of her skin beneath the soft cloth. Her fingers raked through his hair and she arched into him. With a low groan, he worked his way up her body until his lips covered her breast and he pulled a hardened nipple covered in fabric with his teeth.

Cassie tugged hard on his hair. "Oh, God..."

He needed to feel her skin. The bows holding the camisole together were stubborn. His patience at an end, he ripped the garment open to find plump, firm breasts with nipples the color of raspberries. His lips closed around one and he began to suckle.

The splendor took Cassie by surprise. While everything Ty had done to her felt wonderful, the sensations his mouth caused were almost too wonderful to bear. Her whole body trembled, and had he not been holding tight to her hips, she might've fallen—her legs were that weak.

She suddenly recognized the depth of his passion. Yes, his other kisses had curled her toes. But now he ignited a fire deep inside her that set her heart ablaze, burned a path down her stomach, and settled between her thighs. This was more than simple lust. What Ty couldn't seem to say, he revealed in his kiss and his touch. She tried to return that ferocity, telling him with her body what she felt in her heart.

In that moment, she made up her mind.

She and Ty might have no future beyond what they shared now. Her family was going to eventually come between them, and she might well find herself married to a man she abhorred. But there was one thing she could deny that man—one thing she could give freely to the man she loved.

Her virginity.

He offered her nothing but passion in return, and Cassie wouldn't delude herself into thinking otherwise. This wasn't some love story where the lovers found a happy ending. No, she and Ty were star-crossed lovers—like Romeo and Juliet—and their pairing would surely end in heartache or tragedy. She no longer cared.

She would reach for happiness with both hands and deal with the future when it darkened her doorstep.

As he shifted to her other breast, she let her torn camisole fall to the floor. Then she cupped her hands behind his head, urging him to continue his sweet torture. Her breasts felt heavy and full, and her core grew hot and wet—a response that happened often around Ty, especially when he kissed her. Everything was so new, and she wanted to revel in each fresh sensation.

He tugged at her skirt, fumbling with the buttons. She helped. Her pantalets were off just as quickly. The chill in the air touched her skin, raising goose flesh.

Ty let his gaze rake her body slowly. Then he shed his pants.

Cassie couldn't drag her eyes away from his face.

"It'll be okay, sweetheart."

Her voice had fled, so she gave him a curt nod.

"Why are you shaking?"

"I'm cold, Ty."

He wrapped his arms around her. "Then let me warm you up."

His mouth covered hers as the shock of being skin-to-skin with him banished the chill. Her breasts were flattened against his firm chest, and his hot, hard arousal pressed against her lower abdomen, drawing a gasp that was smothered by his lips.

Ty's hands smoothed down her back and settled on her backside. As he moved his hips forward he pulled her against him. Funny how such a simple act could send her thoughts into such a riot.

With no warning, he scooped her into his arms. Balancing her against him, he swept the blanket down before setting her on the ice cold sheets. Before she could even shiver, he stretched out on top of her, blanketing her body with his.

Cassie certainly wasn't cold now. Ty was incredibly hot, that warmth seeping into her skin. She pushed her arms around his neck. "Kiss me, Ty."

With a low growl, he obeyed.

She lost herself in that kiss, closing her eyes and letting her instincts take control. His tongue glided over hers, coaxing her tongue to chase his back into his mouth.

He rolled to his side and pressed kisses along the column of her throat as his palm covered her breast. Arching into his touch, she flitted her fingers over his shoulders. She wanted to touch him everywhere, but when he kissed his way down her chest and licked the valley between her breasts, every thought she held scattered like dried leaves in the wind.

As he drew one of her nipples between his lips, he slid his hand over the flat of her stomach to rake his fingers through the curls on her mound. Moving to her other nipple, he sucked hard at the same time he slipped his fingers between her folds.

Her heart pounded a wild beat. Surely nothing could feel as good as Ty exploring her body. Then his clever finger found a spot so sensitive that a hard rub had her planting her feet against the mattress and crying out.

He snatched his hand away, rising over her with a frown. "Did I hurt you?"

Unable to find a single word to beg him to continue, she grasped his wrist and moved his hand back to her core.

"Liked that, did ya?"

"Don't stop!"

With a satisfied masculine chuckle, he started his delectable torture again. The pad of this thumb quickly found the sweet spot, and he rubbed circles that had her hips rising from the bed. She'd never known such pleasure—until he slid a long finger deep inside her.

Cassie shattered, letting out a shout as her body spasmed with a pleasure she'd never known existed. Her breath came in pants as she opened her eyes.

Ty stared down at her, his gaze full of emotion and a smug smile on his face.

"That was...amazing," she said, her voice breathless.

"Gets better."

She found a grin. "Well, then...show me *better*."

He took her hand and led it to his groin. Then he closed her fingers around his erection.

The skin was silky soft, yet the flesh beneath was hard. And so hot. She ran her hand down to the root then back to the tip, where she rubbed her thumb over the cap.

His body fascinated her. Everything was the opposite of hers—from the rough skin to the depth of muscle. But what she held in her hand was the most captivating. That, and the soft sac she gave a gentle squeeze before returning to his staff.

How in God's name would something so long and thick fit inside her?

Ty gently brushed her hand away.

What if her exploration had somehow hurt him? "Was I doing it wrong?"

He shook his head before gripping her shoulders and easing them back against the mattress. "You touching me makes me want you past waitin'."

Cassie let his words wash over her heart. They might not have been a declaration of love, but they made her core tighten as her desire begin to climb again. She welcomed his kiss, grasping his tongue between her teeth and hoping he enjoyed her boldness.

Ty parted her thighs with his knee and then settled himself between them. He held his erection and rubbed it between her folds, making the burn flare deep inside her. She raised her hips, meeting his teasing strokes.

His hand moved to her hips. "Are you ready, sweetheart?"

She bit his shoulder and wrapped her legs around his hips.

He buried himself inside her in one hard thrust that made her feel she'd just been torn in two. She tried to get him off her, but his weight kept her pinned to the bed. Tears spilled from the corners of her eyes.

Cradling her face in his hands, Ty stared down at her. "Cassie girl...I'm sorry I hurt you."

She'd known it would hurt—her mother had told her as much—but the pain was rapidly subsiding, replaced by a wonderful fullness. She swallowed her fear and hurt. "It's better now."

His gaze searched hers.

"Kiss me again, Ty. Make me forget the pain and remember the pleasure."

The kiss he gave was as intoxicating as champagne. He rubbed his tongue over hers, rekindling the passion that had dimmed with her breaching.

But she wanted more.

She got more when he pulled back and then sank deep inside her. Although she was a little tender, she also felt her body respond each time he repeated the action. When he'd hurt her, she'd dropped her legs from around his hips. Now that he moved in and out of her body, she couldn't stop herself from wrapping them around his hips again, which helped him push deeper inside.

There were no words—only the feel of his body caressing hers as Cassie surrendered to instincts she didn't understand. The rhythm sped as Ty's thrusts became less measured and more forceful. The tension knotted inside her, and this time she knew not to fear it. Instead, she welcomed it, wanting the bliss that only he could give her.

And it burst on her suddenly, capturing her completely as she called to him and raked her nails across his back.

Ty thrust into her—again and again—until he groaned and shuddered. The heat of his seed bathed her insides, setting off a few more tremors deep inside her.

The aftermath was quiet. He rolled to his back, and she snuggled up against his side, rubbing her toes against the tops of his feet. The cold had been banished from their bed, and she dreaded the moment when the blanket would have to be lifted so they could dress. She wanted to stay in the warmth and shelter of his embrace.

"Cassie? Where are you?" a voice called from outside the cabin.

"Caleb," she whispered.

"What in the hell is *he* doing here?" Ty demanded.

There was a knock on the door.

Cassie scrambled over Ty to get to her clothes. He seemed to be in no hurry as he stacked his hands behind his head and watched her quickly try to dress. Her fingers shook so hard, she couldn't even tie the ribbons on her nearly destroyed camisole.

Caleb incessantly pounded on her door. "Cassie! Are you asleep? Wake up! I need you!"

"Get dressed," she hissed at Ty. "He'll know."

Ty merely shrugged.

She tossed his pants at him. "*Please* get dressed and be very quiet."

The door to the cabin opened with a loud squeak. "Cassie?" Caleb called, his voice echoing through the main room.

Since she couldn't seem to dress herself, she whipped the blanket from the bed and wrapped it around her shoulders like a cloak. When she reached for the doorknob, Ty bounded out of the bed.

"You ain't goin' out there to greet him in your underthings," he scolded. Then he glared at the door. "Be out in a minute, Caleb. Go wait outside."

Cassie was horrified. She'd planned to tell Caleb she was feeling poorly and had been resting. Then she would have sent him on his way. Instead, Ty had just announced their intimacy in a voice loud enough that all of White Pines had to have heard.

The door slammed, marking Caleb's retreat.

Chapter Seventeen

Ty couldn't stop scowling at Cassie. Not that he had a right to be mad at *her*. Caleb was the one who'd interrupted them at the worst possible moment.

Well, a few minutes earlier *would have been much worse...*

He smiled at the memory of what they'd shared, thinking about how wonderful her tight heat had felt as it squeezed his cock so tightly. Damn if he wasn't getting hard again.

Not that he could do anything to relieve the ache. She'd be too tender after her first bedding, and then there was Caleb to deal with.

The scowl returned to Ty's lips.

Cassie stomped her bare foot against the floorboards. "I cannot believe you would embarrass me like that." She tossed the blanket from her shoulders and resumed dressing.

Despite the relaxed, sated feeling Ty just experienced, his hunger leapt back to life at the sight of her camisole falling open and revealing her beautiful breasts. The pink nipples were tight buds, and he struggled to tear his gaze away from them.

"We'll be the talk of White Pines now." She yanked on her petticoat and fumbled with the ties.

He probably should've felt bad for sullying her reputation by letting Caleb know they'd shared a bed. But he didn't. Not in the least. His intentions were honorable, and now that she'd given herself to him, her fate was sealed—whether they'd made a child together or not.

She will *be my wife.*

"Get dressed!" she hissed.

With a heavy sigh, Ty threw aside the rest of the covers. The cold immediately raised gooseflesh on his skin as his poor balls pulled tight to his body. He picked up his discarded clothes and started dressing, more to banish the cold than to obey her demands.

Cassie jerked on her skirt, buttoned her shirt fast enough to misalign the buttons, and then slid her feet back into her boots. She was reaching for the doorknob before he could get to his Colt.

"Wait," he scolded as he scrambled for his gun belt.

"Why?"

"Need my gun."

"Whatever for? It's Caleb." She opened the door and stepped out of the bedroom.

Ty jammed his Colt in the holster and followed.

She'd already made her way to the front door. Throwing it open, she slipped through. "Caleb?"

With an angry growl, he grabbed Cassie's coat and slammed the door behind him.

Caleb was leaning against the small fence surrounding Cassie's vegetable garden. He was bundled up against the cold and chewed furiously on a piece of straw sticking out from the corner of his mouth. The heat of his scowl could have set a forest ablaze.

"What's wrong?" she asked.

His gaze still fixed on Ty, Caleb spit out the hay and pushed himself away from the fence. "Drew's asking for you."

"Drew?" Her eyes searched his. "I don't understand. He was going to fetch Gideon and then go to town to work on scenery for *Romeo and Juliet*. Why would he ask for me?"

To hear that Drew was with Gideon wasn't a surprise. Lately, the two men were inseparable. Ty had always understood that Gideon shared the same quirk as Drew, so it hadn't come as a shock that the men had become friendly. While Ty was pleased for them in an odd sort of way, it also meant Drew left Cassie alone at home far too often. A tiny cabin a few miles from town was no place for a woman to be without a man to protect her.

"He was attacked before we got to the Four Aces," Caleb said. "Had Gideon and I not come across the men beating him, could've been real bad for Drew. He's not even worried about himself—he's worried about *you*. Wanted me to be sure you weren't in danger and to bring you to him."

"Attacked? I–I don't understand."

"I do," Ty said. "It was your uncle and that bastard Robert."

He held up Cassie's coat so she could don it. He pulled it closed and fastened the buttons as she looked up at him. The pain in her eyes made him gather her into his arms. He kissed the top of her head.

"Robert?" she asked as she rubbed her cheek against his chest. "You truly believe he and my uncle haven't given up?"

"Yep."

Caleb cleared his throat loudly.

"Where's Drew?" Ty asked.

"Still at the Four Aces," Caleb replied. "Gideon sent for the marshal and Doc while I rode to fetch Cassie." His eyes narrowed. "What exactly are *you* doing all the way out here?"

"That's none of your concern," Ty snapped.

"But it *is* my concern." Caleb put his hands on his hips. "I'm wantin' to court Miss Cassie. Don't want her spending time alone with the likes of *you*."

That sure answered whatever concerns Ty might have had about whether Caleb had any interest in Cassie.

"Caleb..." Cassie shook her head and pushed away from Ty. "We already talked about this many times."

They'd discussed Caleb courting Cassie? That was news to Ty. His temper was rising by the minute.

Ty turned the topic. "Robert had to be the one who went after Drew."

"You don't know that," Cassie retorted, taking his hand and squeezing it tight. "Could've been a robbery, right?"

The woman was grasping air. He draped an arm over her shoulder, but Caleb replied before Ty could find the words.

"It wasn't a robbery," Caleb insisted. "Gideon and I went to help Drew with painting something for the play. When we went 'round back to go in the stage door, we found two men beating Drew but good. Never even tried to pick his pockets. Gideon shot one of 'em. I pulled the other off Drew and pounded him into the mud. He oughta be in the jail by now."

"The one Gideon shot?" Ty asked.

"He's waiting for burial."

Ty nodded. Gideon always was a good shot. "Talk to the other one yet?"

"No time. Came to take Cassie to Drew." Inclining his head at his horse, he reached out to her. "You can ride with me."

"She'll ride with me," Ty insisted. "You go on ahead. I'll get our horses and take her to town."

"H–how bad is Drew?" Cassie asked, his voice a harsh whisper.

Caleb shrugged. "Not good, but he's not gonna die or nothin'." His gloved hand was still extended to her, and he beckoned her with an insistent flip of his wrist. "Come with me. I'll get you there faster."

She didn't let go of Ty's hand.

He shook his head at Caleb. "She goes with *me*."

With a fierce frown, Caleb grabbed his horse's reins and threw himself into his saddle. Then he glared at Ty. "She's not your wife, Bishop. She's a single woman, and she's fair game. I'm aimin' to court her, whether you like it or not." Without waiting for a reply, he dug his spurs into his horse's sides. Hooves churned up snow clumps that flew back at them.

Ty fetched his coat from the house, donned it, and then pulled Cassie to the barn. It only took a few minutes to get the horses ready. They wouldn't be far behind Caleb.

"It's my fault," she said. "Drew was hurt because of me."

Ty lifted her onto her mare's back. Despite his certainty Drew's attack was Robert Putnam's doing, he couldn't stand the hurt in her voice. "You don't know that."

She nodded furiously. "I do. I know this was Robert. Drew claimed to be my husband. Robert could never allow that. He sent those men to kill Drew, then he'd come for me."

Settling himself in his saddle, he directed his horse out of the barn. All Duke needed was a squeeze of Ty's knees and a cluck of his tongue to head down the road to White Pines at a canter. He glanced over her shoulder to be sure Cassie followed. When she prodded Duchess, he eased up the pace to be able to ride side-by-side.

She sniffled.

"Don't you start cryin'," Ty said, trying to keep the bite from his tone. He could handle any of her strong emotions—except sadness. Her tears always hit him far harder than he thought they should, making him want to do anything to bring a smile back to her lips. "Caleb said Drew's gonna be fine."

She gave her head a shake. "He's hurt because he tried to protect me. I should never have accepted his help." Her fingers clenched the saddle horn. "I never should have come here. I've put all of you in danger."

Although she was clearly talking more to herself than him, he wasn't about to let her continue blaming herself. "Stop it."

She knit her brows. "Stop what?"

"Stop talking like you're gonna leave."

"I am."

"You ain't."

"I am. Just as soon as I can make arrangements, I'm going to—"

Ty grabbed the mare's reins and dragged her to a halt. Then he moved

Duke close enough that his thigh brushed Cassie's. "What you're gonna do if you don't stay close to me is find yourself back in San Francisco, standing before a preacher and getting your ass hitched to Robert Putnam."

She tried to turn her head away, but Ty gripped her chin to force her to continue looking at him. "You ain't marrying that bastard, Cassie girl. Not now. Not ever."

Her gaze shifted, and she tried to turn her head again. "I cannot allow good people to be hurt because of me."

He held her fast. Then he brushed his mouth over hers, hoping to wipe away the worried frown. "You're staying put. Promise me."

"Ty...I cannot—"

"Promise me!" He hadn't meant to shout, but she frustrated him almost more than he could bear. The thought of her leaving him—even worse, being married to a rat like Robert—was untenable.

He never got his promise. Cassie pushed his hand away from her face and stiffened her spine. "I shall do what I have to do."

Slapping his reins against his thigh, he shook his head. "You will do what I tell you to do. You're gonna marry me, Cassie. You're gonna let me protect you."

Her gasp frightened some birds from a nearby bush. "You may not boss me around, Ty Bishop. I will not put you in any more danger, and I most certainly will not marry you. Look what Drew's lie about being my husband did to him. A marriage to me would be a death sentence."

He wanted to shake her until her teeth rattled. Since she refused to listen to him, he tried a different tack. "Let's wait and see Drew before we decide anything."

Cassie was content to let the rest of the ride to town pass in silence. Her thoughts consumed her as she fretted over Drew's fate—and over her fears of what her running away from her family had wrought for the wonderful people of White Pines.

If Ty's predictions were true—if Robert had hired men to kill Drew—she'd put as many miles as she could between her and all the people intent on protecting her. Drew had only *pretended* to be her husband. What would Robert be driven to do if he discovered that not only had she given her innocence to Ty, she'd given him her heart?

Ty would be as good as dead.

Robert was cunning, and with the financial backing of her uncle—and her grandfather—there would be no way to stop him from finding her and dragging her back to San Francisco. And he'd surely kill any obstacle to marrying her—her "husband" and the man she loved being the two biggest hurdles.

No, as soon as she could pack a few things, she'd be on her way.

But where?

She hadn't truly decided beyond wanting to put more distance between her and her family. And Robert. While marrying him would end this battle now and forever, she couldn't stomach the thought.

After what she'd just shared with Ty, she couldn't even speculate about having Robert bed her without growing nauseated. How could she ever share that kind of intimacy with anyone but Ty?

If she saw Robert Putnam again, she'd scratch his eyes out. Her uncle and grandfather? She'd spit at their feet and tell them she was no longer a Shay. How dare they hurt Drew!

Dear, sweet Drew. The man was as gentle as a lamb. He'd helped her in her time of need, befriending her and protecting her. And what had he received in return for those kindnesses?

He was beaten.

She choked back a sob, sending up a prayer that he hadn't been hurt too badly.

Ty rubbed her thigh. "You cold, sweetheart?"

The words wouldn't come. Her heart was too troubled to explain all that burdened her.

Her fear for Drew. Her heartache at leaving behind her new friends.

And Ty.

Sweet Lord, how could she leave Ty behind?

"Drew's gonna be fine," he said with a nod.

"You don't know that..."

"Just save the worrying for when we get there." He pointed up the road. "There's White Pines. We'll see for ourselves soon enough."

"What if...what if..." She couldn't spit out her fears, nor could she tell him that she'd be falling apart had it been him that was hurt.

No, her mind was made up. Once she knew Drew would be all right, she would gather some things together and set out on a new adventure.

One that led danger away from the wonderful little town—and the man she loved.

Chapter Eighteen

The moment Cassie saw the damage to Drew's face, she choked back a sob.

Both his eyes were bruised and swollen nearly shut, and red welts colored both cheeks. He smiled at her with a split lip as she came into the bedroom. When he grimaced, she felt as though someone had struck her.

Her mind had been whirling all the way from the cabin to White Pines. Every thought came back to the same problem.

Robert Putnam.

He'd sent someone to hurt—perhaps kill—Drew because he thought she'd taken him as a husband.

Gideon fixed accusing brown eyes on her from where he sat on the bed at Drew's side. They'd taken Drew into one of the upstairs bedrooms that the Four Aces owner—Will Spencer—used for himself, his daughter Emily, and her husband Jake. Cassie saw Jake often when she and Drew rehearsed *Romeo and Juliet* and had watched Jake's daughter, Beth, from time to time, so she knew these rooms well.

Gideon dipped the cloth he held in a basin of water, wrung it out, and then dabbed at the small trickle of blood coming from Drew's nostril.

Drew held a shaking hand out to Cassie. "'But soft! What lies through yonder window breaks? It is the East, and Juliet is the sun!'" His swollen lips and winces with several words made her heart hurt.

"Oh, Drew. I am so dreadfully sorry." She hurried to the other side of the bed and sat on the mattress, taking his hand in hers. She kissed the back of it—grimacing at the bruised and scraped knuckles—and cradled it against her chest. "I'm so, so sorry."

"What the hell happened?" Ty asked as he strode over to stand behind her. He placed his hands on her shoulders, and she drew strength from the connection.

She didn't need Gideon's confirmation. An innocent man—a man that Robert believed was her husband—had been savagely beaten. No doubt her uncle and grandfather had paid for the loathsome venture.

Sadness ran roughshod over her.

She'd known she couldn't stay here in paradise. The time she'd spent in Montana had been heaven on earth—just the way she'd always dreamed the true West would be. Although the Morgans still didn't truly accept her, she genuinely liked them. She also liked Jake and Emily Curtis and their beautiful daughter. And Caleb and Gideon Young were like brothers. Everything inside her told her she belonged here—in this town and among these people rather than among the social elites of San Francisco. The people of White Pines were solid and good folk rather than weak-willed as were all the supposedly superior blue-bloods she'd known.

And then there was Ty Bishop. Leaving him behind would be akin to ripping her heart from her chest. She loved him—more than was probably wise.

The time had come to run away again—this time from what she loved instead of what she loathed. The pain was almost more than she could bear. But she owed it to these wonderful people to make their world safe from the Shays and the evil they perpetuated.

"I'm so sorry," she whispered before she kissed the back of Drew's hand again.

Matthew came striding into the room, his shiny marshal badge pinned to his lapel. "Doing better, Drew?"

"I shall survive," Drew replied before turned back to Cassie. "This isn't your fault, angel."

She couldn't speak for fear tears would choke her, so she didn't bother to correct him.

"Who did this?" Ty asked.

"Two men," Matthew replied. "One's dead."

"Dead?"

"Shot him right between his damn eyes," Gideon said, putting the now stained cloth back in the basin.

"You ain't told me nothing Caleb didn't," Ty said, his voice harsh and rough. "The other bastard?"

"Got him in a cell before Gideon could finish him off too," Matthew replied. "Got winged on the cheek by a bullet, but I didn't think he needed Doc. Drew needs him, though. Victoria helped patch the prisoner up. He won't say much, but I'm going back to try again in a few minutes."

"I'm goin' with you."

Although he frowned at Ty's suggestion, Matthew nodded.

Victoria came into the room, carrying a fresh basin of water. She handed it to Gideon and took the used bowl in return. "How are you feeling, Drew? We sent for the doctor."

"I need no doctor, and I wish you could all stop fussing over me," he replied. Then he flinched as Gideon pressed a wet cloth to his brow.

"Nonsense," Victoria said. "He can give you a look then see to our prisoner."

"It was the Shays," Ty stated. Judging from his clipped and angry tone, his patience had come to an end.

No wonder—so had hers. Her family was dead to her now.

Hearing Ty's accusation aloud filled Cassie's heart with more guilt over the pain she'd brought to these people. Robert had tried to get one husband out of the way before he could take her as his wife to please her despicable uncle.

Drew's gaze found Cassie's. "'From ancient grudge break to new mutiny, where civil blood makes civil hands unclean.'"

"For God's sake," Ty said, taking his hat off and slamming it to the floor. "I've had it with the way you and Cassie talk. What in the hell did you just say?"

"He said the same thing you did," Matthew replied. "It was the Shays."

The marshal stared at Cassie, and she saw the indictment in his eyes.

Or was it her own guilt that plagued her perception?

All she could think was that if she'd never come here so many bad things would never have happened to so many good people.

Drew squeezed her hand. "Stop it, Cass."

A tear spilled from the corner of her eye. "I am so sorry, Drew."

"This wasn't your fault," Ty insisted with a scowl cold enough to make her shiver.

She instinctively let go of Drew's hand and covered Ty's where it again rested on her shoulder. Like her concern for Drew, her fears for Ty's safety ran bone-deep. She couldn't even look at Drew's injuries without panic setting in as she pictured Ty suffering a similar fate—or worse.

And all because a man she didn't wish to marry sought to lay claim to a fortune she didn't even want.

She closed her eyes and straightened her spine as the solution hit her hard enough to make her gasp.

This time, Cassie wasn't running away from something—she was running to it. There would be no new adventure for her. No, there would only be life with a man she despised.

"It's the only way," she whispered.

"Pardon?" Drew asked.

She gave her head a quick shake, sniffing back tears.

"Tell me!" Ty demanded.

Knowing what she had to do now to keep everyone out of harm's reach, she resigned herself to her fate. Force of habit made the Bible's words fall from her lips. "'To obey is better than to sacrifice.'"

"Cass, no," Drew said in a breathless whisper.

If he hadn't already slammed his hat to the ground, Ty would have done so when Cassie said yet another thing he didn't quite understand. While it had seemed like a harmless little game between her and Drew, this wasn't the time or the place for them to toss around stilted quotes. If the Shays were truly trying to get to her again, there were plans to be made. Quickly.

"What in the hell are you talking about?" he asked. "Who is going to *obey* and who is going to *sacrifice?*"

Not surprisingly, Drew replied. "She is planning to sacrifice herself and obey her family to keep me safe." His tone was barely restrained fury—the same fury flowing through Ty at the thought of her doing something so ridiculous.

"The hell she is!" Ty knew Drew was right when Cassie didn't immediately turn around and scold him not only for cursing but for ordering her around. "You're not going anywhere, Cassie!"

Staring at the floor, she said nothing.

He wanted to shake some sense into her. "Not only are you not going anywhere, you ain't getting outta my sight 'til this is all settled."

"What is there to settle?" Her voice was whisper quiet.

The defeat in her voice frightened him. He hadn't given up, why should she? "Lots. There's *lots* to settle. But not yet. Not now."

She shrugged.

The growl rolled up from his chest. He tried to swallow it so he wouldn't take his anger out on her. Snatching his hat from the floor, he donned it as he turned to Matthew. "I want to talk to the other man. Now."

Matthew nodded.

"Stay with Drew," Ty ordered Cassie as he followed Matthew out of the bedroom. "Don't you dare leave. I'll just have to chase you down." When she didn't reply, he lost what control had remained over his temper. "You'll stay, or else."

Her gaze rose, the fire back in her eyes. "Or else what, Mr. Bishop?"

"Or else I'll hop on Duke, ride straight to San Francisco, and have it out with your family now. So will you stay put?"

The threat had merit, but he breathed a relieved sigh when she finally gave him a brisk nod.

Matthew led the way to the jail, stopping right outside the door. "You know this is Shay's man, right?"

"Who in the hell do you think you're talkin' to, Matthew?"

"Fine. I just...I know what they're capable of firsthand."

"You think I don't? If it weren't for Cassie, me and Jake would be dead. You don't need to warn me 'bout the Shays."

Matthew set his lips into a grim line. "As long as she's here, we're their target."

"She ain't going anywhere."

"Ty—"

"She ain't going anywhere." This time the words came out a near roar as he swallowed his panic that Matthew might just be right.

But how could Ty ever survive without Cassie by his side?

"You think you can fight the Shay money? The Shay reach?" Matthew shook his head.

Since the conversation had turned pointless—and since Ty had no intention of letting the Shays win and take Cassie away from him—he opened the door and stepped inside.

The White Pines jail was nothing more than two cells, but it had served the quiet town well. Most of the time, the cells remained empty, unless the marshal was forced to bring someone who'd gotten a bit too rowdy at the Four Aces in for a night or two. Seldom did the town have to deal with a person as sinister as the one glaring at Ty through the bars.

A jagged gash ran the length of his cheek. Since it didn't appear to be bleeding any longer, the wound was only superficial. The man had no idea how lucky he was. Gideon Young was one of the best shots in Montana. The prisoner's tan shirt was stained with dried blood when it easily could've been blood-soaked.

Stepping up to the cell, Matthew put his hands on his hips. "Time to talk."

"Ain't got nothin' to say to you," the man replied.

"Who sent you?"

The prisoner's dark eyes shifted between Matthew and Ty a few times before settling on Ty. "You be Ty Bishop?"

"Who's wantin' to know?"

The prisoner sat on his bunk as though relaxed. "So you *are*." His smile was reptilian. "Lots of people want you dead. Lots of *important* people."

"Who?" Matthew asked. "Who sent you here? Derrick Shay?"

"Ain't sayin'."

Matthew smacked the bars with the back of his hand. "You might as well talk to us, 'cause you're here for a good, long while. I'm pretty damn sure the judge'll throw the book at you."

The man shrugged.

"Why Drew?" Matthew asked. "Who sent you after Drew?"

Stepping closer to the cell, Ty let him temper get the better of him. "Did Robert Putnam send you?"

This time the prisoner chuckled. "When's the judge comin' to town? It's my right to post a bond and get outta this pissant town."

"Judge will be here in a few days," Matthew replied. "Maybe even a week or more. Might as well cool your heels. You're my guest 'til then."

Another shrug. "Been in worse. I'm wantin' some vittles."

"You'll eat later," Matthew snapped. With a sigh, he went to his desk, sat down, and started sifting through papers.

Ty turned his temper on Matthew. Striding to the desk, he slapped his hand on the surface. "That's it? The man near to beats Drew to death and that's *it?* You know he would've snatched Cassie up."

"Cassie's fine, Ty. He won't be bothering her now."

A snorted laugh came from the prisoner.

This time, when Ty went to the cell he swept his vest aside and set his hand on his gun. "When you get outta here, I got a message for you to take back to Robert Putnam."

"Don't know no Robert Putnam."

"Sure you don't," Matthew said, setting his jaw.

"Tell you what," Ty continued, "give the message to Derrick Shay while you're at it. You tell them that Ty Bishop will kill them if they touch one hair on Cassie's head."

The prisoner snorted another laugh.

"You hear me, you piece of shit? You tell them. Don't care how long it takes. Don't care how much it costs. They hurt that lady, and they're both dead men. Got it?"

"Don't know no Robert Putnam. Don't know no Derrick Shay."

"The hell you don't!" Wrapping his fingers around the cold metal bars, Ty gave them a hard shake. "You tell them! And know this—you lay one hand on her, and I'll end you, too."

Matthew's hand grabbed Ty's upper arm. "C'mon. Time for you to go."

Ty shook the bars once again before backing away. He narrowed his eyes. "You tell them, damn you." He reluctantly followed the marshal out of the jail.

Matthew launched into him the moment they were outside. "You can't threaten the man, Ty."

"You know damn well he came here for Cassie. He was told to kill Drew 'cause they thought he'd married her. Then they'd haul her ass back to San Francisco."

"I believe you. Trouble is I can't prove it."

"You don't give a shit 'bout her at all, do you?"

When Matthew didn't reply, Ty knew he'd hit a bull's eye. Bringing Cassie home had been a horrible mistake. Not because she was a Shay, but because the people Ty loved could never accept her. "I'm taking Cassie and we're leavin'."

"Leaving? C'mon, Ty. Where do you think you're gonna go?" He shook his head. "Trust me. Doesn't matter how far you run. The Shays will find you."

"Won't find me."

"You don't know them like I do. Grace and I ran for near to twenty years."

"So?"

"Twenty years, Ty. Cassie's uncle found us almost every damn town our long drives ended up in. Every. Damn. Time."

"You just want Cassie gone."

Using his knuckle, Matthew pushed the brim of his hat up. "Not denying it."

"Where she goes, I go."

"Not surprised."

Ty had heard enough. There were plans to be made to keep Cassie safe, and at that moment, that was all he cared about. If these men were sent by the Shays, more would soon follow. "I'm taking Cassie, and we're leavin'."

"Just exactly where do you think you'll go?"

All he could do was shake his head. Right now, he wanted to get Cassie out of White Pines and somewhere—*anywhere*—safe. "Keep an eye on her. I'm heading to the ranch to grab a few things for me, then going by her place and getting some of her clothes. I'll be back for by nightfall."

"Ty…"

"Don't let her leave, Matthew. I'll be back as fast as I can."

***

The house was only beginning to take shape. Not that Ty had found much time to work on it. Between his duties at the ranch and spending so much time in White Pines, he'd only put down a good foundation and raised two walls.

Stepping into what would be the bedroom he'd share with Cassie, he inhaled the smell of fresh cut pine. Damn, but he wished he had time to show her the place before they left. Although he still wasn't sure where he was taking her, he knew it wouldn't be forever. The Shays would give up once he married her because he could protect her. Drew was a friend, and he meant well. But he was weak, and the Shays knew that. Hell, their detectives probably knew everything there was about everyone in Cassie's life—which meant they had to understand Ty would kill anyone who got close enough to hurt her. The would-be kidnappers had surely delivered their message as well.

Hoof beats drew his attention, and Ty wasn't at all surprised to see Adam riding up. The man he considered his father reined his bay to a stop next to Duke, threw himself out of the saddle, and strode to Ty's side.

"Got a good start on the house." Adam nodded at the walls. "Won't finish before the snow flies."

"Considering the snow's already flying…" Sarcasm wasn't Ty's usual way of handling things, but his nerves were stretched as tight as Grace's clothesline.

"Are you sure running is the right thing to do? If you stay here, I can help. So can Jake and Matthew."

"Matthew's made it pretty clear what he thinks of Cassie."

"He's got a right."

Ty gave his head a disgusted shake. "She's not one of them."

"Much as I hate to be unkind, I gotta agree with Matthew." Adam put his hand on Ty's shoulder.

For the first time since Adam had saved Ty and Jake from a life on the streets, Ty thought Adam was wrong. Hell, he'd practically worshipped the ground the man walked on, thinking each and every piece of advice was nothing short of sage.

This time, however, Adam was wrong. Very wrong. "Cassie's innocent in all this. She's every bit as much a victim as Grace. She's suffered too."

Adam rubbed the back of his neck. "I can't tell you who to love, son."

There was that word again. Love. Ty was getting damn sick and tired of having it thrown in his face all the time.

Love didn't matter.

Her safety did. "I'm takin' Cassie away."

Shuffling in his pocket for a moment, Adam pulled out some folded bills. He shoved them at Ty. "Take this."

"I ain't takin' your money."

"Take it. Please. If you need anything, send a message."

"Adam…"

"Take the money, Ty. It's not charity. You can pay me back later if that makes you happy."

With a frown, he took the money. "Just for Cassie."

"Fine. For Cassie." Adam clapped him on the shoulder. "It's near dark. You best be going." He nodded at the house. "We'll keep putting time in on this while you're gone. You'll want a place to bring her to when you return." His stern expression eased into a slow grin. "Are you going by the church on your way out of town?"

Ty had been asking himself the same question. "If I have my way, yes."

"You usually do, son. You usually do."

Chapter Nineteen

"She's *what?*" Ty resisted the urge to grab Matthew and pound him into a bloody pulp—friend or not. All unleashing his frustration would do was get him thrown in the jail when he needed to find Cassie. Quickly.

"She's gone," Matthew replied. "I'm sorry, Ty."

With a disgusted shake of his head, Ty brushed off the snow clinging to the shoulders of his coat. Shoving the door to the bedroom open, he marched right up to Drew. "You let her leave? After what happened to you, you let her leave?"

Drew had been reclining against the pillows, but rose up on his elbows. "You should realize by now, sir, that no one *lets* Cassie do anything. And I will have you know that I was asleep at the time."

Since Gideon suddenly seemed very busy fiddling with the things on the nightstand, Ty knew exactly what had happened. "Damn you, Gideon. You knew she was taking off, didn't you?"

Drew turned to gape at Gideon. "You knew Cassie would leave town—and you let her?"

Gideon dropped the cloth he was folding and heaved a sigh. "Yes, I let her leave. It was the best thing for everyone."

Ty set his jaw. "It sure as hell wasn't best for *her*. The Shays will find her."

"That's what I mean—it really *is* the best thing. She should be back with her family, not here, living with–with… She should go home."

"You don't want her here," Ty said. "With Drew. Ain't that right, Gideon? You're jealous 'cause Drew said he'd marry her." When Gideon didn't answer, Ty took a threatening step closer. "You'd leave her to those vermin just 'cause you want Drew for yourself?"

"I'll leave you three to discuss this in private." Matthew didn't make eye contact with anyone before he stepped outside the bedroom, closing the door as he left.

Pushing himself up to lean back against the brass headboard, Drew fixed his blackened eyes on Gideon. "You shouldn't have let her go."

Gideon drew his mouth into a hard line but didn't reply.

"Did she at least give you some idea where she's headin'?" Ty asked.

Gideon clearly wanted to guard Drew every bit as much as Ty protected Cassie, and whatever there was between Gideon and Drew was none of his business. But at that moment, all that mattered was getting to Cassie before Shay's hirelings did. It also didn't help that dark, heavy clouds had gathered, meaning more snow was on the way—a lot more than she was prepared to deal with.

The woman didn't even have a warm pair of gloves.

"Gideon…" Ty tried to soften his tone. "Just tell me this—where was she going?"

"Didn't say. Only said she needed to go and to tell you and Drew to respect her wishes."

"You should have woken me, Gideon." Drew struggled to throw off his quilt, hisses of pain falling from his bruised lips.

"Where in the hell do you think you're going?" Ty asked.

"We should go after her." Bare feet on the floor, Drew tried to rise. After standing for a few moments on shaky legs, he dropped back to the bed, panting for breath. "I fear... I might not be—"

"For God's sake, Drew." Gideon helped Drew get settled against the pillows again. "You're not going anywhere."

"Where was Cassie going?" Ty demanded again. While he appreciated that Drew was worried about her, all the man would do was slow him down.

"She didn't really say. Just used one of those quotes."

"What did she say?" Drew asked.

"I can't remember exactly. Something 'bout loving with words was bad, then something about acting. Figured she was talking about not doing the play with you."

After a moment of thought, Drew quirked an eyebrow. "Perhaps 'let you not love with words or tongue but with actions'?"

Gideon nodded.

"Another *Romeo and Juliet* quote? What's it mean?" Ty asked.

When he found Cassie, he would burn her ears for a good long while—not only about her habit of running away, but also for constantly tossing around words that made little sense.

"It's not Shakespeare. It's a Bible verse," Drew replied. "John, chapter three, verse eighteen. It means actions speak louder than words. If my guess is correct, it means that she has decided to return to her family."

With a low growl, Ty clenched his hands into fists. "Why would you think she'd do something that foolish?"

"She wants to show us who she truly loves—to sacrifice herself to keep all of us safe." Although his breathing had returned to normal, Drew's face was still contorted. "I cannot go with you, Ty. You have to bring our girl back. This time, I shall truly marry her. I will not allow those bastards to harm her."

"Lotta good it did *pretending* to marry her," Gideon said, his eyes narrowing. "You're lucky you're alive."

"A true marriage will offer her protection," Drew countered. "No doubt the Shays found no proof of her being married and assumed it was a ruse. They came for her and punished me. I refuse to bow to them. I shall marry her and announce it in the San Francisco papers. Then they will finally leave her be."

Gideon stood up and walked to the door. Throwing a harsh scowl at Drew, he left, slamming the door behind him.

Ty had heard enough. "Get one thing straight—Cassie ain't *our* girl. She's *my* girl. If anyone's gonna marry her, it's gonna be me. We both know you ain't husband material."

"My, that was blunt," Drew drawled.

"Cassie deserves a husband, a family."

"And you plan to give her those things?"

"Damn right." A brusque nod punctuated Ty's vow.

Heaving a sigh, Drew said, "I love her too, you understand. Perhaps not with the passion you feel, but I could be her husband. I could give her children."

Even though Drew stared at him with abused eyes that stood as testament for his love for Cassie, Ty would never let another man claim her. "She's *mine.*"

After a few stilted moments, Drew gave a conciliatory nod. "You damn well better be good to her."

"I will be. Now…where do you think she's headin'—back to California?"

"Absolutely. She will be going back to her uncle so she can offer herself in return for our safety."

"To hell with that!" Stomping to the door, Ty stopped to glance back at Drew. "You get healed. Hear me?"

"Why, Ty… You really do care."

"You care 'bout Cassie, and she cares 'bout you." He shrugged. "Guess it just rubbed off."

Gideon was waiting at the bottom of the stairs. He leaned against the wall, arms folded over his chest. When Ty came down the staircase, Gideon pushed himself away and glared, his face full of anger.

"Drew's not going," he insisted.

"Had no intention of taking him," Ty retorted.

All the anger seemed to drain out of Gideon. "Good."

Done with placating the man, Ty headed to the kitchen to pack supplies for his search.

Gideon followed.

Without another word, Ty grabbed a burlap bag and filled it with jerky, cheese, crusty bread, and a few apples. His mind still whirled as he thought of where he could take Cassie that would be safe—someplace isolated. Someplace no one would think to look.

But he had to find her first.

"You good at tracking?" Gideon asked, handing Ty a canteen.

"Damn good."

"You'll find her?"

"I will." Then the perfect place came to mind, and his lips twitched into a grin.

"What in the hell are you smilin' about?" Gideon demanded.

"Tell Adam I'm getting Cassie, then we're going to the trapping cabin."

"What trapping cabin?"

One high enough in the mountains no one other than Adam and Jake would know to look. "Just tell him. Adam will understand."

***

Drew was right—she *hadn't* seen a real blizzard before.

Cassie huddled close to the small fire as though it would help her plight. The snow was falling at an astonishing rate, coming down so thick and blinding, she'd had no choice but to stop riding. Within an hour, the fire would be buried.

And she would freeze to death.

If only there'd been time to prepare better for her journey. When she'd made the decision to leave, she'd found herself in a panic, unsure of how quickly Ty would return. Gideon was the only person who saw her frantically donning her coat and hurrying to the kitchen to grab a few things to eat on her trip. His silence had confirmed her suspicions that the man wanted her out of Drew's life. He'd uttered not a single word to stop her flight, merely accepting what she told him and letting her go.

She'd ridden until she feared for Duchess's wellbeing, the snow so thick she couldn't see past the horse's ears. Leading her mare into a thicket, Cassie made camp by gathering kindling and starting a fire the way Ty had taught her on their trip to White Pines.

Little good it would do her now. The snow had turned it into nothing but a hissing pile of ash.

Her heart ached simply thinking of Ty. By now, he'd know she was gone. She prayed he wouldn't come after her.

Who was she trying to fool? He wouldn't. Just like Gideon, Ty would see her leaving as a blessing. He would no longer be burdened by her troubles, and he would be free to live a wonderful life with his family. Yes, he'd bedded her, but there had been no words of love and affection.

Ty didn't want or need her love. The man didn't even realize he held her heart in the palms of his hands.

She closed her eyes against the memories of their lovemaking. She'd never expected it to be so fulfilling—so consuming. Her love for him only made what they'd shared all the more bittersweet and heartbreaking. There was no way she'd ever be able to offer herself to another man in the same way—especially someone as reprehensible as Robert.

God, she was conflicted. Her prayers to keep Ty away easily changed into prayers that something—or someone—would save her from the fate she'd chosen. Even freezing to death was preferable to marrying Robert Putnam. She'd read once it was an easy way to die—a person simply fell asleep and never woke up. Rather romantic...

"I am too young to die," she whispered. While being Robert's wife might be a fate she despised, it was still a fate better than death at such a tender age.

Her teeth began to chatter. "But I shall if I don't find warmth."

And now I'm talking to no one.

Forcing herself to her feet, Cassie looked around for a way to shelter both her and Duchess—any shelter in the storm. Her poor pet shouldn't have to suffer. While she'd assumed she could simply start a fire and camp amongst in the thicket for the night, the blizzard insured that another plan was necessary.

A scream slipped out when a rider burst through the trees. Although she quickly recognized Ty staring down at her from Duke's back, she couldn't seem to get her heart to settle back into a normal rhythm.

He came for me!

"Don't you *dare* smile at me!" he snapped.

She couldn't help it—the grin refused to budge.

He *did* care. Despite his gruff exterior and words of duty rather than love, he cared enough to hunt her down.

After dismounting, Ty left Duke next to Duchess. Then he stomped over to Cassie, grabbed her upper arms, and slammed his mouth down on hers.

Tears stinging her eyes, she threw her arms around his neck and kissed him back, letting out a moan when his tongue invaded her mouth. His hands settled on her backside before pulling her tight against him. She wanted to be surrounded by his warmth, to feel his hot skin against her own. Ty would banish the cold.

Ty couldn't make himself end the kiss. It was possessive. Primitive. Erotic. The whimpers coming from Cassie were fuel to his fire. Had they been someplace warm, he would have had her naked in a heartbeat.

It wasn't until she started trembling that he was able to regain some control and remembered that they were in the middle of a snowstorm.

Easing back, he was pleased to see her panting for breath until he realized he was every bit as affected by the kiss. The woman had him bewitched.

Then his anger took the reins.

"Damn it, Cassie. Do you know how dangerous it is for you to be out here all alone?"

She bowed her head, but he refused to let her off without a stern lecture.

"There's a blizzard brewing, and here you are in the middle of the woods. Not even a blanket! You could have died, woman!"

All she did was give him a curt nod as she continued to stare at his feet.

"Do you know how selfish you are?"

Her head snapped up. "Selfish? I left to protect you!"

God, how he preferred her angry than seeing her so defeated. "You were gonna protect me by freezing to death in the wilderness?"

"I will admit I should have planned better, but—"

"Better?" Ty shouted. "You didn't plan at all!"

The relief that had swept through him when he found her evaporated. He'd kissed her because he'd been so damned happy to find her hale and hearty, but right now he wanted to scare some sense into her.

He took her hands in his, rubbing them for warmth. "We need to get you to shelter."

"Shelter?" Her gaze scanned the trees. "I fear there is no shelter near here. I've seen nary a barn or a lean-to since I left the town."

Ignoring her protestations, he picked her up and carried her to his horse. After setting her on the saddle, he climbed up behind Cassie and grabbed her mare's reins. "There's a trapping cabin about two miles east of here."

"Trapping cabin? I saw no cabin."

"You went due south. It's a place Adam, Jake, and I use when we're hunting and trapping. We've got two of 'em."

"Where's the second cabin?"

"You'll know soon enough."

She turned her head to stare at him over her shoulder. "When?"

All he did was grunt.

They rode in silence through the snow that fell so heavy their clothes were both soaked. The chattering of her teeth and the way she shivered so violently made Ty worry, but the best he could do to help her was open his jacket, lean her back against him, and hold her close to share his heat.

He was grateful to find the cabin and its small barn still closed tight. From time to time, they'd find that someone—or *something*—had made a home there. Anything from simple squatters to a family of raccoons. Now, it looked exactly as it had when he and Jake had hunted before their ill-fated trip to San Francisco. The wood they'd chopped was still piled high.

Ty swung down from the saddle, lifted Cassie to the ground, and gave her a gentle push toward the door. "Go inside. Get outta those wet clothes and wrap yourself in a blanket. I'll get the horses taken care of, then I'll get a fire going."

She obeyed, stumbling through the knee-deep snow.

After he bedded down Duke and Duchess, he went inside, shaking like a wet dog to get the snow off his coat. Cassie had lit a candle, but she was still shivering in her wet clothes.

"Damn it, Cassie…" Striding over, he started stripping her. "Sometimes you ain't got the sense God gave a goat."

Whatever response she tried to give him was lost to her chattering teeth. Only when he'd stripped her bare did he stop. Snatching a thick blanket from the trunk full of linens and spare clothes, he wrapped it around her and set her in one of the two chairs he'd pulled close to the stove. Then he went about getting a fire going.

Before too long, a roaring fire was warming the interior, and Ty was ready to shed his own sodden clothing.

Cassie watched with wide eyes as he stripped, something he found entirely too erotic. The blanket was wrapped around her, but from where she held it together against her chest, he could see a fair amount of her breasts. Unfortunately, the cold did nothing to make him appear manly. His cock might as well have been a frightened turtle. Since there was no remedy for it except getting warm, he quickly got linens on the bed and returned to her.

Ty pulled her to her feet and then swept her into his arms. He carried her to the bed, jerked off the blanket, and waited while she scrambled under the covers. After he spread the blanket over the rest of the bedding, he slid in beside her and hauled her up against his side.

She still shivered, so he dragged her on top of his body, trapping her legs between his and trying to touch as much skin as he could to share his body heat. Before long, she let out a sleepy sigh and rested her cheek against his shoulder.

His cock had hardened, but she didn't mention it and he didn't think now was the time to be pawing at her.

Later. When they were both warm and rested.

"Warmer?" he asked in a soft voice in case she'd drifted to sleep.

She nodded against his chest, her breath tickling his skin. "Much. Thank you, Ty."

He grunted and hugged her tighter. "I'm still madder than a hornet at you."

"Be mad at me in a few minutes."

"Why a few minutes?" he asked, straining to peer down at her face. It was tucked too tightly under his chin for him to see if that familiar, mischievous twinkle was in her eyes.

"Because I shall be asleep and won't hear you scolding me."

Fatigue bore down on him hard, so he let her have her way.

There would be plenty of time to scold her tomorrow. For now, he'd hold her, get some rest, and then let her know what he expected of her.

Marriage. And nothing less.

Chapter Twenty

Cassie woke with a start. Her mind took long moments to clear, and the strange surroundings did little to alleviate her confusion. She was warm, rested, and hungry according to her rumbling stomach, but the room was dark and unfamiliar.

A fire burned low, the orange embers glowing through the slits in the stove's door. Although the fire needed stoked, she didn't want to drag herself from under the covers. Then she heard a soft snore rising from Ty and everything came flooding back. He'd come for her to stop her from going back to San Francisco, which meant there were some tender feelings hiding behind that gruff exterior.

Memories of their encounter at her cabin brought a smile to her lips, and she realized now that the tingles spreading over her skin and filling her core with need were desire. No wonder since she was draped over him. Naked. Her passion ignited and quickly turned into an inferno that made her want to wake him and have him ravish her again.

Or perhaps this time *she* would ravish *him*.

I have turned into a wanton.

That thought pounded through her brain until she dismissed it as bothersome. Ty had shown her the joy of making love, and she would revel in that joy. She wrapped her fingers around his soft—*what was the word he used?*—cock. A bit bemusing how different it was in a resting state. Yet after only a few strokes, it began to grow hot and hard against her fingers and palm. With a grin, she kissed his chest and giggled when a low growl rumbled against her lips.

"Good morning," she said from under the blanket.

He lifted the edge to stare at her.

"What are you doing?"

"This." She answered him by giving his budding erection a caress from root to tip and then circling her thumb around the crown. His responding moan made her feel powerful.

"Cassie…"

"Hush, Ty. It's my turn to make love to you."

Exploring his body was the most erotic experience she'd ever known—everything about him was utterly fascinating. Thick muscle moved like knotted rope beneath his skin. Coarse hair covered him, starting at his chest and tapering until it fanned around his erection. Even his legs were hair-roughened.

His masculine scent excited her almost as much as touching him. Rubbing her nose in the hair on his chest, she shifted to flick her tongue over his nipple.

"You're killing me," he said with a groan.

"But I believe you shall die happy."

She kissed his navel, loving how his stomach muscles contracted and he gulped in a breath.

"Cassie…you don't have to—"

Flipping the blanket away from her face, she tried to give him a stern glare. "I already told you…it's *my* turn to make love to *you*. I denied you nothing and let you touch every part of my body. Show me you trust me by giving me the same consideration."

His lopsided grin touched her heart. "Well then… Go right ahead."

"What would please you?"

"You. *You* please me."

The compliment was most welcome, but she needed some instructions in the art of loving a man. "What do you wish me to do with…*this?*" She stroked him.

"Kiss it," he said, his voice husky before he tugged the blanket back up. "Please."

The near darkness made her bolder, and she pressed her lips against the tip of his cock before tracing the ridges of the crown with her tongue. The strangled sound he made frightened her.

"Did I hurt you?" she asked, drawing back.

"Don't stop!"

The touch of desperation in Ty's voice made her core clench in need. Without hesitation, she took him into her mouth.

Although she felt awkward, she hoped he enjoyed what she was doing. She swirled her tongue around the cap before swallowing him deep again, sucking hard. He responded by lifting his hips, starting a rhythm in and out of her mouth as his hands fisted in the linens before moving to tangle in her hair.

She wanted more, to discover all his secrets. Trailing her fingers lower, she cradled his soft balls in her palm.

The blanket was suddenly tossed aside, letting cold air wash over her skin. "Stop," he said with a grunt.

"But I want to—"

He shook his head as he put his hands under her arms and dragged her up his body until she straddled his hips. "Now, Cassie girl. Take me inside you *now.*"

Unsure how the new position would work, she lifted her hips and took hold of his staff. Then she tried to guide him inside her. After a couple of clumsy thrusts, Ty buried himself to the hilt.

Cassie hissed her approval, leaning down to press her palms against the mattress. The angle let his cock glide over her sensitive nub, and she tried to find a cadence that would please them both. She couldn't seem to get it right.

His hands settled on her hips and he lifted her and then thrust up hard at the same time he pulled her down. The pleasure cleared her mind of everything except the building pressure inside her.

"Sit up, Cassie."

She pushed herself back up. "Now what?"

"Now…*this.*" He thrust deep.

She whimpered. "Do it again."

Ty wondered if he could die from the bliss Cassie was giving him. Her body was paradise—hot, wet, so very tight. He took greedy advantage by sitting up, bending her back over his arm, and drawing a hardened nipple deep into his mouth.

Her fingers tunneled into his hair as a gasp fell from her lips.

He suckled before shifting to her other breast. Her body was perfection to him—her firm breasts, her slim hips, her long legs. Her skin was as sweet as honey, and he could never get enough of her taste, of her scent.

Of *her*.

When her head dropped back in surrender, he laid back and raised his hips to push into her again and again. Her breath caught and her eyes squeezed shut just as her body began to contract around him. With a rumbling growl, he let his orgasm wash through him at the same time Cassie called his name.

A contentment he'd never known settled on Ty, a sated and happy feeling. The world could have ended then and there, and he would be still be content—simply because he had Cassie in his arms. Her happiness was his, and when she hurt, he did too.

His whole body stiffened as he suddenly recognized the new emotion—a feeling that he'd only heard about but had now fallen victim to.

I love her.

Damn it all, that wasn't how things were supposed to go.

He gave his head a shake just as she flopped forward to sprawl over him. She was humming happily as she rubbed her cheek against his shoulder.

"That was…stupendous," she whispered. "I had no idea I would enjoy making love so very much."

The smile in her voice would have made him smile in return if he hadn't been in such a panic over his revelation.

Love was for women, not cowboys. It ruined lives—of *that* he was sure. Everyone he knew who fell in love ended up miserable.

Adam had suffered something terrible when Grace had been kidnapped by Stephen Shay. Victoria had fussed over Matthew when he'd been wounded in his job as marshal—twice, he'd taken a bullet. Both times, she'd helped him in her typically efficient manner. It wasn't until Matthew was patched up that she fell apart. Ty comforted her as she wept, lamenting how horrible it would have been to lose Matthew. Only Jake and Emily seemed immune to disaster, but how long would their luck hold out?

His parents had been in love a long time ago, or so they said. Their "love" had produced a brood of children far too large for them to care for, which meant Ty ended up in an abusive orphanage, discarded and unwanted.

Love?

No. No blasted way.

"Pardon?" Cassie raised her head to look into his eyes. "No blasted way what?"

He sure as hell hadn't meant to speak. Just another way love was going to ruin his life—making him spit out whatever was on his mind. "No blasted way…I'm letting that fire die."

Her body trembled. "It is growing cold." With a resigned sigh, she rolled off him and jerked the blanket over her body as Ty scrambled out of the bed.

The chill helped sober him. Tugging on his pants, he went to the woodpile and tossed a couple of fat logs in the stove. After using the poker to stoke the flames back to vivid life, he turned back to the bed.

Cassie was staring at him over the edge of the blanket, her brow furrowed. "Ty? What's wrong?"

Since he had no intention of explaining what was truly bothering him, he turned his anger at himself on her. "You were damned stupid. Ain't you got a brain in your head? Riding off before a snow storm."

She bowed her head. "I am sorry to have put you through so much."

"You'd be dead if I hadn't tracked you." Snatching up his shirt, he donned it, all the while trying to keep her sad expression from getting to him.

Anger was good. He could feel it and still be in control. He had a right to his anger anyway—unfortunately, he couldn't direct it toward himself. He'd been an idiot, thinking he could do nothing but bed and wed her and never feel anything but desire.

But love?

Never that.

So he kept his anger directed at the person who'd dared to touch his heart.

After jerking on his socks and boots, he put on his coat. "I'm checking the horses. If the snow's ended, we can head back to town."

She shook her stubborn head. "I shall *not* go back there, Ty. You best understand that now. I refuse to put the people you love in jeopardy."

"Get this straight right now," he snapped. "I don't love no one. Got it?"

"B–but what about Jake and Adam and—"

"They're family. That's it. Just family. I don't *love* them. Don't love no one, and that's that."

"Not Victoria or your mother or Grace or—"

"No one!" His bellow bounced off the cabin walls.

Her lip quivered. "I see…"

Ty had to stop looking at her if he was going to bluster through this. He might have been foolish enough to develop tender feelings for the woman, but he'd be damned if he let her know that. Hell, she'd turn him in to milk toast, snapping her fingers to get him to dance to her tune.

Fuck that.

"Get dressed," he ordered. "I'm getting the horses ready, then we're heading back."

She had the balls to shake her head again. "I already told you, Ty…I will not—"

Stomping over, he put his hands on his hips and glared down at her. "You will do as I tell you, woman. Understand?"

At least the hurt in her face changed to anger. Anger, he could handle. "Don't you dare order me around, Ty Bishop. I don't belong to you."

"You will."

Damn him, he was still going to marry her. She needed a protector, and even though his feelings for her complicated things, he made a vow to bury that love so deep inside himself, it would never resurface. He'd take care of her, protect her, even honor her.

But he wasn't going to *love* her.

On that pronouncement, he opened the door, hoping the snow didn't have them buried inside for a few days. Thankfully, it wasn't too deep and must have stopped not long after they'd come to the cabin. With some work, they'd be able to leave within the hour.

"We're leaving soon, Cassie. Get dressed." He slammed the door behind him.

Cassie kept staring at the door, blinking and trying to figure out exactly what had happened. While men as a gender were normally moody and unpredictable, Ty had been neither. Two of the things she loved most about him were his steady temperament and reliability.

There was nothing reliable about him now, and his temperament was far from steady.

The stove did a good job of warming the interior, but when she got out of bed, her bare feet felt as though she'd just stepped on a block of ice. She dressed quickly, still pondering what was wrong with Ty.

She'd pleased him when they'd made love. Naïve though she was about bed sports, she understood that he'd enjoyed himself. The way he'd shouted in pleasure and the sticky feeling between her thighs confirmed it.

Then why was he suddenly so angry?

After dressing, she folded the blankets, waiting for Ty to return and tell her how the horses had fared through the storm. Her gaze wandered the stark cabin. There was nothing that she could use to help them break their fast, not a scrap of food. Perhaps his sour mood came from hunger.

More likely from chasing me…

Pulling one of the two chairs closer to the stove, Cassie sat and warmed her hands. Everything was different this morning, not just because Ty had followed her and stopped her from returning to her family. While that meant more to her than he could ever know, it was the way he made love to her that convinced her once and for all that she would never be happy without him in her life.

A marriage to Robert Putnam—or any man except Ty Bishop—would be a travesty. If she couldn't make Ty love her, she'd live the rest of her life alone.

If he was serious about marriage, she decided then and there that she'd exchange vows with him. While there would always be the worry that Robert and Uncle Derrick would come after him the same way they'd sent someone to hurt Drew, Ty could defend himself much better.

Maybe her original plan—to disappear in an unsettled area—would work now. He could help her carve a new home in the wilderness.

She frowned. To start over with her someplace new, he would have to leave his family behind. Even though they didn't truly accept her, Cassie might one day have been able to make a place for herself in White Pines. If they left, he would lose Adam, Grace, Jake, and Victoria. Matthew seemed close to him too, as did Emily and many of the other people in town.

"What am I to do?"

The door opened, thankfully bringing an end to her troubled train of thought. Ty stepped in, holding a burlap bag. "Here's some food."

She hurried to him and took the bag. All she recognized of the contents was dried meat. She held up a stick of the shriveled brown jerky. "Is this venison?"

He shook his head. "It's deer."

There was no need to correct him, especially in his bitter mood. Sitting back in her chair, she pulled more items out and set them on her lap.

Ty dragged the other chair over, and they ate the hard bread and tough jerky in silence. He'd brought a bucket of snow inside the cabin that was melting next to the stove. Although she needed a drink to get the dry mixture down, she wasn't about to beg for anything like a cup. After all she'd put him through— and judging from his continued scowls—he would be put out by her asking.

He tugged a tin cup from his pocket, dipped it in the bucket, and offered her water.

With a grateful murmur, she drank all the water before handing him back the cup.

Unable to take the silence any longer, Cassie swallowed hard and then spoke. "I am sorry that I inconvenienced you."

All he did was grunt in response.

"I appreciate that you came after me."

This time he shrugged.

She'd had enough. "Will you kindly stop scowling at me? I simply don't understand how you can go from holding me in your arms to treating me like...like...this!"

He stood, gathered the uneaten food and shoved it in the bag, and headed toward the door. "We're ridin' out in a few minutes."

Indulging herself in anger, she stomped her foot hard against the floorboards after he left. Not only did it do nothing to ease her anger, but pain shot through her foot, feeling like bee stings. She sat down, popped off her boot, and rubbed her abused toes, muttering to herself the whole while about the frustrating male gender.

A small squeal slipped from her lips when the door opened again. Ty was back, holding something in his hands.

"What happened?" he asked, nodding at her discarded boot.

"My foot was cold," she fibbed, not wanting to worry him. She snatched the boot up and put it on.

He came to stand in front of her. "Get up."

Since he was snapping at her like a military leader, she jumped to her feet and gave him a sassy salute. "Yes, sir!"

At least her antics made him grin. He picked up her coat and helped her slide her arms in the sleeves. After buttoning her up, he unwrapped a long woolen scarf from around his neck and started putting it on her.

"Won't you be cold without your scarf?"

"Got another." He tucked the ends in the front of her coat. "Victoria made this one for you."

"Then why were you wearing it?"

Instead of answering her, he pulled a pair of wool gloves from his pocket. "These, too."

"That was very kind of her."

He shrugged. "Told her you were suffering from the cold."

Cassie rose on tiptoes to give him a quick kiss.

His brows gathered as a frown spread over his face.

To have him give her show of affection such a horrible reception ended her self-control. Tears blurred her vision as she lashed out at him the only way she could. With words. "I wish you had never come to find me."

"What?"

God, she sounded pathetic. She simply couldn't make sense of why he'd cooled toward her so abruptly. "You should have let me go back to my family."

"You'd have died of exposure before you got to the next town."

"I was fine," she insisted, knowing it was a lie—just as he had to know. "I might have already made my way to a rail station by now."

His snort made the threatening tears finally fall.

"Why did you make love to me?" she asked, her voice shrill. "If you hate me so much you treat me this cruelly, why did you make love to me? Why did you even come after me?"

Ty's expression softened. "I don't hate you, Cassie."

When he tried to brush his hand over her cheek, she stepped back. "Yes, you do. You take me to bed as though you…as if you… And then you…"

The words wouldn't come. How could she possibly ask if he loved her? Humiliated, she couldn't go on.

Why couldn't he love her the way she loved him?

Chapter Twenty-One

Cassie had a hard time holding her tongue.

From the moment she and Ty had arrived at the ranch, a debate over his future—and *hers*—had raged.

Adam and Grace were both home when Ty led Cassie into the kitchen. While their greeting was cordial, it was also brusque enough to reveal their unease. Matthew and Victoria had come for a visit and were sharing supper with the Morgans. Their reaction to Cassie's arrival was far less reticent.

Both of them frowned.

Although she was voraciously hungry, Cassie didn't dare ask for some of the sumptuous smelling food. It wasn't until her stomach loudly proclaimed its empty state that Grace asked if she and Ty wanted something to eat.

Ty replied with a nod and a grunt, tossed off his coat, and sat down to start helping himself to the bounty.

Cassie considered declining the less-than-hospitable invitation until Adam smiled at her and asked her to sit by him.

No matter how hungry she'd been, the meal held little appeal. She'd eaten merely to satisfy her hunger, and there had been little conversation, which ended when the meal did. While Grace and Victoria seemed grateful that she helped with the clean-up, Cassie knew when Ty told them his plans, the women would wish her a thousand miles away.

Now, she sat in a stiff chair as Ty, Adam, and Matthew argued over whether Ty should marry Cassie and take her north to an isolated cabin that—if he was correct in his foretelling—would be buried under snow for a good three months.

Adam drew her back from her thoughts when he placed a gentle hand on her shoulder. "You'd definitely be safe there, and if you pack enough staples, you'll get through the worst of the winter with no problem. But it will be just the two of you." He smiled down at Cassie. "What do *you* want to do?"

I want to marry Ty, have you all accept me, and live happily ever after.

She considered what she would reply aloud much more carefully. "I do not wish any of you to be threatened by my family any longer."

Matthew snorted. "Then you shouldn't marry Ty."

His wife shot him a glare. "You don't have to be so blunt."

"It's the truth," he replied with a shrug. "The only way to keep all of us out of the Shay's reach is for Cassie to go home." A heavy sigh slipped out as he faced her. "I'm sorry, Cassie. I truly am. I like you, and I think you're good for Ty, but—"

"It's *my* life," Ty countered. "I ain't letting her family haul her back to California. Do you know anything about the bastard they want her to marry?"

"I can imagine," Grace replied, her voice whisper-soft. "If he's anything like Stephen..." A shudder ripped through her. "We should try to protect her."

"I agree." Adam squeezed Cassie's shoulder before his hand fell away. He must have heard the same tremor in Grace's words because he sat on the arm of her chair and grabbed her hand. "Stephen's dead, Gracie. He can't hurt you anymore."

"I know." She gave him a hesitant smile. "The fear is an old one and hard to shake even now."

Cassie hung her head. Ty might win the day if he kept pressing his argument, but there was one thing—one secret she'd held close—that would forever end any chance she had of being happy here with these people.

She owed them all the truth, even if it cost her a joyful future. Drew wasn't here to stop her this time, and although her heart was breaking, she had to set the misassumption of her parentage straight. A marriage couldn't be based on a lie, especially one of such magnitude.

"I have something to say." She stood and smoothed her trembling hands down the front of her skirt, gathering her courage and fighting the overwhelming desire to wail at the unfairness of the situation. Her father's legacy was pain, and this would be his final torture.

All their curious faces were on her, overwhelming her and sending her courage fleeing. Once she told them the truth, her future with Ty would disappear. While he might still feel obligated to protect her, she would never allow it. She loved him too much to tear him away from his family.

Using Drew's advice from when they'd rehearsed on stage to look past the faces and focus on an object behind them, Cassie fixed her gaze on a window, letting the bright sunlight reflected off the snow blind her to everything else.

After a deep breath, she said what needed to be said. "Stephen Shay was my father, not my uncle."

The immediate reaction was silence, followed closely by everyone talking—more like *shouting*—at once. The only one she was concerned with was Ty.

He didn't say a word, settling his gaze on her. The surprise she saw there was quickly replaced with anger.

"I'm sorry, Ty," she said, ignoring the myriad questions being fired at her. "I should have set you straight when we first met."

A mask of calm settled on his features, one she knew well. Whenever his emotions were getting the better of him, Ty hid behind a face void of emotion. She knew better. He was furious. But he'd always reserved the stoic façade for others, showing her what he truly felt.

He was shutting her out.

"I am so very sorry." Tears blurred her vision. She needed to get out of there. "I should go to Drew now."

"I can't believe you'd lie to us about something that important!" Matthew shook his head. "After everything your father did to Grace, how could you—"

"You were all so set against me!" Her temper was rising, and her heart was breaking. "I wanted you to accept me—I wanted to be with Ty. I know I should have said something, but Drew warned me not to and—"

"Drew?" Ty's voice was a roar. "You told *Drew* and not me?"

With teeth tugging on her bottom lip, she gave him a curt nod.

"I cannot believe you're his daughter." Grace wrung her hands as she kept looking at Cassie and then at her husband. "He was so...evil. And you are such a sweet girl."

Victoria's kind eyes had hardened. "I cannot abide lies, especially about something so important. You shouldn't have let us believe he was your uncle, Cassie."

His face fixed in a scorching frown, Matthew stomped over to where Cassie sat.

She tried not to be intimated by his height and his strength, and she straightened her spine to try to show him so.

"Do you have any idea what your father put Grace through?" he bellowed. "He raped her! Then he hunted her like an animal for near to twenty years!"

Since she had no defense for her father's reprehensible actions, she held her tongue.

"Matthew…" Grace's voice was surprising calm considering how agitated she'd seemed. "Cassie isn't to blame for her father's sins."

He whirled toward his sister. "The man tried to destroy you!"

"And he didn't succeed," she countered.

"I should go." Cassie stood and took a few steps toward the kitchen. She would go to Drew. Perhaps together they could plan what she would do.

She'd donned her coat and the scarf Victoria had so thoughtfully made before anyone tried to stop her.

It was Adam who came to her, not Ty. "Someone should take you to town."

Even her only ally was lost. She vowed not to cry. Not here. Not yet. "There is still plenty of daylight. I am going to Drew." Then she could decide how to rebuild the life she'd just destroyed.

"There might be danger."

"The men my uncle sent have not reported their failure to him yet. No one new will come until then." She tugged on her gloves.

"Cassie…"

With a shake of her head, she reached for the doorknob. "I must go, Adam. I know it, and so do you. I thank you for the kindness you've shown me. I shall never forget you."

"Ty will—"

She shook her head again. "You must make him understand. No matter how much…" She swallowed hard. "He mustn't come after me. Please don't let him come after me. Ever."

Adam nodded. "God go with you."

No one followed her when she left, no matter how many times she glanced over her shoulder as she rode away.

***

Drew pushed himself higher up on the pillows. "What's wrong?"

Cassie tossed him a derisive snort. She'd ridden straight to him after leaving the Twin Springs, needing to know there was someone in the world who loved her. "Everything." She took off her coat, scarf, and gloves and tossed them on the foot of the bed.

With a sympathetic smile, he patted the mattress next to him. "Well, then… Sit down and tell me what 'everything' is."

Sitting was impossible. Instead, she threw herself into his open arms and let the tears fall that she'd valiantly kept at bay.

Drew rubbed her back. "Come now…it cannot be that terrible."

"It is!" she wailed.

God, she sounded pitiful, but it couldn't be helped. Her heart had shattered into a million pieces. Without Ty, it would never be whole again.

"Tell me what could possibly cause you this kind of anguish," Drew said as he stroked her hair.

She tried to explain, although her words were hesitant and punctuated with sniffs and sobs. "Ty and I are…no more. We shall…never marry. It's simply…not possible."

"Now, now." He gripped her shoulders and eased her back. "Dry those tears. We shall come up with a plan to win back your Romeo."

While all she wanted to do was weep some more, Cassie mopped her tears with her sleeves. "I can never be with Ty, not after I told him the truth."

"The truth?" His gaze searched hers until understanding dawned. "You told him about your father, didn't you?"

A sob bubbled up as she nodded.

"Why?"

She sat back, swiping away the rest of her tears with the backs of her hands. "I had to tell him, Drew."

"Why?" he asked again, his tone incredulous.

"He wanted to marry me, and I had agreed."

He knit his brows. "I still don't understand. Why would you marrying the man require you to explain your parentage? He knew you were a Shay. That should've sufficed."

"Surely, you jest," she scoffed before a small hiccough slipped out.

"Not at all. There was no reason for you to tell him—or *anyone*—about your past. All that should matter is your future together."

With a sigh, she turned to lean back against the headboard next to him, stretching her legs out on top of the quilt. "A good marriage cannot be based on a lie."

He took her hand. "My darling girl, you are a Shay, which means—if you'll forgive me for saying so—you have never seen a good marriage."

She was amazed she could even smile, but a grin tickled her lips. "Touché." Reality quickly sobered her. "I couldn't let him bind himself to me for life and not tell him who I really am. I might hate my father and all he's done, but I am still his daughter. After the way Grace suffered at his hand…"

Drew squeezed her hand. "What happened was not your fault, angel."

"I will not marry the man I love and base that union on a lie of omission," she insisted.

"I gather their reaction wasn't good."

Dropping her chin, she stared at their joined hands. "I am as good as dead to all of them."

"Even Ty?"

"*Especially* Ty. When I left, he made no move to follow me."

"So no wedding?"

She shook her head.

The door opened, and Gideon strode into the room with Caleb on his heels. The brothers looked to where Cassie and Drew lounged against the headboard and frowned.

"Why is *she* here?" Gideon demanded.

When she tried to get out of the bed, Drew draped his arm over her shoulder and anchored her next to him. "Gideon, we have discussed this before. Cassie is dear to me, but she is no threat to what we share. You cannot forbid me to spend time with her or give the poor girl a hug when she requires one."

Gideon's expression softened. "I'm sorry...I just... To see you so close will always be...difficult."

Caleb was less diplomatic. "That's 'cause you can't claim Drew in public. You don't want his name tied to someone else."

As if her soul wasn't already in enough pain. Now she hurt for Drew and Gideon. They were obviously in love, but no one would ever accept them together.

Caleb marched over to the bed and set his hands against his hips. "You've been crying."

Drew spoke before she could figure out how to explain why she was such a mess. "T'would seem our Cassie is now a free woman."

Eyes wide, Caleb gaped at her. "What about Ty Bishop? I thought you two would marry soon."

"You thought wrong," Cassie snapped. She shrugged Drew's arm off her shoulder and stood. "I believe I have come up with a solution to all my problems." She heaved a sigh and explained the only choice she had remaining. "I shall get myself to Sacramento as quickly as possible. I cannot let my Uncle Derrick send more ruffians after the good people of this city."

"Why Sacramento?" Caleb asked.

"Cass..." Drew's voice was low and full of concern.

She skirted around Caleb so she could breathe. He'd moved close enough to make her feel crowded—a feeling she despised. "I shall go to my Uncle Simon and ask for sanctuary."

"I thought you only had one uncle," Drew said. "And are you not under the guardianship of your grandfather?"

"Uncle Simon is my mother's brother. He isn't a Shay. He's a Randall. While he might not have the political connections of my grandfather and uncle, he is not without influence. If I go to him and beg for his protection, I might still be able to avoid having to marry Robert."

When she reached for her scarf, Caleb grabbed her upper arm. "Wait. You can't think to travel all the way to Sacramento by yourself—especially now that winter is here?"

"I have no choice," she insisted. "I must leave this place before any more people come to drag me back to San Francisco."

"I'll take you," he insisted. "All the way to Sacramento."

Gideon joined in. "He'll get you there quickly and safely. Never seen a man who can hide as well as Caleb and still move miles and miles in a day."

After everything her family had put Ty and his family—and Drew—through, she was reluctant to accept help from anyone else. "If you escort me, I fear it will put you in danger. I cannot ask that of you, Caleb."

"Wouldn't be for nothing." He took her hand. "I'd want something for my help."

She quirked an eyebrow, although she had a pretty good idea what he would want.

"You have to marry me first."

"Caleb!" Drew slapped the mattress. "You can't ask that of her! She's trying to escape an unhappy marriage, why would she—"

"Who says it would be unhappy?" Caleb asked. "I've been wantin' to court her. I like her." His gaze found hers. "I could make you a good husband."

"I fear I cannot marry you, Caleb," Cassie said, "for all the same reasons I must leave this town."

His eyes narrowed. "I don't know what you mean."

"If we marry, where shall we live?" She didn't give him time to reply. "You want to stay on the farm with your brother. Should we marry and live here, I would still be within my Uncle Derrick's reach. I would be putting you and your brother in danger—just as I put Ty and his family in danger."

Ty. Saying his name brought fresh tears to her eyes. She refused to let them fall.

Now that she had a plan, she wanted to implement it with all haste. "I will be fine. I shall dress as a boy and take a train to Sacramento. Then I will find my Uncle Simon."

All three men started yelling, but they expressed a similar theme.

They all thought she was out of her mind.

Cassie held up a hand to silence them. "My mind is made up. I'm going to Sacramento. *By myself.*"

"I won't let you go out on your own." Drew tossed the cover aside and got out of bed. While he appeared to have more strength than he had the last time she'd seen him, he was clearly too weak to travel.

"She won't be on her own," Caleb said. "I'm goin' with her."

"I cannot allow that," Cassie retorted. "I cannot marry you, Caleb."

His lips thinned to a grim line.

"I will be fine on my own," she insisted.

"Tell you what…" Caleb picked up her coat and held it out to her. "I'll get you to Sacramento. By the time we get there, I'll have convinced you to marry me."

"But—"

"No, buts." He helped her into her coat. "We're going back to the farm, packin' a few things, then we're leavin'."

She looked to Drew. After a few long moments, he nodded. "At least you won't be alone."

"Gideon?" Caleb asked. "Can you handle things on your own?"

"For a while," his brother replied. "But you'll be back?"

"Not sure."

Stomping her foot, she tried again. "I cannot let you—"

Caleb pressed right on as though she hadn't spoken a word. "Once Drew is stronger, he can help you."

"How long will you be gone?" Gideon asked.

"Depends on whether Cassie marries me or not."

"And if I don't?" While she might be railroaded into letting him accompany her to Sacramento, she had absolutely no intention of marrying him. She might welcome his escort, but she wouldn't ruin her friend's life by becoming his bride.

Besides, there was only one man she loved—one man she could be with as a true wife.

"If you don't…" Caleb shrugged. "I'll come back here, I s'pose."

Those words only firmed her resolve. He would help her escape to the only sanctuary left to her. Then she'd be sure to send him back to his life here in Montana.

Drew gave her a hug. "This is for the best, Cass. Let Caleb help you since I cannot."

She rubbed her cheek against his shoulder. "We shall meet again?"

After squeezing her tight, he kissed the top of her head before turning her loose. "Absolutely. I love you."

"And I love you." She rose on tiptoes and kissed his cheek. "Farewell my knight in shining armor."

With the future she had planned—as well as the future that waited for him with Gideon—Drew was wrong. Not only would she never see him again, when she left Montana behind, it would be for good.

Ty will come for me.

No. There would be no rescue this time. There wasn't any reason for him to seek her out. While she loved him—with every ounce of her being—he would never forgive her. Although she knew that was for the best, her heart simply didn't understand.

I love him.

If only he'd loved her in return. Then there would be a reason to struggle for a future together.

Her future—bleak though it was—now rested in the hands of Caleb Young and her Uncle Simon.

Chapter Twenty-Two

Silence reigned after Cassie left. Ty didn't trust himself to speak, afraid in his rage he'd lash out at the people he'd always considered his true family.

Letting her go had been difficult, but he wouldn't have to chase her down this time. She was going to Drew, and she'd be safe there until Ty could get to her and soothe her.

Right now, he needed to straighten everyone out about what his future held. He'd let Cassie leave solely to prevent her from hearing anymore hurtful things when he clued Adam, Grace, Matthew, and Victoria in on his plans. He'd be sure to straighten out Jake and his wife when he fetched Cassie from town.

They were sure to rebel when he told them that she was his future—whether they approved or not. He'd made his choice. No matter how much he loved them, this woman had become his everything. He refused to live his life without Cassie in it.

"What did we just do?" Grace asked, her tone full of regret.

"What you *did*," Ty replied, "was punish an innocent girl—one who's never done none of you wrong—just 'cause she's the daughter of a cruel bastard." He let his accusing glare settle on each person—even Adam, though he was less to blame than the others. "She can't help who her pa was, and she ain't nothing like him."

"We know that," Victoria said. "It's only…after what happened to Grace—"

"I know all about what he did to Grace," Ty snapped. "But what the hell does that have to do with Cassie? She's a victim of that family too."

Adam nodded. "He's right. We should all be ashamed of ourselves."

Crossing his arms over his chest, Matthew didn't appear the least bit contrite. "It's not just about the girl, Ty. This is about the danger that goes with her. She's nice enough, but she's still a Shay. Where she goes, her uncle will follow, exactly like his brother did—hunting anyone who gets in his way 'til he gets her back. You *know* that, you just won't *accept* it."

"He can send as many men as he wants, and I'll fight to the last one." Ty snatched up his coat.

"You're going after her, aren't you?" Grace asked. "Are you sure that's what's best?"

"I don't give a damn if it's what's best," Ty replied. Then he let his anger swell until it ruled his words. "I care for that woman, and if she'll have me, I'm gonna marry her. If you can't accept that, then know this—where *she* goes, *I* go. You ain't gonna welcome her into our family? Then you ain't never gonna see me again. I'll drag her up to the huntin' cabin and stay buried in the snow for the next three months. Then we'll be on the next stage outta town and take the danger with us."

Adam sat down and wrapped an arm around his wife's shoulder. "There's no need for you to leave, Ty. Marry your Cassie. We'll all help protect her."

After giving Adam a grateful nod, Ty stared at Matthew—his biggest obstacle and the friend he'd counted on to help guard Cassie.

Ty had underestimated how much Matthew hated Stephen Shay. He'd always assumed Grace had suffered, but he hadn't realized exactly how much the nightmare of Stephen's dogged pursuit had affected Matthew.

The man was the town marshal, and if Ty couldn't sway him, the danger to Cassie in White Pines would be too hard to handle. Adam would give some assistance, but Ty needed Matthew—or he and Cassie would have to move on.

Victoria took her husband's hand. "He's right, you know. Since when have we ever been the kind of people to turn away an innocent who needs our shelter?" She smiled. "We have three cats in a two-room home because you couldn't stand to see them go hungry."

Matthew's sigh gave Ty hope. At least the man was considering things rather than dismissing Cassie without a moment of thought. God, he hated the idea of three months snowed in at that cabin. Sure, she'd be safe—but could she still want him after that much forced isolation? Hell, he couldn't even read. She'd surely figure out how much higher she could reach.

If Matthew would come around to protecting Cassie and accepting her as part of Ty's life, they just might be able to stay in town—or at least closer than up the blasted mountain.

Grace's gaze bored into her brother. "I have come to terms with my past, Matthew. Stephen paid with his life for the crimes he committed against us both, and for having Ty beaten. Why should his daughter be forced to accept our blame and disdain? She's a sweet girl with a big heart. She obviously loves Ty."

"*What?*" Ty shook his head. It couldn't be true. Not a miracle like that.

"Grace is right. That girl loves you," Adam said.

"She ain't said so," Ty insisted.

Could she really love him? Could God truly be that merciful?

"Are–are you sure, Grace?" His voice squeaked.

Her smile was genuine and a bit sassy. "You can't see it?"

"How could I possibly see love?"

"It's in her eyes every time she looks at you," Grace explained. "Accept it."

"She's right, Ty," Adam added. "Cassie adores you."

Ty suddenly felt reborn—cleansed in heart and soul.

She loves me.

And oh, how he loved her! He'd loved her from the moment she rescued him.

He wanted to run after her and show her with his lips and his body just how much… But things needed to be decided first.

"I–I love her," he confessed.

"You love her?" Grace asked, a tear slipping down her cheek.

"I do."

She gave him a weak smile and a nod.

"Matthew?" Ty arched his eyebrow. "Up to you. Do we stay and count on your help? Or do we hightail it outta town?"

"*After* a visit to the preacher." Adam smiled with that command.

Ty nodded but kept his gaze on Matthew.

After pressing a kiss to her husband's cheek, Victoria stared deeply into his eyes. "Please? You know it's the right thing to do." Her plea was a whisper.

Matthew stared at his wife for a few, long moments before he heaved a weary sigh. "Fine."

"Meaning?" Ty had to be sure. If he and Cassie were going to head north, they needed to leave immediately. Snow had already fallen, and the threat of more—*much* more—scented the air and tinted the clouds an ominous gray.

"Meaning you—and Cassie—will have my help." He offered Ty his hand.

Giving it a shake, Ty threw in a grateful nod. "I'm goin' after her. When I get back—with my wife—we'll move into her cabin until I can get our home ready."

"I imagine we can speed things along with your place," Adam said. "Go on now…go get your bride."

***

Ty was getting damned sick and tired of chasing Cassie all over the Montana Territory. He unloaded all his anger on Drew and Gideon. The men sat at a table in the theater, staring into their glasses of beer.

Ty knew guilt when he saw it.

"I expected this of Gideon," Ty accused. "But you, Drew? You let her go when you know she's in danger?"

Drew's head snapped up, the anger clear in his eyes. "I let her go because I wanted her *out* of danger. Cassie has a good plan. Caleb is taking her to—" He took a long drink and slammed the glass down. "Never mind. It's not for you to know."

Ty's temper flared hotter. These men knew where she was. Didn't they know how much she needed his protection? That, and the thought of her alone with Caleb ate at him. "Where? *Where* is Caleb taking her?"

With a shake of his head, Drew glanced to Gideon.

"Not telling you," Gideon replied. "She's got a plan—a good plan. Caleb will take good care of her just fine."

"He's got no right!" Ty insisted. "She belongs with me."

"You ain't her husband," Gideon retorted. "She's a single woman. Caleb likes her and—"

"But I *love* her!"

Rolling his eyes toward the ceiling, Ty took a deep breath. At the rate he was confessing his new feelings he might as well post flyers around town, proclaiming his love. The only person he hadn't told was…

Cassie.

The one person who deserved to know.

He had to find her.

When Gideon started to speak again, Drew put his hand over the one Gideon rested on the table. "Wait." He considered Ty for a long moment. "You love her?"

Since he'd shouted it in Drew's face, there was no reason to deny it. "I do. And I want to marry her. Today."

"It'll put you in danger." Drew pointed at his bruised face. "They'll send more next time since they didn't get the job done when they attacked me. No doubt they'll learn soon that I lied about being married to her and that you are her real husband."

Gideon sputtered. "He can't marry her! What about her promise to Caleb?"

Ty clenched his hands into fists. "What exactly did she promise him?"

"She's gonna marry him when they reach their destination."

"The hell she is!" Insides twisting into tight knots, Ty slammed his fist on the table, sending the mugs of beer jumping. "Where's he taking her?"

"Not telling you that." With a shake of his head, Gideon glared at Drew. "Neither are you."

"Gideon... Ty loves her," Drew insisted. "Doesn't she deserve to know that before she marries your brother?"

"Doesn't my brother deserve a wife? He ain't never gonna get one out here. Cassie came to him for a reason, and I say Caleb deserves her every bit as much Ty."

That ridiculous statement was enough to make Ty want to take a swing at Gideon. The man had always been his friend, but if he didn't tell Ty where Caleb had taken Cassie, he was going to get a broken nose.

He took a threatening step toward Gideon. "Tell me, damn you!"

Gideon stood up so fast, his chair went flying behind him. The sound echoed through the cavernous theater. Holding his fists in front of him, he looked ready for a fight. "Or what, Bishop?"

If he wanted a fight, Ty was damn well ready to pound him into the floorboard. "Or I'll beat it outta you."

Drew stood—grimacing in pain as he rose—and held an arm against Gideon's chest. "There will be none of that." He settled his gaze on Ty. "You really do love her, don't you?"

Damn it, he was tired of being asked that. "For the love of... Yes! *Yes*, I love her!"

Drew nodded. "They're going to Sacramento. They only left a few hours ago. You can probably catch them if you're a good tracker."

"I am."

Gideon dropped his hands to his sides. "Drew...what about Caleb?"

"Caleb will get by. Besides..." He tossed Ty a lopsided smile. "He doesn't love her—not like Ty does. She deserves a man who truly loves her."

Ty marched toward the door, ready to track the Caleb and Cassie down. Then he was dragging her ass right back to White Pines.

"Ty?" Drew called.

Whirling to face him, Ty didn't even try to hide his impatience. "What now?"

"You'll bring our girl back?" The worry and pain were etched on Drew's features.

"Damn right I will."

Chapter Twenty-Three

Ty caught up with Cassie and Caleb at sunset. They hadn't been hard to track, which meant Caleb wasn't properly trained in hiding his trail, or he didn't believe they'd be followed.

He was wrong.

The tightness in Ty's chest eased the moment he saw Cassie emerge from the shelter of the trees. She walked over to where Caleb worked to start a fire and tossed an armload of kindling at his feet.

Ty eased Duke back into the trees, hoping neither of them would see him. His errant emotions needed to be controlled first—controlled and discarded so he could talk to Cassie without shouting a string of profanities over the fright she'd given him.

She'd dressed in men's clothes again. When would the woman learn that she'd be tempting in a potato sack? Her shape was so clear to him. Or was that the memory of running his hands over her gentle curves?

Damn if he wasn't physically reacting to the erotic images of her flashing through his mind.

Ty let his anger sweep aside his desire. It was time to let Cassie know her destiny. He urged Duke out of the trees. "Goddammit, woman! Why can't you stay where I put you?"

Rising, Caleb let his hand edge toward his gun.

"Don't even think about it," Ty said, swinging down from his saddle.

"Ty!" Cassie took some running steps toward him before stopping abruptly. "What... how..."

"I'm getting sick and tired of chasing you down." He closed the distance between them, grabbed her shoulders, and pulled her to him. Then he kissed her—a kiss that let her know in no uncertain terms he wasn't letting her get away.

Never again.

At first, she was stiff as a board in his arms. But when Ty swept his tongue into her mouth to mate with hers, she relaxed. Holding tight to his coat, she sagged against him in surrender.

Caleb stomped over to them. "Leave her be."

"Ain't gonna," Ty replied. His gaze found Cassie's. "You're going back to town with me. *Now.*"

"Ty..." Her sigh was ragged. "I–I cannot. I must go—"

He took her hand and started dragging her toward Duke.

She dug in her heels. "I must go to my uncle and—"

Whirling on his heel, he glared down at her. "If you think I'm letting you go back to that bastard, you got another think coming."

"My *other* uncle," she explained. "Uncle Simon—my mother's brother. He's in Sacramento. I believe he will listen to my plight and help me."

As if he'd let her near her family, especially when she wasn't even sure anyone would truly help her.

Only Ty could protect her. "C'mon, Cassie. Full moon tonight. We can get back to town before too late."

Caleb snaked his arm around her waist and tried to pull her back.

She tugged his hands away and twisted until he stepped back. "Stop it. Both of you. I am not a prize to be fought over!" Striding away, she crouched by the fire and fed the growing flames more kindling. "I have made up my mind." Her voice quavered. "I–I shall go to Uncle Simon alone. I do not need either of you to put yourselves in harm's way for me."

Caleb sputtered in obvious anger while Ty took a different approach. He marched over to her and put a hand on her shoulder. "I know you love me."

Her sharp gasp echoed through the camp. "Why I–I do no such thing!"

"Cassie girl...I know you do. And I... I..." He tossed a glance back over his shoulder. Why did Caleb have to be there? It would be hard enough to confess what was in his heart to her. He didn't need a witness. "And I'm takin' you back." He pulled her to her feet and scooped her into his arms. "End of discussion."

She didn't struggle, which came as a surprise. She did, however, look to Caleb. "I suppose it was a foolhardy plan..."

Ty snorted at that obvious statement. "I got a better one." He tossed her onto Duke's back, then he went to where Duchess was tied and led her to his horse. He tied the reins onto his saddle. "You comin'?" he asked Caleb.

Caleb had busied himself with putting out the fire. "I should fight you, Bishop. I should beat you bloody."

"You can *try*."

He shook his head. "Why fight when I already lost the war?"

"What are you talking about?"

"She loves you," Caleb replied. "I lose." He kicked some snow and dirt over the smoking embers and retrieved his horse. "Let's get going. I wanna sleep in my own bed. Alone."

Ty swung up behind Cassie. Rubbing his chin against her cheek, he whispered, "I'll get you home to *your* bed."

And then I'll join you in it.

She trembled in his arms. "Then let us be off."

He turned Duke toward the road north, ready to get Cassie back where she belonged.

***

They reached the cabin after midnight.

Cassie shivered. Not from the cold. Ty had wrapped his arms around her the whole ride, and even through his thick coat, he radiated heat. The shelter of his embrace had made the trip seem far too quick.

No, the way she trembled was in anticipation for what would happen when they reached their destination.

She wanted him. From the moment he'd come to her—chasing her down again to bring her back to his side—she'd wanted to show him exactly how much she loved him and how grateful she was that he wouldn't let her run away.

Could he love her? Or was he merely acting on his honor—wanting to keep the promise he'd made her to protect her?

The cabin was empty. Drew would still be recuperating in town—or at

Gideon's. She and Ty had parted ways with Caleb several minutes ago as he'd headed toward his home, leaving them alone for the last part of the trip.

Ty hadn't said a kind word since they'd left the campsite, so she guessed he was still angry. From time to time he'd shudder, hold her hips, and gruffly demand she stop wiggling. Not once did he explain his odd statement about her loving him.

How could he possibly know that?

I'm a fool.

Of course he knew. She'd all but said the words. He had to understand that by giving him her virginity she was declaring her love.

Lifting her under the arms, Ty gently set her on the ground. "Go inside. Get a fire going. I'll tend your horse."

She gave Duchess a stroke on her velvet muzzle and obeyed. A yawn slipped out as she opened the door. With a glance over her shoulder, she said, "I am so weary. I shall sleep the moment my head hits the pillow."

Why couldn't she bring herself to ask him to stay? Couldn't he see how much she needed him to hold her—to make love to her again?

"A–are you weary as well?" she asked.

"Nope." He'd slipped from the saddle and was untying the mare's reins from the back of his saddle. "Go on inside, Cassie girl. Get warm."

"Shall I see you in the morning?" After all the trouble he'd gone to fetch her—again—she shouldn't be asking any more favors. "I–I mean to say…I would be pleased to share our morning meal. I–I can cook for you. Will you be here for breakfast?"

His smile puzzled her. "I promise you, I'll be here for breakfast."

The man was simply too obtuse to understand, and her pride wouldn't allow for her to beg him to share her bed again.

Why had he come after her and Caleb? She'd thought—she'd *hoped*—Ty felt affection enough to want her to remain by his side. Why else had he gone to so much trouble?

"Good night then…" She watched him lead Duchess into the barn, not even sparing her a glance.

Had she not been freezing, she wouldn't even have bothered with the fire. She had it lit in no time and stood next to her bed, wondering if she should even bother removing her clothes.

Tears stung her eyes, but she refused to let a single one fall. Her life was a mess—in every aspect. Crying about it wouldn't change a thing. It wouldn't make Robert Putnam disappear, nor would it make Ty love her the way she loved him.

Lord, she was tired. She excused her silly, girlish fantasies, using fatigue as an excuse. Straightening her spine, she swallowed hard and tossed her coat on Drew's empty bed. Then she went on her side of the wall and lit the lamp.

Ty said he had a plan. She would put her faith in him.

Even if he had no faith in her.

Just as she pulled back the covers, the door opened and Ty stepped through.

"Ty! I–I thought you were going to return home."

Without a word, he crossed the cabin, gathered her into his arms, and kissed her.

Ty couldn't believe Cassie thought he was going back to the ranch. He'd just chased her down and brought her back, yet she thought he'd simply drop her off at the cabin and leave her alone?

Not only would that place her back in danger, he wanted to make love to her again. Desperately.

How could she not know that?

Because he hadn't found the courage to tell her what was in his heart...

Framing her face in his hands, he stared into her eyes. "You know I'll protect you. No matter what. I won't leave you. Ever."

He brushed his lips over hers. Once. Twice. Then he settled his mouth on hers and deepened the kiss. There was no hesitation from Cassie. She returned his passion by stroking her tongue over his.

Being with her was so different than any other woman he'd ever taken to bed. Those interludes were fine but unmemorable. They usually ended in him leaving some money on the dresser on his way out. Never once had he slept a full night with a woman he truly cared for, let alone loved.

Each touch, each caress was so raw he had to close his eyes against the rush of emotion. He was the only man who'd ever touched her soft skin, kissed her sweet lips. Possessed her body.

He'd kill any other man who dared touch her—with his bare hands. And he'd make him suffer before he died.

"Ty..." She unbuttoned his coat while he toed off his boots.

He wanted her naked. *Now.* But he let her take the lead. Her cheeks were bright with color. Even in the dim light of the lamp he could see her blush. Yet she didn't stop undressing him.

His coat hit the floor, followed by his shirt. He stood before her, bare chested with his hat still firmly on his head.

"Oh...my..." Her words were breathless as she slipped off her shirt. Then she unbuttoned her pants and pushed them over her hips and down her legs. She'd already removed her boots. All that remained was a camisole and thin pantalets.

He was out of his clothes in two blinks of an eye, discarding them like so much trash. He needed to feel her skin against his.

As she reached for the ribbon of her camisole, he eased her hands away. "Let me." His voice was ragged as the winter wind.

He pulled the ribbon and opened the garment. Her nipples had tightened into hard pebbles that he had to taste. Dropping to his knees, he put his hands on her hips and covered her breast with his mouth.

Cassie arched her back. She touched his head, groaned and then plucked his hat off and tossed it aside. She tunneled her fingers through his hair and whimpered when Ty sucked hard on her nipple.

Lavishing his attention on her breasts, he untied her pantalets and pulled them down. The sweet scent of her arousal made his cock twitch. With a groan, he stood and lifted her off his feet. He carried her to the bed, laid her in the center, and stretched out on top of her.

"Cassie girl..." He buried his lips against her neck, loving the fast pulse he found there. Trailing his kisses down her chest, he reverently touched his lips to each breast before moving lower. His tongue circled her bellybutton, then he rubbed his nose through the soft hair on her mound.

"Ty...you can't mean to—"

"Oh, I mean to all right."

Nudging her thighs farther apart, he kissed the heat of her, separating her folds with his fingers before stabbing his tongue into her.

Ty lost a few locks of hair—or at least he thought he had from the way Cassie pulled at it. She writhed as he loved her with his mouth, drawing her knees up and squeezing her thighs tight against his head. He simply eased them apart and swirled his tongue around the bud he hoped would drive her wild.

"Don't... stop..." She panted for breath before lifting her hips off the bed and trembling with her release.

His own passion demanded his attention. He rose over her, bracing his weight on his arms as he kissed her, loving how she sighed against his mouth.

"You tasted like honey," he murmured.

Her face was even brighter with color. "Oh, Lord... Do we have to talk about...*that?*"

"Are you embarrassed?"

"Of course I'm embarrassed! You just... I mean..."

Ty kissed her again. One hard kiss before he thrust his hips to rub his cock against her core. "Don't be ashamed of—"

"I never said I was *ashamed*. I'm simply...*embarrassed*. I did not realize a man could love a woman that way."

"Then be embarrassed, so long as you let me do it again when the mood strikes."

Her smile was broad. "I'd die should you refuse to...gift me with such attention again." She wiggled her hand between their bodies and wrapped her fingers around his shaft. "Make love to me, Ty. I want to feel you deep inside me again."

Ty almost came simply from hearing her declaration. A few deep breaths helped him regain some control. He pushed inside her slowly, wanting to savor each sensation.

Cassie would have none of it. Ty had to know he was driving her mad by teasing her so. She pressed her palms against his backside and raised her hips to force him more deeply into her body.

He growled, a sound she hoped meant he would give her what she wanted—a rough, fast ride toward fulfillment.

"I'm trying to go slow," he whispered, his teeth clenched tight.

"Go slow *later*, Ty."

He must have taken her words to heart as he sped his rhythm, thrusting into her again and again. She gave herself over to him completely, surrendering to the storm that was gathering inside her. It hit like a lightning strike, sending jolts of pleasure from her core to her limbs. She cried out his name as she rode the waves of delight.

Ty thrust into her several more times before he groaned out three words.

"I love you."

Then he shuddered as he held her tightly.

It wasn't until he rolled off her, tugged the quilt over them, and hauled her up against his side that Cassie allowed herself to think about what he'd said.

Her heart wanted to sing, but she snuffed her happiness back down. Words said in the heat of passion weren't something she could count on in the stark light of day.

His soft snore told her there would be no discussion tonight, which was for the best.

Her fatigue weighed heavily, drugging her with sleep. She'd think more on his declaration when she was rested and no longer lost to the afterglow of making love.

There'd be time to ponder the problem later.

Chapter Twenty-Four

Ty woke to the sound of Cassie's rooster announcing the dawn.

He'd slept like the dead. Normally, he heard every sound and woke several times during the night. But holding her close—in the aftermath of lovemaking—gave him such contentment...

She sighed and snuggled closer to his side. He never wanted her to leave his arms. Here, she was safe from harm—from her family.

And from Robert Putnam.

Ty frowned.

Damn it all, the woman needed to marry him. *Today.* Then he could set his plan in motion to rid her of the threat from her family. Perhaps her Uncle Simon could be included once Ty learned more about him from Cassie.

First things first. It was time to stand before the preacher.

"Good morning," she murmured, still sounding more asleep than awake.

"Mornin'," he gruffly replied.

Her lips brushed against his collarbone. "Don't be grumpy with me. It's such a beautiful morning."

All Ty did was grunt.

"What's wrong?"

"You and me need to come to an understanding."

Pushing up on one elbow, she stared down at him. Her hair was in lovely disarray, locks of it resting on her cheek as long curls swirled around her shoulders. The glint in her eyes made his body tighten with need.

While he would have thoroughly enjoyed tumbling her again, he tamped down his desire and focused on the more important goal.

"What understanding are we to come to, Ty?"

"We're getting hitched today. Got it?"

"I beg your pardon?"

"Hitched. Married. We're getting *married*. Today." He tossed the blanket aside and stood. Had he not found some self-control, the chill in the air would have done the trick just as well. At least his clothes were close.

Cassie quickly jerked the cover back around her and watched him as he dressed. Her quiet ate at him.

"Did you hear me, Cassie girl?"

"I heard you quite well, Mr. Bishop."

He couldn't help but roll his eyes because she had to know she was tweaking his temper. "Get up. We'll have some breakfast, then we'll go to town. We can stop and get Jake and Emily to stand up with us." His clothes were nothing more than heavy work wear. A shame he couldn't fetch his Sunday best.

No. No stalling, not even to dress in finery. He wouldn't be able to relax until Cassie Shay traded her last name for his.

"Have you lost your senses?" She'd pulled the covers up to her chin, and she had the most incredulous frown on her face.

He wanted to kiss it away. "Nope."

"I couldn't possible marry you," she insisted. "Drew—"

Fully dressed, Ty stomped back to the bed. "Listen to me, and listen good.

We're gettin' married today. Only one thing could change my mind."

"Then tell me that one thing, and I shall use it to prevent you from making such a horrible mistake."

Leaning closer, he stopped when his lips were only inches from hers. "I won't marry you if you can honestly tell me you ain't in love with me."

Sweet Lord, that was the one thing Cassie couldn't say. No matter how hard she tried to lie to him, Ty would see right through her. She loved him with all her heart and soul, and he knew it.

She muttered a curse.

He grinned.

"Whether I love you or not is irrelevant. After what happened to Drew, I can't marry you."

Without a warning, he yanked the covers off her, tossing the quilt on the floor.

Not only did the cold steal her breath away, Cassie wasn't ready for Ty to see her body. It was one thing to allow his hands—and his mouth—to touch her skin. To have him see all her flaws in the stark light of day?

Unthinkable.

"Damn," he said, drawing out the word.

Cassie hung her head. She was well aware of her flaws—her grandfather, her Uncle Derrick, and Robert had berated her about them often enough. She was too short, too skinny, and lacking in feminine curves. Because of her penchant to run around like a boy, she had sleek muscles rather than the softness of a gentle, desirable woman. The notion that Ty looked upon her with the same disdain as those horrible men near to broke her heart.

His finger under her chin forced her gaze up. "Ain't never seen a woman half as pretty as you, Cassie girl."

She had trouble letting his praise sink in. "Truly? You think I'm...pretty?"

Leaning down, he kissed her—a sweet, simple kiss that left her wanting more. As he pulled back, she cupped her hands behind his head, knocking his hat from his head as she laced her fingers through his hair. She rose on her knees and gave him the kind of kiss she needed, sliding her tongue between his lips and stroking his.

Ty growled deep in his chest and embraced her roughly. The kiss seemed never-ending until he finally eased back and stared into her eyes. "Marry me? Today?"

At least he'd changed from demanding to asking...

While she wanted nothing more than to accept and marry the man who owned her heart, she hesitated. Not only would she be putting him in danger, she was fighting back the fear that she'd be tying down a man who simply had no desire to be wed. Was he proposing out of responsibility or affection?

She had to know. "Do you love me, Ty?"

A slow smile curved his lips, which came as a shock. Most men refused to even consider let along answer such a question.

"Do you think I'd be marryin' a Shay for another other reason?"

"Y–you love me?"

"Listen carefully, woman." He held her chin firmly. "I love you. Now will you marry me?"

"Yes." She nibbled on her bottom lip, battling happy tears. "Yes, I'll marry you."

Ty marched away, stopping at the door to glance at her over his shoulder. "Today?"

"Today."

After tossing her a nod, he left the cabin.

***

Although it wasn't the wedding of her dreams, Cassie beamed through the entire ceremony.

While there were no sprays of flowers and her dress was nothing but a simple calico, she would have it no other way. She didn't need a church full of people or a reception with the finest cuisine. All that mattered was that she was marrying Ty Bishop—and that his friend stood by his side and his family behind them.

Jake had immediately agreed to be witness, which eased some of Cassie's fear of rejection. But when Emily insisted Jake ride to the Twin Springs to fetch Grace and Adam, Cassie's stomach had knotted. Worse, while Jake made the trip, Emily went to the marshal's office to tell Matthew and Victoria about the wedding and bring them along.

Instead of arriving and trying to talk Ty out of marrying her, they all welcomed her with hugs and kind words. If they'd had reservations, they'd set them aside—for Ty and his happiness. Jake even called her "sister" and seemed happy to know their new familial status.

Ty had been thoughtful enough to get Drew, and Gideon arrived with him.

Caleb was nowhere to be found.

The preacher cleared his throat.

"I'm sorry." For shame. She'd been caught daydreaming in her own wedding. "I...um...could you please repeat..."

"Do you promise to love, honor, and obey this man?" the gray-haired reverend asked.

"Obey?" She arched an eyebrow at Ty.

His smile eased her worries. "I ain't a man who expects blind obedience."

"I promise to love, honor, and obey—so long as he is reasonable in his orders," she vowed, her voice steady.

"This is...highly unusual." The preacher glanced to Ty.

"I accept your terms," Ty replied, still grinning at her.

He knew her well. Just another of the reasons she loved him.

The rest of the ceremony flew by in a happy whirl. Ty kissed her before he was torn away by the men so they could slap him on the back. Then the women wanted to embrace him.

When Grace gave Cassie a hug, she whispered in her ear, "I'll bake a cake for you. Soon. We'll have a big supper and—"

"A generous offer," Cassie said. "But I don't wish for you to go to so much trouble for me."

"Not just for you," Grace said. "For Ty as well. We'll celebrate your marriage." A smile spread over her face. "You're my daughter now, you realize."

Happy tears formed, but Cassie tried to blink them away. "I consider it an honor that you would consider me such."

"So formal?" Adam said, his hand on her shoulder. He turned her and gave her a heartfelt embrace. "Welcome to the family, Cassie."

She closed her eyes, willing the tears aside. "Thank you, Adam."

Drew tossed her a lopsided smile. "'Tis better to have loved and lost than never to have loved at all.'"

"Tennyson." Rising on tiptoes, Cassie gave his cheek a kiss. "You shall never lose me, Drew. Never."

Ty scowled, wrapped his arm around her shoulder, and pulled her close. His lingering jealousy forced a smile she tried to hide by turning her head.

"You are a lucky man, Mr. Bishop." Drew offered his hand.

Ty shook it. "Damned lucky." Then he looked to Adam. "We need to talk. I'm takin' Cassie to San Francisco and—"

"*What?*" Cassie couldn't contain her shout.

Grace seemed every bit as dubious. "Ty, what in the devil—"

Drew sputtered but couldn't seem to get a word out.

Adam held up his hand. "Ty and I have a plan to end this nonsense with Cassie's family."

"But to go straight to their lair?" Grace shook her head. "Better to stay out of their reach."

"That's the problem," Ty said. He signaled for Jake to come closer.

Not only did Jake draw near, so did the rest of the family.

Ty went on. "The Shays' reach is too damned long to stay out of it our whole lives. Adam, Jake, and I talked this out. There's only one way to keep Cassie safe. Jake and me are taking her back to San Francisco. Jake's getting a document that says he's gonna wash his hands of all the Shay money. Cassie'll do the same. Once that jackanapes Putnam knows she's married—and that she ain't a virgin no more—he'll give up."

Cassie whole face flushed hot, spreading down her neck. She elbowed Ty in the ribs to let him know her displeasure with him parading their intimate life in front of his family. "He thought I'd married Drew."

"He didn't believe that for a minute," Ty retorted. "Otherwise Drew would be dead and not just bloodied up. No, he knew he'd still get a virgin if he married you. Not now that we slept—"

"Ty!" Grace scolded, hiding her chuckle behind her hand. "Can't you see how embarrassing this is for Cassie?"

Victoria wasn't so subtle, poking her finger into his shoulder. "Shame on you!"

"Such matters should be private," Cassie murmured.

Unfortunately, her words were drowned out by the loud laughter of the men.

While she was concerned about this plan of Ty's, she knew it wasn't foolproof. Her family might be pleased she was tossing aside any claim she had to the Shay fortune, but Robert was a man with enormous pride who wouldn't take the blow they'd given him well. No, he'd want revenge.

They needed the support of someone with influence to help protect them from Robert.

"I believe the plan is sound," she said. "But I also believe a visit to my Uncle Simon first might be beneficial."

"How so?" Adam asked.

"Uncle Simon has separated himself from the Shay family," she explained. "He was...displeased with my grandfather and his rather...cruel way of handling business matters. He also resented how my mother was treated."

Matthew nodded. "I'd heard he and your other uncle...the one in New York City... What's that uncle's name?"

"My Uncle Theodore," Cassie replied.

"I'd heard Theodore and Simon were disgusted with your father and—"

"Matthew..." Ty's voice took on a hard edge. "It ain't Cassie's fault her dad was such a bastard."

"I'm not blaming *her*," Matthew snapped. "I'm just saying...her Uncle Simon might be able to help you. He knows what the Shays are capable of— maybe he can help Cassie break free. Doubt you'd be able to get much help from a man in New York City, though."

Cassie nodded. "Uncle Simon is the only one we need. He's a lawyer. He can help us prepare documents eschewing the—"

"A-chewing? What's a-chewing?" Ty asked.

"Eschewing," Victoria corrected before Cassie could. "It means Cassie and Jake will forfeit any claim to the Shay fortune."

"This uncle's in Sacramento?" Ty asked.

Cassie nodded. "He is an aide to the governor of California."

Adam grinned. "Always nice to know people in high places."

"It's a sound plan." Jake turned to Ty. "You should leave now—before they have a chance to send someone after you."

"Let 'em." Ty let out a snort. "I can handle anything they throw at me."

Leaning harder against his side, Cassie shook her head. "I'll not have you hurt because of me."

Emily sidled up to her husband, and he draped his arm around her shoulder. "Will you be leaving soon?" The worry was as clear in her voice as it was in Cassie's mind.

The reply came from Ty. "He ain't goin'. Just me and Cassie for now. Jake can do his papers later when we know if the Shays will accept 'em."

"When are you and Cassie leaving?" Emily asked.

"As soon as we can pack and get goin'."

"Well, then..." Grace took Cassie's hand and gave it a squeeze. "It appears as though you'll be spending your honeymoon in Sacramento."

Chapter Twenty-Five

Ty held tight to Cassie's hand. He hated that she trembled and wished he could do something to ease her fears. Then again, she might be walking straight into the lions' den rather than simply into her Uncle Simon's home.

While part of him still wanted to pack her up and take her to the mountain cabin, he also knew hiding away wasn't going to solve anything. Derrick Shay and Robert Putnam needed to be dealt with and then pushed to the past, existing in Cassie's life as nothing more than bad memories.

She hesitated at the door, nibbling on her bottom lip. "Perhaps this is not as wise as I had hoped."

"What's got you worried? You said Simon ain't like Derrick. He'll be glad to see you, right?"

"That is my wish. He was always my savior when I was a child. It's just...it has been many years since I confided in him—now I fear he might not want my problems set upon his shoulders."

Since Ty's own kin had abandoned him, he could easily understand her concern. Yet even within his own wretched family, there were good people—siblings who'd come to find him after they grew up. Many had stories of their youths as gloomy as Ty's own, yet they'd turned out to be honorable and kind people.

With a little bit of luck, Simon might be their saving grace. "Trust your gut, Cassie girl. You'll know what to do."

She turned her face to his, her gaze searching for something.

He tried to show her confidence, then he touched his lips to hers—a quick kiss that added to his frustration. They'd left the afternoon of their wedding and had done nothing but travel since. There'd been no privacy, no place appropriate to make love to his beautiful new bride. In the back of his mind rested one concern—they hadn't properly consummated their marriage.

Once they were in their room at the inn, he'd remedy that problem immediately. While Cassie had wanted to stay at the Western Hotel, Ty had chosen an inconspicuous inn just north of the city, hoping that Simon's home wasn't being watched by Pinkertons who hoped to catch her and drag her back to San Francisco.

He wasn't taking any risks with her safety, and his Colt rested reassuringly against his hip.

After a bracing breath, she used the brass knocker, hitting three times and then easing a step back.

Ty took her hand in his and gave it a squeeze, but he kept his guard up.

The door opened to a reed-thin man in a dark suit and white gloves. "May I help you?"

"I am...um...is Uncle..." Cassie closed her eyes and took another breath. Then she opened her eyes and leveled her gaze on the butler. "I am Cassandra Shay. I am here to see my Uncle Simon."

Opening the door wider, the butler motioned them inside to a cavernous foyer. "Please wait here, and I will inform Mr. Randall of your arrival." He marched along the long foyer, headed toward the back of the house.

The place wasn't a *home*—it was a *palace*. Even the Shay mansion in San

Francisco couldn't hold a candle to the marble floors, carved banisters, and crystal chandeliers of Simon Randall's home. A peek to Ty's right revealed a dining room with padded chairs for twenty people. The room to the left had a grand piano that was surrounded by upholstered sofas. Portraits in gilded frames stared down from every wall.

He nervously snatched his hat from his head. Even in his Sunday best, he felt as out of place as a donkey at a horserace.

A tall and rather heavyset man in a dark suit came lumbering back up the foyer, the butler scurrying behind. "Cassandra! I have been so worried!" He spread his arms wide.

"Uncle Simon!" Cassie hurried to him.

"I cannot believe you're here." Simon all but swallowed her in a bear hug. He kissed the top of her head, which barely came to his collarbone. "I had heard you'd left San Francisco." His dark eyes settled on Ty, narrowing in obvious anger. "I was told you'd been taken against your will by two men— one matching the description of your companion. Should I call a constable?"

Ty held his gaze, refusing to be intimidated. "She ran away on her own."

Simon arched an eyebrow. "Then how have you come to be in her company?"

Cassie pushed back from her uncle and took Ty's hand. "This is my husband—Ty Bishop."

"*Husband?*" Simon's incredulous tone and thunderous voice accompanied his fierce frown. "Oh, Cassandra... Why would you make such a horrible mistake? Your family doesn't even *know* this man. We cannot allow you to do something so foolish."

Not liking the way this conversation was heading, Ty took a threatening step forward. He wasn't about to let Cassie's family take her away from him.

She put herself between him and Simon. "I've made no mistake, nor have I done something foolish."

"But this man is clearly one of your abductors," Simon insisted.

She shook her head. "I was never *abducted.* Ty and Jake Curtis helped me leave before Uncle Derrick forced me to marry a horrible man."

Simon's curt nod wasn't expected. "So I'd been told. A Robert Putnam, if I'm not mistaken. He's Derrick's right hand man."

Letting out a snort, Ty said, "Putnam don't deserve Cassie. That bastard hit her." Even talking about it, although long past the fact, still made his blood boil.

Simon gaped at his niece. "Cassandra? Is this true?"

"Yes," Cassie replied. "Ty's giving you the truth. He and Jake were my protectors. Ty insisted on staying with me as I fled, even though he was putting his own life at risk."

"And for that, I am truly thankful." He extended his hand.

Although he wasn't sure he trusted the man as much as Cassie did, Ty shook his hand.

With a sweep of his arm, Simon invited them to follow the butler back down the foyer. They ended up in a room that reminded Ty of Adam's large library back at the Twin Springs.

Adam had always loved books, often reading to Ty and Jake when they'd been boys and trying to teach them the skill. Jake had taken to reading like a duck to water. But Ty had struggled. He loved to hear stories, but to try to read them himself was next to impossible. Even when Victoria tried to help, he'd never been able to learn. The words just didn't look the same to him as the way others described. The letters were tricky, often twisting and turning and making him feel stupid.

So he'd finally given up.

Cassie hadn't, though. There weren't too many days that slipped by that she didn't sit him down with her copy of *Romeo and Juliet* and make Ty read some of the words. While the letters still liked fooling him, he was finally getting the way of it.

Simon moved behind an ornate desk while Cassie led Ty to two chairs facing the desk.

"James," Simon said to the butler, who was still following them, "please bring us all a spot of tea." He grinned at Cassie. "Perhaps that will help banish the cold."

With a nod, the butler left the study, closing the pocket doors behind him.

Simon stared at Ty. "Tell me, Mr. Bishop...what do you do to earn a living?"

"He works on a ranch," Cassie replied before he could. "He's a true cowboy, Uncle!"

"A cowboy, you say?" Simon tapped the cleft in his chin with his index finger. "And does being a cowboy provide a good income, Mr. Bishop? You know, of course, that Cassandra will one day be a very wealthy woman."

Thankfully, Cassie jumped in again before Ty could respond to the insulting statement meant to get a rise out of him, which it did. "He works for—"

With a raised hand, Simon stopped her. "I am speaking to Mr. Bishop at the moment, Cassandra. I need to know his intentions."

"Intentions? But I am his wife and—"

"*That*," Simon said, "has yet to be decided. If it's discovered that the man you chose isn't acceptable to your family or is simply taking her as a wife to get his greedy hands on her fortune, a marriage can be easily dissolved."

Horrified at the thought, Ty jumped to his feet. "The hell it can! She's my wife!"

Cassie held tight to the back of Ty's jacket. Only her trembling kept him from heading around the desk to show Simon just what he thought of him. "Uncle Simon...there is no need to talk of ending this marriage."

"Oh?" Simon's eyebrow arched. "Then the marriage has been duly consummated?"

Hating the way the conversation had turned and having never expected such a personal question from her own uncle, Cassie stammered out a response. "Um...no. Err...yes. I...um... Should you even be asking this?" Then it dawned on her what Simon was implying. No wonder Ty was enraged when he'd mentioned dissolving their marriage. "There will be no annulment. Ty is my husband in every sense of the word."

Her face felt hot enough to burst into flame, and she hated the lie she'd just told. But true consummation was merely a technicality. They might not have slept together since the ceremony, but they had thoroughly consummated their passion. That they'd made love before they'd spoken vows rather than after meant nothing to her.

"She's my *wife*," Ty said, thumping his thumb against his chest in some sort of masculine gesture of possession. "Mine, and you ain't taking her away. Got it?"

The smile on her uncle's face eased her concerns. "I was merely hoping to discover whether you truly desired my niece or had set your sights on her wealth. I can see now that it is Cassandra you want, not only in your rather forceful claim but in the fact you've not once inquired to her fortune."

"I don't want her damn money." Ty's grimace told her that not only did he mean what he said, she'd probably be hard-pressed to ever get him to use any funds that came to her from her family.

So be it.

She had no use for wealth, especially from a family who didn't love her. All she'd ever wanted she'd found in the simplicity of White Pines—and in the arms of her husband.

Simon settled his gaze on her. "Now, young lady, we must see what we can do to be sure Derrick Shay cannot put asunder that which God has joined."

Cassie nodded. "I was hoping perhaps you could help draw up a document that would help me surrender any inheritance in turn for Uncle Derrick leaving me in peace."

"He has bothered you since you left?"

"Very much," she replied. "Once he had me abducted until Ty came to rescue me. He also took Grace Morgan—"

Simon gathered his brows. "Grace. But her name is Morgan? I believe your father had a rather strong...attachment to a woman named Grace, but her family name was Riley, as I remember."

Ty had just settled back in his seat. Suddenly, he was back on his feet. "Stephen Shay raped Grace when she was nothing but a girl. Chased her all over the country too."

"So it *is* the same woman." Simon gave his head a shake. "Stephen always was a bit...obsessive about things he believed belonged to him. From what I've heard, she murdered him."

"Not murder," Ty insisted. "The man deserved killing."

"I'll remind you," Simon said, his voice growing hard. "Stephen was my brother-in-law."

Afraid the anger in their voices would cause a rift, Cassie shook her head. "He was a bad man, Uncle Simon. Can you not recall the times you protected me from him and from Uncle Derrick?"

Her uncle's features softened as he nodded.

"Can you help me?" she asked. "I also believe my half-brother would like to be sure the family never harms him again."

Simon's eyes widened. "You bring me so much news, Cassandra. First, I'm told you've married. Now you tell me about a brother? I suppose the child is Grace's?"

Cassie nodded. "But he's no child. He's older than I am. Grace never told my father. After he...assaulted her, she was left with child. His name is Jake

Curtis and he's my husband's dearest friend. Grace gave him up for adoption when he was born. She never wanted him to know about my father's attack."

"But he knows now?"

"Yes," she replied. "Uncle Derrick knows too. He sent for Jake. When he and Ty went to San Francisco, Uncle Derrick and Robert tried to have them both killed. I overheard their plan and helped them escape."

He chuckled. "So you married your savior, Mr. Bishop?"

Ty grinned as he took Cassie's hand in his. "Yes, sir. I surely did."

When he kissed her fingers, Cassie's insides did a little flip flop. The man had her under his spell, and she wanted nothing more than to make their excuses and head to the inn they planned to stay at tonight.

A knock on the door was followed by the butler wheeling in a tea cart. Little was said as James poured tea into china cups and handed them to Cassie and Ty.

"Anything else, sir?" the butler asked.

Simon waved him off. "I'm fine. Thank you, James. You may go."

James plucked a paper from his pocket. "A telegram was delivered for you, sir."

Taking the message, Simon read it as a deep frown settled on his mouth.

"What's wrong?" Cassie asked, worried at his dark expression.

He let out a heavy sigh before holding the telegram out to her. "I'm afraid, Cassandra, that your grandfather has died."

"What?" She bolted out of her chair and snatched the paper from his hand. She was too agitated to even read it. "Grandfather is dead?"

His answer was a curt nod.

While she should be mourning her grandfather's passing, she could only fret over the implications. She looked to her husband, clenching his hand as her own trembled. "This will make things worse. *Much* worse."

"Why?" Ty asked. "Now they'll leave you be. Derrick's got his money."

She shook her head. "Grandfather always told me he would provide well for me in his will. Uncle Derrick will want me back so Robert can claim anything Grandfather left me."

"I fear there is worse news," Simon said. "Read the message, Cassandra."

"Worse?" Ty asked. He set his hands on her shoulders as she read the telegram.

Then the words registered. "No. No, this cannot be."

Simon gave her a brusque nod. "Derrick has been appointed your guardian."

Chapter Twenty-Six

"Calm down, Cassandra."

Her Uncle Simon had repeated that phrase more times than Cassie could count. She simply couldn't stop pacing the length of his study and back again, thinking about the horror facing her should she not pull free of the Shay's reach.

Simon was right, of course. She truly needed to get her fears under control. But calming down just wasn't possible—not when it seemed as though there would never be a way to be free of her Uncle Derrick and Robert Putnam.

Ty's hand grasped hers. "Cassie girl... Ain't nothing they can do to you. Not anymore. I'm your husband now. Derrick can't be your guardian." His gaze went to Simon. "Right? Ain't that what you said? She's a married woman, and that trumps Derrick's claim."

Simon nodded. Then he addressed Cassie. "Did you two happen to bring along your marriage certificate? That would be helpful when we draw up the paperwork, and it could sway the judge we'll speak to in San Francisco. I still believe you are doing yourself a disservice by renouncing all the money that was put aside for you and your husband. You're a Shay. You should share in the Shay fortune."

She snorted. "The only reason there is money for me is because my grandfather meant for Robert to control it. Were there no fortune, I would not be in this pickle. Robert would have no use for me, and Uncle Derrick would have no care for what I chose to do with my life." She shook her head. "No, I'm sure about this. I don't want any money, Uncle Simon. How many times must I repeat myself?"

His chuckle was warm. "It would appear *that* was the last time. I'm merely serving as your legal advisor and cautioning you against forfeiting such a large sum. You have let me know how adamant you are to pursue this course, therefore I shall help you steer the choppy waters of negotiating with our family. Should Mr. Curtis wish to pursue a similar tactic, I would be pleased to help him as well. The two of you should share the money your father left in your grandfather's care."

She opened her mouth to launch another protest, but Simon raised his hand.

"But I understand why you've made this choice. Seeing as your brother was all but murdered when he reached out to his new family, I would not be surprised if he made the same choice."

"Thank you, Uncle."

The only guilt Cassie felt about turning down the money was that Ty could have enjoyed a life of leisure if they had those funds at their fingertips. His life would change for the better. There would be no more hard work trying to hack a living out in the wilderness.

Now she was being fanciful. White Pines wasn't truly "wilderness" any longer. Ty might work hard, but that was only one of the many traits that made her fall in love with him. While he would never change from the dependable man he was simply if given money, there was no doubt that should she be given her inheritance, he wouldn't ever touch a penny of it.

If turning down the fortune freed her from the clutches of her family, good riddance.

A yawn slipped out, and weariness settled on her. They'd traveled hard after the wedding, trying to get to Sacramento before any news of her true marriage reached San Francisco. Now that she'd learned of her grandfather's passing, she held out hope her Uncle Derrick was too occupied dealing with things needing his immediate attention to worry about her whereabouts.

Ty squeezed her hand. "Are you tired, Cassie girl?"

"Very." Another yawn made her whole body shake. "Pray forgive my rudeness. We should be traveling to our inn soon, Ty, or I fear I will not be able to stay awake for the trip."

"Nonsense," Simon said, rising from his desk. "You have no need to leave. I insist you be my guests for the time you're in our fair town."

"Don't wanna put you out," Ty said, giving her a worried look.

Cassie understood his trepidation. She, too, worried if they should stay in a place where she could be so easily found. "That is a generous offer, Uncle Simon, but—"

"No buts," Simon insisted. He went to the door and opened it. "James!"

A few moments later, the butler stepped into the study. "Sir?"

"Have some bedrooms prepared for—"

"*Bedroom*," Ty insisted. "My wife sleeps with me."

Simon laughed as he nodded. "Of course, my boy. I merely forgot. Forgive an old man who will always view Cassandra as a young girl. She is, indeed, your wife, and you should share a bed." He held up his index finger to his butler. "*One* bedroom, James."

"Sir," James replied with an easy smile, "I have already taken the liberty to prepare the large suite in the west wing. I had assumed you'd wish to keep your visitors close." His words were weighted with meaning—something more than the humor he obviously found in the situation.

"Uncle Simon?" She cocked her head. "What are you not telling me?"

Patting her shoulder, he sighed. "I should have remembered how perceptive you are, my dear. I had hoped you wouldn't notice, but there are a number of men watching my home. I believe they're here to return you to your Uncle Derrick."

Ty swept his jacket aside and put his hand on his gun. "The hell they will."

"Easy, my boy," Simon cautioned. "So long as you both remain here, you are under my protection. My own men are guarding every entrance and will not let anyone inside without my direct instructions to allow it."

Cassie's fatigue had vanished, replaced by the rapid pounding of her heart. Just as she feared, her Uncle Derrick had found her and had every intention of forcing her into a marriage with Robert.

She might be married to Ty now, but Shay money had a way of making things change—even something as difficult as a lawful wedding. If her family couldn't buy an annulment, they would have no reservations about making her a widow.

A shiver raced through her.

Ty wrapped his arm around her shoulder. "You cold, sweetheart?"

"Yes," she fibbed, not wishing to tell him what really upset her. "And tired."

"We're safe here."

"I know." She offered her uncle a hesitant smile. "Thank you for protecting us."

Simon's lips drew into a thin line. "You are safe here, Cassandra. But the danger will not be over until we are able to present the forfeiture papers to Derrick and have the judge set aside your guardianship."

She nodded.

"That's why I shall accompany you to San Francisco. Both of us should pay our respects to your grandfather, and the judge and I go back to law school. He's a fair man and will help us."

The last thing in the world she wanted to do was go back into the Shay estate. Her uncle was right—she *should* be there out of respect to her grandfather. Yet she didn't want those evil men to have another shot at harming Ty. She'd never forgotten their first meeting in that cave and how frightened she'd been for the two men bound and left to die when the tide came in.

She'd fallen in love with Ty from that very first moment as she'd watched how he'd faced his own death with humor and aplomb. How could she not love him?

Just as she'd protected him that day, Cassie would protect him now. Even if it meant going back to hell alone.

Yes! That was the answer. Ty would stay in Sacramento!

Now she just needed to convince him that was the best solution.

"If you'll follow me..." James swept his arm toward the hallway.

Holding her husband's hand, she followed the butler up the ornate staircase, turning left down a long hallway. The door James opened was the last on the left.

He led them into a suite decorated in pleasant blues. At the center of the room was a large four-poster bed on a dais. The velvet curtains had been pulled back and tied, and the covers were turned down to reveal fresh, white sheets.

Even though she would be sharing that bed with her husband, she couldn't stop a hot flush from spreading over her face.

James's friendly smile put her mind at ease. "The bathroom is to the right. I trust you'll be comfortable. Should you need anything..." he brushed his hand over a rope next to the door, "...pull this and it will alert me to return." Hand on the doorknob, he bowed. "Sleep well. I will bring up a breakfast tray at seven." He shut the door behind him.

Before Cassie could even say a word, she found herself swept into Ty's arms. He strode to the bed, tossed her on the mattress, and then blanketed her with his body. "God, I've been wantin' you all day."

His mouth found hers, his tongue thrusting inside. There was desperation in his kiss, the same fear she'd felt when her Uncle Simon had told her of Derrick's despicable move in making himself her guardian.

Guardian, indeed.

Before anger could take hold of her again, Cassie gave herself over to the passion Ty sent racing through her. She put her arms around his neck and held him close, letting him take her away from the worries of the world.

His tongue stroked her mouth, his hot breath mingling with hers as each struggled to breathe without ending the incredible kiss. She chased his retreating tongue into his mouth, where his teeth grasped her tongue and gave it a gentle tug.

"Make me yours," she whispered, not surprised to hear the huskiness in her own voice. Desire swept through her, making her breasts tingle and her core tighten. "Please, Ty. Make love to me."

"To my *wife*," Ty replied. He pushed back and pulled off his jacket, tossing it off the bed. Instead of unbuttoning his shirt, he merely jerked it open, sending buttons flying. His boots hit the floor before he tugged at his pants.

She was every bit as eager, trying to pull off her own clothes while also helping him remove his. All she wanted was to be skin-to-skin with Ty, to not only consummate their marriage, but to once again show him how much she loved him.

His cock sprang forward as he removed his pants. Instead of taking off the rest of her garments, she was more interested in touching him. She wrapped her fingers around his hot shaft and stroked, loving how he growled deep in his chest.

"I want to see all of you." He brushed her hand away and pulled her to her feet.

Kneeling in front of her, he eased her petticoats down her hips. His gaze held hers as he untied her pantalets and pulled them down. She stood before him, naked and unashamed. He was also bare, showing her every inch of his incredible physique.

Hands on her hips he moved her forward, nudging her thighs apart and pressing his mouth to her core.

Cassie dug her fingers into his hair, trying to keep her knees from buckling under his tender onslaught. Her head fell back in surrender.

Ty's hands smoothed over her buttocks and around her thighs. Then he lifted her, dropping her back to the mattress. As she writhed beneath him, he tortured her—his tongue teasing her sensitive nub as he drove a finger deep inside her again and again, mimicking the act she so desperately wanted.

"Ty...*now*. Please!"

He gave her no quarter, driving her higher and higher until she shattered, bucking beneath him as he smothered her cries by covering her mouth with his as he again stretched out on top of her.

Before she could even come back down to earth, Ty nudged her thighs farther apart, rubbing his cock between her folds.

His hands framed her face, forcing her to look into his eyes. "You're mine, Cassie. Forever."

She nodded.

"Say the word. Forever."

"I've always been yours, Ty. Forever."

He thrust inside her and was buried to the hilt. The fullness in her body had never felt so right. She wanted to give him the same pleasure he'd given her. Wrapping her legs around his hips, she pulled him deeper inside.

With a groan, Ty withdrew and then pressed back into her. With each stroke of his body, the word "mine" slipped from his lips, making her heart swell with love.

Ty couldn't understand the strength of the feelings flowing through him.

Making love to his new wife had changed their connection, strengthening it with the commitment they'd made as they'd exchanged vows to stay with each other through thick and thin.

She was truly his. A miracle, that.

Her sheath was so tight, so incredibly hot. And Cassie held nothing back, turning into a wildcat in his arms, raking her nails across his back as her hips rose to meet each of his thrusts.

He tried to hold back his climax, wanting this moment—where it felt as though their hearts beat as one—to last forever. But she was so giving, so free with herself he could do nothing but give her equal measure.

"Ty!" His name slipped from her lips in a breathless cry as her body clenched around his cock, pulling him along with her as she came.

With a shout, he poured his seed into her for what seemed like forever. He buried his face against her neck, drawing each new breath in a big gulp. Her scent, now mingled with his, pleased him.

"I love you, Cassie girl," Ty whispered before kissing her neck.

"Sweet Lord Almighty. That was...so...so..." She squeezed her legs tighter. "I love you too, Ty."

Although he didn't want to leave her, he figured he had to be crushing her. Rolling to his side, he dragged her up against him, needing to hold her close.

"We'll be leaving in the morning." She tucked her head under his chin and threw her slender thigh across his. "I would ask you to stay here and wait for Uncle Simon and me to return."

Ty strained his neck to glare down at her. "Have you lost your mind?"

She let out a heavy sigh. "I *want* you to stay, but I know you'll have none of that. Promise me you'll take every precaution and won't take any chances."

While he should've been insulted that his wife didn't think he could take care of himself, Ty was touched by her concern. No one had ever worried about him the way Cassie did. It was downright flattering. "You'll be in danger too," he reminded her.

"Yes, but... I cannot lose you, husband."

"Husband?" He smiled. "I like the sound of that, *wife.*"

"You'll take every care?"

"I'll keep you safe, Cassie girl."

"Keep yourself safe too, Ty."

Chapter Twenty-Seven

Cassie held tight to Ty's hand, trying to draw courage from their connection. Uncle Simon stood to her left. He must have sensed her unease because he took her free hand in his and gave it a squeeze.

Everyone was staring at them. The church had fallen as silent as a graveyard when they stepped through the double doors leading to the sanctuary. The crowd was smaller than she expected considering her grandfather's wealth and influence.

All of the Shays were there. Dressed in black and gaping at her, her family was an intimidating bunch. Cassie avoided eye contact with any of them, keeping her gaze settled on the polished coffin resting below the marble altar.

A low snarl gained her attention. Robert Putnam stood next to Uncle Derrick. The two were talking in whispers, but judging from Robert's red face, he was angry.

She didn't give a damn. Once this ordeal ended, she'd never have to see him again.

After what seemed like an eternity, Cassie swallowed hard, pulled her hands free, and strode down the long aisle. Head held high, she strode past the pews, trying to ignore the whispering in her wake. Simon and Ty fell in step behind her but stayed close enough to make her feel protected.

Derrick stepped in front of her before she could reach her grandfather's coffin. "Well, well. You've finally returned."

She knew that look. He wanted to slap her.

She refused to be intimidated. "I have only returned to say goodbye to my grandfather."

His hand gripped her upper arm. "You must come with me. *Now, Cassandra.*"

She jerked her arm away and held it out to stop Ty from going after her uncle. "I have come to pay respects, then I shall return to my *home.*"

Robert took up his normal place—at Derrick's side. The anger was etched clearly on his face, and he, too, probably itched to give her a few hard hits. "So you've finally come to your senses." As if just noticing that his voice was echoing through the cavernous church, he dropped his voice considerably. "You'll pay dearly for the humiliation I've suffered. When we're married—"

Cassie cut him off with a slash of her wrist. "You misunderstand. I will return to Montana. That is my home now." She let Ty take the last step forward so he was by her side. "This is Ty Bishop—my *husband.* From this day forward, neither of you will have a say over my life."

Face flushing darker red, Robert sputtered in anger. "You will marry *me.*"

"No, Robert. I won't. I'm a married woman now."

"You think we didn't know what you've done?" His rueful chuckle didn't come as a surprise. "This...this...*debacle* will be annulled." He inclined his head at Derrick. "We've already begun the petition."

They knew about her marriage. Hardly a surprise, but now she knew which plan to use. She, Simon, and Ty had rehearsed exactly how today would unfold depending on what Derrick and Robert knew about her and Ty.

She launched the first volley. "This is a legal marriage between two adults.

You have no standing to challenge it."

"I'm your guardian!" Derrick insisted.

"A twenty-year old woman don't need no guardian," Ty replied. "Especially one the likes of you."

Cassie slipped her arm around Ty's waist. She could feel him tremble in anger, but he held himself in check. She glanced over her shoulder and gave Uncle Simon a curt nod.

He entered the fray. "Cassandra's marriage is quite legal. Of that, I assure you." He handed the form his judge friend had signed on the couple's behalf the night before. "Quite legal, and quite permanent."

After Derrick read it, he handed it to Robert.

Robert read it and ripped it in two before dropping it to the floor.

Simon let out a chuckle. "You think I wasn't intelligent enough to have more than one copy?"

Taking a threatening step forward, Robert clenched his hands into fists. "Then I'll make her a widow."

Derrick set his hand on Robert's shoulder as he leveled a haughty smile at his brother. "Why, Simon... How odd that you would suddenly take an interest in Shay family affairs after shunning us for so long."

"Where Cassandra is concerned, I will deign to deal with you, reprehensible though it is."

If the barb struck home, Derrick didn't show it. "Cassie might be of legal age, but she is a bit...flighty. I could easily convince one of many other more powerful judges that her mental competency is in question. Trust me, this sham of a marriage will be easily set aside." A hard stare at Ty. "I assure you, sir, that you might have escaped me once. But even a cat eventually runs out of lives. If you're wise, you'll go right back to your backwater little town and leave Cassie to her family."

Ty snorted. "*I'm* her family."

The reverend loudly cleared his throat. "If we may begin..." He marched up the stairs to the altar.

Battle lines drawn, Cassie let Ty escort her to a pew. Once the service was over, she would have Simon present her surrender papers to Derrick. Once he knew she didn't want a penny of the Shay money, the war would finally end.

***

Ty had sworn he would never set foot in the mansion again. He'd never thought he'd go back on that oath. Only one thing made him enter the devil's den.

Cassie.

My wife.

For her, he'd go—even if the last time he'd been there, that bastard Derrick had tried to murder him.

Just as soon as the service had ended, Derrick had been confronted with his father's lawyer. Despite Derrick's objections, the man demanded the will be read immediately since every beneficiary was in attendance—an event that wasn't likely to happen again without great effort.

Now, Ty escorted Cassie to her grandfather's study with Simon close on their heels. He'd convinced them to wait and see what happened with the old man's will before Cassie made her move. While Ty wasn't happy with the plan—wanting to get the hell away from there as quickly as possible—he understood Simon's logic. If the senator had cut her out of the will, the papers they'd drawn up last night wouldn't be needed.

Without her money, Robert would no longer be a problem.

When they reached the large doors, the lawyer had the attendees enter single-file, checking off each name on his list. Cassie hesitated after he checked off her name, her face turned to Ty's.

"This is my husband, Ty Bishop. He should be at my side," she insisted before the lawyer could ask his name.

"Your husband?" he asked in an incredulous tone.

"Yes, sir. My husband."

"Then he is *required* to attend."

"Required?"

"Of course." He looked at Simon. "And you sir?"

Cassie answered for him. "He is my legal counsel."

All the man did was give her a terse nod before returning to his list.

The room reeked of stale tobacco and was every bit as dark and intimidating as Senator Shay had been. Servants were arranging chairs of all shapes and sizes in a large semi-circle around the oak desk as fast as they could to accommodate the people there to hear the man's last wishes.

Once that distasteful task was done, Cassie could present the papers that forever released her from these vultures.

Damn, but Ty was proud of her. How many women would walk away from that kind of fortune? But she hadn't even hesitated. Hell, the woman had *demanded* that she no longer be considered a Shay.

When he'd sat her down and told her the truth—that all he'd probably ever be able to give her was a home with very few luxuries—she'd kissed him gently and told him that he was all she'd ever need.

Why God had blessed him with the love of a woman with such a pure heart was beyond his understanding. He simply sent an awkward prayer to his Maker and accepted the gift he neither deserved nor would ever give up.

The lawyer finally took a seat at the senator's desk and opened his leather case. From it he pulled two papers, then he cleared his throat. "I am here to let it be known that these are the last wishes of Hiram Shay. This last will and testament was written by his own hand and duly notarized." He cleared his throat again and started reading.

Ty had little interest in what the lawyer was saying. He wanted nothing more than for Simon to shove Cassie's papers at her family and drag her all the way back to Montana. He did, however, enjoy some of the grimaces, groans, and growls coming from each of her relatives as the late senator got in some last licks in the form of insults and ridiculously small sums of money.

Cassie had chosen to sit on the arm of Ty's chair, and she kept a tight grip on his hand. Every now and then her gaze would drift back to where Derrick and Robert sat, which usually made her tremble.

Trying to will some of his strength to his wife, Ty kissed the back of her knuckles.

She gifted him with a smile and stopped shaking.

The lawyer shifted to the second paper, giving Ty hope that the ordeal would be over soon.

"Because I still mourn the death of my beloved Stephen," the lawyer read, "I feel honor bound to give special mention to his two children."

A gasp slipped from Cassie.

"What?" Ty whispered.

"I am his only child, except... He can't think to name—"

"To Jake Curtis," the lawyer said, increasing his volume as everyone in the crowd began to whisper to one another, "I leave the sum of one dollar. I choose that sum for him and instruct him to use it to reimburse his mother for her sexual services to my son. The whore..." he tugged on his collar as though it suddenly became too tight, "...murdered my son. I will not allow hers to inherit a single penny of my fortune."

Then he directed his dark eyes to Cassie. "Now, I have special instructions for my beloved Stephen's only legitimate child—his daughter, Cassandra. Her fortuitous marriage has been finally been arranged, and I want to provide well for her new family. Once her marriage is blessed and consummated, I bequeath to her husband the sum of five-hundred thousand dollars."

The room fell deathly quiet for a few long moments before all hell broke loose.

"*What?*" Robert was on his feet as he hurried to the desk.

Derrick was stammering and couldn't seem to get a coherent word out.

The rest of the Shays alternated been shouting and shaking their heads—with the exception of Simon.

He was grinning as he set his hand on Cassie's shoulder after she jumped to her feet. "'Twould seem your grandfather has finally made a mistake, and it was of epic proportions. He was a bit...negligent in his specificities."

She looked up at him, wide-eyed as Ty stood and wrapped an arm around her waist. He had no idea why everyone was reacting as though everything had changed. It was clear the senator had meant that money for Robert since he was the one who would've married Cassie.

Why was everyone so damned upset?

"What do you mean, Uncle?" she asked. "What specificities?"

His grin grew. "What I mean, my darling Cassandra, is that your Mr. Bishop just inherited half a million dollars."

Chapter Twenty-Eight

"Have you lost your mind?" Ty couldn't accept what he was hearing. "That ain't my money."

"It is now," Simon insisted.

Cassie's kept shifting her gaze between the two men, looking far too dumbfounded to say a word.

Voices, most of them angrily raised, filled the room. Ty instinctively pushed Cassie behind his back when someone smashed a vase against the wall.

Francis Middleton stood and motioned for everyone to sit. "Please! Please! We must finish the reading of the will!"

No one paid him any heed as they either argued with one another or simply left the room.

Robert and Derrick shoved their way toward them.

Cassie tried to step around him, but Ty kept her sheltered with his own body. They'd have to go through him to get to her. He swept aside his coat and set his hand on his Colt, giving them fair warning.

Both men stopped, glaring at him with red faces and clenched hands. Neither had a weapon, which gave Ty the advantage. For now. He was still on their land—something he would remedy just as soon as possible. Unfortunately, Hiram Shay's will had now complicated things something fierce.

"That's my money!" Robert's bellow made the rest of the crowd fall silent.

While Ty didn't give a shit about the money, he couldn't help but rub salt in Robert's open wound. "Can't help but notice that you're a mite more concerned about that cash than about Cassie not being your bride no more."

"I want my money!" Robert demanded.

"It ain't your money now. It's mine—just like Cassie's mine."

That statement set the crowd to shouting again.

Ty could care less about them. His focus was on the enraged man he suddenly feared he'd have to kill to keep his wife safe. Unlike Robert, however, he wasn't a murderer. He'd simply have to stay on his guard. Robert would surely come for them, then Ty could settle accounts once and for all.

"Please!" Francis was still on his feet. "If everyone will take their seats we can—"

"*Mine!*" Robert wagged his finger. "Understand, you half-wit?"

"I don't want your damned money," Ty snapped. "And if you touch me again, you'll pay for it."

Cassie tugged on his coat. "Ty...please be careful."

Derrick found his voice. "If you think I'll let you get away with this travesty—"

"The boy has done nothing to bring this about," Simon said. "This was your father's doing."

"That money was meant for Robert," Derrick insisted. "He should be Cassie's husband."

"Well, then..." Simon cuffed Ty on the shoulder. "It would appear that Robert was bested in the quest for Cassandra's hand *and* her money."

"The money is mine!" Robert took a step forward. The man was practically foaming at the mouth.

A gunshot followed by breaking glass made Ty pull his gun. He quickly realized the shot came from Francis, who now held a smoking Derringer after shooting out the window.

Despite the chaos, Ty's lips formed a smile at the lawyer's pluck.

"Now that I finally have your attention," Francis said, "I would ask everyone except Cassandra Shay and her husband to leave this study."

People whispered, but few moved.

Francis pointed his gun at Robert. "I shall not ask again."

The room cleared as fast as a saloon after the whiskey ran out.

Just as Simon was leaving, Cassie put her hand on his arm. "I would like my uncle to stay."

"I act as her legal counsel," Simon added.

The lawyer gave her a curt nod.

Ty still held his Colt, although he was more at ease now that Robert was gone. Not that the man would simply let them be. So long as Robert still drew breath, he'd be a danger to Cassie.

Francis sat back down and once again cleared his throat. "It would seem we have a dilemma."

"That's an understatement," Ty quipped. He held a chair for Cassie and moved one closer to hers as Simon sat on her other side.

There was no doubt what Shay's lawyer would say. Now they'd all hear exactly why that money would be going to Robert Putnam.

So be it.

The Shay money never bought anything but misery for far too many people Ty loved. He didn't want a penny of it.

Cassie thoughts whirled. She still couldn't believe her grandfather had been so foolhardy. The man had controlling down to an art form.

"I still don't understand," she said. "Why would grandfather leave the money to my 'husband' rather than name the man? He was always so...*precise* in all his dealings."

A knowing grin spread over Francis's face. "I put that same question to your grandfather when I helped him draw up this will. He informed me that Robert Putnam was his choice for a husband, but he believed the man to be a bit too arrogant for his taste. The gesture was meant to remind him that *you*, my dear, were the Shay, and that the only reason Robert would have any of the Shay fortune was because he'd married you."

Simon jumped in. "That being said, the money is now legally Ty's, correct? The will never named her husband, so the money belongs to her legal husband—Ty Bishop?"

"Exactly." Francis grinned.

Gathering her brows, Cassie had questions of her own if she was ever going to make sense of this turn of events. "Do you know why he had you draw up his will? I mean no offense, sir, but both Uncle Derrick and Robert are attorneys. Grandfather had several others on his staff. Why didn't he have any of them see to the task?"

His grin grew. "The senator told me it was never wise to keep all your eggs in one basket. While he and I had little affection for one another, having faced each other in court on many occasions, he claimed I was an honest man and would see his wishes through regardless of any pressure brought to bear by his family. I must say, this has been a rather entertaining venture thanks to your impulsiveness, young lady." He gaze became serious. "I must know for a fact that your marriage to Mr. Bishop is legal and consummated as your grandfather requested."

Her face flushed hot, but she refused to be embarrassed. "Yes, sir."

"Yes, it is legal? Or yes, it was consummated?"

"Both, sir."

Simon chuckled. "I have a copy of their marriage certificate, and after they were guests in my home last night, I can assure you, their marriage bed is quite *lively*. Even my servants commented on the ruckus they made."

Cassie gasped her outrage. "Uncle Simon! Jesus, Mary, and Joseph, how could you say something so–so–personal?"

Ty put his hand over hers where it lay on the armrest. "The old man underestimated you, Cassie girl."

Though grateful for the turn of topic, she quirked an eyebrow. "I fail to see how putting Robert in his place could be seen as him underestimating me."

His smile made her stomach flutter. "He never thought you'd defy him. But you did. You ran away, and thank God for that."

Her eyes stung with tears. "I do."

"Do what?"

"Thank God. Every day, I thank Him for sending you to me to save me from the hell my family had planned for me."

Ty caressed her cheek with the back of his hand. "*You* are the blessing."

"Now we must make arrangements," Francis said. "The money must be placed in your name, Mr. Bishop and—"

"Don't want it," Ty said with a shake of his head.

"I beg your pardon?"

"Don't want any of it."

Cassie blinked at her new husband, wondering what was flying through his mind. "You would walk away from that much money?"

"In a heartbeat."

"Why?"

He took her hand back in his. "I don't want anyone coming after you again. So long as you have that money, you're nothin' but a target."

"Think of how your life would be," she cautioned. Perhaps she needed to enlighten him as to the ease of living that came with a fortune that size. He needed to understand before he made any decisions. "You could be a man of leisure. You could have things you've never thought possible. You could—"

He was shaking her head before she could even finish. "I like my life, Cassie. I ain't got need for money. I got me a home I love. I got the mountain air. And I got you. Don't need nothin' else."

The tears were back, blurring her vision. "Oh, Ty..." She leaned over and kissed his cheek. "I love you so."

Francis looked dumbfounded. "You truly don't want the money?"

"Nope. Not a penny," Ty replied.

"Then the money passes to Cassandra."

Since Ty had shown the courage to leave the trappings of luxury behind, Cassie followed suit. "I don't want it, either."

"You cannot be serious," Francis protested.

"I assure you, sir, I am quite serious. If my husband believes the money will only cause us more trouble, then we are better served to leave it behind."

"Then it will be returned to your grandfather's estate and—"

"If you'll pardon my interrupting," Simon said. "I might have a solution to this little problem."

Cassie wasn't at all pleased with her Uncle Derrick getting his hands back on the money, which would surely happen should it be returned to her grandfather's estate. He'd most likely put right into Robert's greedy hands, so she was more than willing to hear Simon's suggestion.

"By all means, tell us," she said.

"Perhaps the bequeath could be placed in a trust for any children that come from your marriage."

"A trust?" Ty asked. "What's that?"

"The money will be held for your children. Should they decide later they would like to pursue their educations or perhaps travel, they would have access to those funds."

"Would you be willing to manage the trust?" Cassie asked.

"Of course, Cassandra."

"A good choice," Francis said. "Everyone who knows Simon realizes he has a knack for investments. Why, I'd wager by the time your children are grown, the profit will eclipse the original funds."

"Ty?" She couldn't tell what he was thinking. While she thought Simon had an excellent idea, she wasn't about to speak for her husband. Although she'd never be an obedient wife, she wanted this marriage to begin with sharing this enormous decision. "What do you think?"

His face, as usual, revealed nothing. "I don't know about this kind of stuff, Cassie."

She leaned closer. "The money would remain in Uncle Simon's care. He would invest it wisely to keep it growing. When our children are older, they can use the funds to go to college or visit Europe."

Still, he hesitated.

"Think about your own childhood, Ty. This money would insure that even if something happened to us, our children would be provided for."

Judging from the pain that entered his eyes, the memories were unpleasant.

Cassie couldn't change his past. But she was damned well going to make sure he had a wonderful future. "It's the best choice. Not only will we know our children's future is safe, but that money will never be in Robert's hands."

"Then that's what we'll do."

***

Ty led the way out of the study, keeping his hand on his Colt. Just in case.

Instead of Derrick and Robert being there to confront them, the hall was empty. Simon led them through the corridors to the front door of the Shay mansion. With the exception of a few servants, the rest of the Shays had disappeared, most likely licking their wounds after the senator's rather insulting will.

No one spoke until they were inside Simon's carriage heading back to his home. Simon sat on one side, stretching his long legs out until Cassie had to move her skirts to give him more room. Ty wrapped his arm around his wife's shoulder to pull her a little closer, which gave Simon even more room.

"Well, well." Simon grinned as he set his leather case aside. "This was truly a day of surprises." He leaned forward to glance out the window one last time. "The biggest of which is how we were able to escape without Robert and Derrick having another explosion."

"Where do you think they went?" Cassie asked. "Do you think they've accepted the loss—"

The loud guffaw from Simon stopped her cold. It took him a moment to get himself under control. "I'm sorry, my dear. I couldn't help myself. The mere notion of Derrick ever walking away from money simply set me to..." He started laughing again.

All Simon's amusement did was affirm what Ty already believed.

This was far from over.

Chapter Twenty-Nine

Ty's nerves were stretched tighter than barbed wire fencing. Even lying in bed with his wife sleeping contentedly at his side, he found his thoughts churning into a whirlwind.

In the month since he and Cassie had returned to White Pines, he'd spent almost every waking hour on alert, sure that Robert would be coming to get his revenge. Only exhaustion had allowed him to sleep at night, but even then, he felt as though he slept with one eye open.

Thankfully, Simon had decided to stay in San Francisco to keep an eye on Cassie's family. He sent a telegraph message daily to keep Ty apprised of the turmoil in the Shay household. Unfortunately, his last message had been several days ago, and Ty worried something had happened that Simon was afraid to tell him.

Not that Cassie even noticed, nor would he tell her about the messages. His wife had been so busy preparing for the coming performance of *Romeo and Juliet*, she hadn't had time for worry. At least when she was in the Four Aces with Drew and the rest of the cast and crew, she was safe. Ty used the time where she was busy to continue working on their new home.

Winter had slowed his progress significantly. With the help of Adam, Matthew, and Jake, the frame was complete. Then the snows came. No true blizzard. Yet. But the bone-chilling cold made construction crawl.

He'd resigned himself to staying in the cabin on Gideon's property until spring—maybe even summer—but at least the newlyweds had privacy since Drew had finally given up his pretext of living with Cassie and moved to Gideon's farmhouse. Ty let them both know how grateful he was to be able to be alone with his new wife.

With a sleepy sigh, she snuggled up against his side. He pulled her tight against him, wondering if she'd wake up soon. He had chores to work on. The sun was already rising, but he was content to hold Cassie close and let her have a few more minutes of sleep.

Of course if she opened her eyes soon, he might be able to make love to her before he had to brave the cold. That thought brought a smile.

"You're up," she murmured against his neck. Then she brushed her lips over his sensitive skin, sending heat rushing straight to his groin.

"I'm *up* all right." Beneath the covers, Ty led her hand to his hardening cock.

"Oh my..." She rubbed him through his longjohns before her hand slipped between the buttons. Her fingers circled his shaft before she slid her hand from root to tip and back.

Letting out a rumbling growl, he decided chores could wait a little while longer.

Cassie let go, ducked under the covers, and started working on the buttons, opening them from the neck down and pressing kisses against each new patch of skin she revealed. She only stopped long enough for him to yank her flannel nightgown over her head.

Her lips smoothed over his chest, down his stomach, and to his navel.

Ty tensed when she freed his erection.

She combed her fingers through the hair around his cock as she continued to stroke him. About the time he was convinced she wouldn't follow through, her lips touched the crown.

A hiss slipped through his clenched teeth.

"You like that, husband?" Her voice was muffled by the quilts, but he understood her words.

"God, yes, I like that."

"Well then...how about *this?*"

He barely had the self-control to keep himself from coming when the wet heat of her mouth completely surrounded his head. Beneath the covers, he tangled his fingers in her hair.

His response seemed to fuel her own. She was awkward but thorough, and she pleased him more than he'd ever be able to tell her.

Knowing he was about to come, he slipped his hands under her arms and dragged her up his body. She straddled his hips, obviously knowing what he wanted. Once she guided him to her entrance, he drove deep inside her. Each time he entered her, he felt as though he'd come home—to the place he belonged.

Cassie arched her back, moving her hips in a teasing rhythm that he put a stop to by holding tight to her waist and thrusting into her again and again, needing the release that only she could give him. When her body squeezed him tight, signaling her climax, Ty sped his movements. He poured his seed into her as she whispered his name in a husky voice full of wonder.

Collapsing against his chest, Cassie hummed. He smiled, knowing he'd pleased her.

"This gets any better, and you're gonna lay me in an early grave," Ty said.

"I shall take that as a compliment."

He swatted her bare backside. "The day's wasting away. I gotta get you to town. You've got a play tonight. Remember?"

"As if I could forget." She brushed her lips against his neck. "But I thank you for the pleasant diversion."

***

Cassie stood in the wings of the stage, staring at the tables and chairs that were rapidly filling with people.

She was ready. Drew said so. She shouldn't be worried about anything.

But she *was* worried, and her stomach felt as though she'd swallowed a jar of the fireflies she used to capture as a child. If she stayed this nervous, she'd surely be ill before the performance.

Comforting hands settled on her shoulders and gave her an affectionate squeeze. "Having jitters?" Drew asked.

She nodded. "Ty's not here yet."

"Ah...I would venture to guess that when he arrives, you'll relax and enjoy yourself."

"Relax?" A snort slipped out. "Never. But I would take courage from his presence."

"You really love the cowboy, don't you, Cass?"

Cassie turned and smiled. "With all my heart."

Leaning in, he kissed her forehead. "My fair Juliet has lost her heart. I will admit to having some misgivings about Mr. Bishop. Now that I know the man behind the gruff exterior, I believe you will be happy."

"*Very* happy."

Drew's gaze was fixed over her head—out to the audience. "Then take heart, dear Juliette, for your Romeo is here."

Her velvet skirt clung to her legs, almost tripping her, as she whirled around to see for herself.

Ty was hanging his coat on a chair at the table to the far right of the stage, a place she'd reserved for him and his family. Thankfully, all of them were there as well. Adam. Grace. Jake. Emily. Even, to Cassie's surprise, Victoria and Matthew. There was another man at the table, but his back was to her, and his heavy coat and hat blocked his—

Recognition came swiftly. "Uncle Simon!"

She hadn't meant to shout. The raucous audience actually quieted as they turned to stare at the side of the stage where she hid.

Cassie didn't care if they saw her of not. She stepped from behind the curtain and waved.

Her uncle gifted her with an enormous smile and waved back.

"Cass." Dragging her back into the shadows, Drew clucked his tongue. "You're in costume. You may greet your uncle *after* the performance."

"Of course." How odd that her nerves had settled considerably just knowing everyone—especially Ty—was there to support her.

Ty couldn't stop staring at the place his wife had stood. He'd heard her recite her lines time and time again. The story was touching, though he doubted he'd ever admit that to anyone. No, what drew his attention was how beautiful his wife looked in her costume.

Her dress was a dark red velvet, and her long, brown hair had been arranged so she could wear a delicate lace cap. She seemed so young, so like the Juliet from the story. And he felt so unworthy of her.

Simon clapped him on the shoulder. "I can see you are still lovesick over my niece."

Ty shrugged.

"I've never seen him like this," Matthew added. "Follows her around like an unweaned puppy trails his ma."

While everyone at the table chuckled, Ty fought the need to growl at all of them.

On the other hand, their teasing meant they'd finally accepted Cassie as his wife. If they wanted to give him guff because he'd lost his heart to her, so be it.

Leaning closer, Simon said, "We must talk after the play. There are...changes you should know."

"Changes?"

Simon nodded as his smile faded.

The news clearly wasn't good. "Tell me now."

"Derrick Shay is dead. He was murdered in his home."

"Bein' as he kept company with nothing but rats, he was bound to get bit."

"It gets worse... Robert Putnam is believed to have been the murderer, and the authorities have been unable to apprehend him."

"Apprehend?"

"It means catch," Matthew interjected. He leveled a hard stare at Ty. "He'll come here, won't he?"

Simon was the one to answer. "That is my fear. When Derrick's body was discovered, the servants insisted that Robert was the culprit. He and Derrick had quarreled, and Derrick had given him the cut direct, ordering Robert to leave the mansion and never return. The quarrel was about Cassie. Robert insisted if he could bring her back, he could still have the trust money. Derrick told him that money was lost forever."

"He'll come," Ty said. "Since he can't get that money back, he'll want to punish Cassie."

Their conversation was interrupted as Will Spencer stepped to the middle of the stage, motioning for the rather rowdy crowd to calm down. "Thank you for comin' out to the Four Aces' very first honest-to-God play!" He waited for the applause to die down. "I hope you all enjoy the show."

To Ty's surprise, Caleb was one of the actors. He took the stage to begin the show.

"'Two households, both alike in dignity...'"

***

Cassie swallowed hard, listening intently for her cue and whispering her first line over and over. "'How now! Who calls? How now! Who—"

A hand cut off her words as it covered her mouth. She struggled against the arm that wrapped around her middle and pulled her back hard against a man's chest.

"Miss me, sweetheart?" Robert whispered in her ear.

Chapter Thirty

Heart slamming in her chest, Cassie reacted like a trapped animal. She made a fist and slammed it into Robert's groin as hard as she could. Then she pulled her knee up and stomped on the instep of his foot.

He released his hold, letting out a howl that would've done a banshee proud.

Bolting, she blindly ran onto the stage, colliding with the kind, plump woman who was playing her nursemaid. They ended up sprawled on the stage.

Cassie's gaze frantically searched for the one person she knew would protect her. "Ty! Help!"

She struggled to her feet, fighting the thick skirts that had tangled between her legs. Footsteps slapped against the stage, alerting her that Robert had recovered from her assault and was in pursuit.

"I'll kill you, you bitch!"

His gait was awkward, but it wasn't slow enough to give her time to escape. When his hand slid inside his thick coat, she knew he was armed. Flipping to her back, she tried to scoot away, making very little progress and praying for a miracle.

Ty's heart was also slamming in his chest. He'd leapt to his feet, scrambling to the stage to get to Cassie. Although he saw no danger, he could taste her fear. It wasn't until Robert Putnam stumbled onto the stage that Ty realized exactly what had sent his wife frantically bolting out of the shadows.

"You bitch! You cost me everything!" Robert jerked a gun from his coat.

Ty drew his Colt, aimed, and fired before his adversary could even get his firearm entirely free.

Dropping the gun, Robert clutched at the front of his coat, trying to snatch it open. With a strangled cry, he collapsed to his knees. He turned to stare at Ty, eyes still full of fury. Then Robert pitched forward to land on the floorboards. His death rattle echoed through the now silent theater.

Then bedlam ensued. It seemed as though everyone started shouting at the same time.

Ty vaulted onto the stage and quickly kicked aside the gun Robert had dropped. Although he was sure he'd killed the man, Ty knelt down and checked for signs of life.

He found none. It took all his self-control not to spit on the corpse as a final insult. Instead, he gave a satisfied grunt.

Some men just deserved killing.

When he stood, he was nearly knocked down as Cassie threw herself into his arms. He held her tight. "It's over now, sweetheart. He can't hurt you anymore."

"Truly, Ty?" Her voice quivered.

"Truly."

Matthew crouched by Robert. "Good shot, Ty. Clean through the heart."

Cassie pulled away and put herself between Ty and Matthew. "He did nothing wrong, marshal. Robert was trying to kill me and—"

Holding up a hand, Matthew cut her off. "There's no crime here, Cassie. We all witnessed what happened."

"So you won't arrest him?"

"No, ma'am. I won't arrest him."

***

Damn if it wasn't the most entertaining thing Ty had seen in his entire life.

Once Robert's body was removed and the rather unfazed crowd loudly insisted the show go on, the people of White Pines were treated to a great performance of Shakespeare's *Romeo and Juliet.*

While the words didn't always make sense, Ty understood the story well enough to follow along. So much joy. So much sadness. Drew and Cassie brought the young lovers to life in a way Ty had never dreamed possible. And in the final scene, where Cassie had pretended to plunge the dagger into her body, he hadn't been surprised to feel the burn of tears forming in his eyes.

Not that he'd *ever* admit that to anyone...

If there were more stories like this one out there, maybe reading might be something he could come to enjoy. Since Cassie was intent on helping him improve the skill, he'd give in and let her.

An image formed in his mind of her sitting in a chair, reading to a circle of children—their children. She'd be a wonderful mother, the type a child deserved. And he'd be the father they needed.

Together, he and Cassie could do anything.

He watched her as she was greeted by the awed members of the audience who'd crowded the stage at the end of the performance. She seemed genuinely surprised at how much everyone enjoyed not only the show but her as Juliet.

Content to wait, he considered his wife. It was no wonder that he'd fallen in love with her. She was not only beautiful in face, body, and soul, but she had not an ounce of vanity. Her mother must have been a wonderful person to have kept Cassie so untainted by the Shays, and he thanked God for that blessing.

She finally came to stand at his side. "I fear I'm exhausted now. There was far too much excitement today. I will sleep for hours and hours when we get home."

"That's a shame. I'll have to save your surprise for tomorrow."

"Surprise? What surprise?"

Ty pressed a kiss to the lace cap on the crown on her head. "Tomorrow."

"'O wilt thou leave me so unsatisfied?'"

"That's Romeo's line, not Juliet's."

Her smile was radiant. "You *did* listen. I thought for a moment or two you might have nodded off during my performance. Did you enjoy the show?"

"It weren't half bad. Maybe one day that Shakespeare guy will write another play."

***

"Oh, Ty. It's beautiful. Absolutely beautiful." Cassie stared at the frame of what would be her new home, filled with awe and wonder.

It was everything she'd ever dreamed. A cabin in the middle of the mountains that she could share with the man she loved. One day, their children would romp on the green grass while she hung out their laundry and Ty herded their cattle.

"You really like it?" His tone betrayed his worry.

She turned to wrap her arms around his waist and rest her cheek against his chest. "I *love* it." Glancing up, she gave him a kiss and a smile. "I cannot believe you were able to keep all this work a secret from me."

He shrugged.

"Where will the cows be?" she asked.

Ty quirked a brow. "Cows? You want cows?"

"Of course! 'My bounty is as boundless as the sea. My love as deep; the more I give to thee, the more I have, for both are infinite.'"

"In other words..."

"In other words, I love you Ty Bishop."

"I love you too, Cassie Bishop." Ty let his gaze wander the home before it returned to her, his eyes full of emotion. "'I'm afraid all this is just a dream, too sweet to be real.'"

Cassie gaped at him. "You remembered that line?"

He nodded. "And a bunch more. How about... 'And what love can do, that dares love attempt.' I did all this for you, Cassie. My love for you made me strong."

"Just like your love for me made me strong enough to do exactly what I'd always wanted to do?"

"To act?" Ty asked.

She shook her head.

"To run away?"

Again, she shook her head.

"Then what did my love give you the strength to do?"

"To capture a cowboy."

A white cloud rose from his mouth as he chuckled. "And am I your cowboy?"

"Oh, yes. My very own genuine cowboy.

The End

ABOUT THE AUTHOR

Author Biography:
Sandy lives in a quiet suburb of Indianapolis, where she teaches psychology. Published through Grand Central Forever Yours, Carina Press, and indie-published, she has been an Amazon #1 Bestseller multiple times and has won numerous awards including two HOLT Medallions. Please visit her website at sandyjames.com for more information or find her on Twitter and Facebook. Represented by Danielle Egan-Miller of Browne & Miller Literary.

Other Books by Sandy James:

Damaged Heroes Series
Murphy's Law (Book 1)
Free Falling (Book 2)
All the Right Reasons (Book 3)
Faith of the Heart (Book 4)
Twist of Fate (Book 5)

Safe Havens Series
Saving Grace (Book 1)
Runaway (Book 2)
Redeemed (Book 3)
Hideaway (Book 4)
False Pretenses (book 5 ~ Coming soon!)

Ladies Who Lunch Series
The Bottom Line (Book 1)
Signed, Sealed, Delivered (Book 2)
Sealing the Deal (Book 3)
Fringe Benefits (Book 4)

Alliance of the Amazons
The Reluctant Amazon (Book 1)
The Impetuous Amazon (Book 2)
The Brazen Amazon (Book 3)
The Volatile Amazon (Book 4)

Single Titles
Turning Thirty-Twelve
Rules of the Game
The Seeker

Nashville Dreams Series
Can't Walk Away (Book 1)
Can't Let Her Go (Book 2)
Can't Fight the Feeling (Book 3)